THE RETURN OF HIS PROMISED DUCHESS

Lauri Robinson

MILLS & BOON

First Published in Great Britain 2022
by Mills & Boon, an imprint of HarperCollins*Publishers* Ltd,
1 London Bridge Street, London, SE1 9GF

www.harpercollins.co.uk

HarperCollins*Publishers*
1st Floor, Watermarque Building,
Ringsend Road, Dublin 4, Ireland

The Return of His Promised Duchess © 2022 Lauri Robinson

ISBN: 978-0-263-30172-4

05/22

MIX
Paper from
responsible sources
FSC™ C007454

This book is produced from independently certified FSC™ paper
to ensure responsible forest management.
For more information visit www.harpercollins.co.uk/green.

Printed and Bound in Spain using 100% Renewable Electricity
at CPI Black Print, Barcelona

To two of my nieces, Denise and Kari.

I have such fond memories of our trip to Atlanta
all those years ago.

Chapter One

1861

Grey skies. Mist. Cobblestoned streets. So chilly a shiver rippled her spine.

Annabelle Smith wasn't sure if this was what she'd expected or not. Then again, she'd never expected to be in London. Ever.

She closed her eyes, forced the tears to stay at bay and swallowed the indignation that was pressing hard to come forward. Having been deposited on to a ship like a sack of feed—tossed over a shoulder and carried up the gangplank and shipped away from her homeland—was enough to fill anyone with indignation.

More than indignation.

She was still so hurt that merely thinking about it made her eyes sting.

She'd never expected her father to treat her like that.

But he had.

For her own safety.

Hogwash.

That's what it was.

Hogwash.

Yet, here she was, in London, on her way to her grandfather's house. A man she'd never met. Hadn't known he existed. She'd been an infant when her mother had escaped to America.

That could be why she was chilled to the bone. Because of the things she'd learned during her trip across the ocean. The most devastating was that Arlo Smith wasn't her father. He was her stepfather.

A great sense of *woe is me* washed over her again.

Having seen enough of London, she released the heavy curtain hanging over the window and leaned back in the seat of the rocking coach, listened the clip clop of the horse's steps echo off the cobblestones.

The coach wasn't like the stagecoaches in America, where the leather curtains were rolled up, letting in the sunshine and fresh breezes. The coaches back home were also brightly painted.

This coach was painted black. Inside and out.

Even the heavy curtains covering the windows were black and the interior was dark and gloomy, much like she felt inside.

She adjusted the small wooden chest sitting on her lap, held it closer against her stomach, as if it might provide a tiny amount of protection, or at least familiarity. The chest had been her mother's and, as a child, she'd thought it was a tiny treasure chest.

The contents of the box had come as a surprise. Not a wonderful one.

There were jewels in it. A necklace.

Also in the box was a tiny infant bootie and a diary.

During the sea voyage from Virginia, she'd read the diary and examined the necklace several times. Set in gold, the emerald stones of varying sizes were connected with gold links in a distinct one large stone, two small stones pattern, and six teardrop-shaped pearls dangled from the larger stones. The pearls were of varying sizes, with the largest connected to the largest emerald in the centre. She had never seen her mother wear it. Had never known that the necklace existed until she'd opened the box. Some might consider it a lovely piece of jewellery, but the story behind it was not.

She'd learned that story from her mother's

diary. Another thing she hadn't known existed. Between the pages of the leather-bound book was a dark, brooding story that had left her questioning if she even knew who she was. She certainly wasn't the Annabelle Smith she'd always known herself to be. And Arlo Smith, the man that she'd grown up calling Papa, was not her father.

Her true father had been a duke. Archibald Fredrickson, Duke of Compton, had been more than four decades older than her mother and, according to the diary, not a nice man.

'Excuse me, miss, but we will soon arrive,' said Captain Berland, sitting stiffy in his seat facing hers. 'I've been instructed to inform you that if you find the situation you've been placed in to be hazardous, you should contact this man. He is here in London.'

Annabelle took the slip of paper he held towards her. The Captain, though pleasant enough, was most likely chomping at the bit to get rid of her. He'd not only captained the ship that had brought her from America, he'd also accepted the responsibility of delivering her to her grandfather, which had included a long train ride to London from where they'd docked following their sea voyage to England.

Opening the blue silk and black lace pouch that matched her dress and was hooked on her wrist with a ribbon, she deposited the still folded note inside and pulled the drawstring tight. 'Thank you.'

'I do wish you the very best, Miss Smith,' he said.

'Thank you,' she said again. 'I wish you a speedy return to America.'

'I won't be leaving for a few weeks. If you're unable to find the man on the note, you may feel free to search me out in Southampton.'

Annabelle nodded. 'I appreciate that.' However, she knew the Captain would not return her to America, which would be her only reason for contacting him. Her father—stepfather—had bid strict instructions she was to remain overseas. In London. With her grandfather. Even as she'd cried and begged him not to send her away.

'I do not know your grandfather, the Earl of Westerdownes, but have heard of him and am inclined to believe that he'll be pleased to have his family reunited.'

That they had in common. Annabelle did not know Lawrence Thomas Harding, the Earl of Westerdownes, either, and wasn't looking forward to meeting him. From her mother's diary, it sounded as though her grandfather wasn't any nicer than the old Duke he'd forced his only child to wed.

The coach rocked as the horses were pulled to a stop and she swallowed against the dryness of her mouth, knowing they'd arrived.

Captain Berland lifted his cap off the seat beside him, tucked it under his arm. 'I will escort you to the door and then oversee the unloading of your trunks.'

She could tell him that wasn't necessary, but knew the man was honour bound to deliver her to her grandfather's door, so merely nodded while adjusting the ribbons holding her navy-blue hat in place.

The coach door was opened by the driver and Annabelle waited for the Captain to step out first and then accepted his hand to assist her in stepping on to the hanging step and then the ground. Sucking in air, she took her first look of her grandfather's home. It was quite large. Three storeys. But rather narrow, tucked closely to other like homes built on each side. The bricks constructing the house were brown, wide and rough looking, and the steps leading to the front door were made out of the same bricks. The yard between the house and street was well manicured, but there wasn't a single flower in sight.

That made her sigh heavily and once again glance at the grey sky. Perhaps the sun never shone here, therefore flowers couldn't grow.

She wasn't certain about that, but that was how she felt. Everything around her appeared to be a gloomy, nearly colourless world.

The Captain took her elbow to guide her along the pathway towards the steps. Still clutching the box against her person, she walked forward, feeling as if she was walking the plank on some pirate's ship, facing nothing but impending doom.

Not ready to meet her grandfather, she startled slightly when the door of the home opened. A man exited the house and hurried down the steps, paying more attention to the hat in his hand than to her and the Captain. He was quite smartly dressed, wearing a dark brown coat hosting long tails in the back, but open in the front, revealing a shimmering gold waistcoat, white shirt and brown trousers, along with tall brown boots.

Perhaps she noticed all that because she was overly relieved that he was much too young to be her grandfather.

When he noticed them, he stepped one way, which happened to be the same way she and the Captain stepped, attempting to give him room to pass. That happened again when they all stepped in the opposite direction.

Huffing out a breath, he stepped on to the grass and waved a hand for them to move forward.

'Thank you,' Captain Berland replied.

The man nodded and Annabelle noticed that his hair was as brown as his coat—so were his eyes, but they also held specks of gold nearly the same shade as his waistcoat.

Said eyes narrowed and his lips puckered before he gave her a nod and stepped back on the pavement as she and the Captain walked past him.

She withheld the want to look at him over her shoulder, wondering why he seemed so disgusted. Unless that was how all Londoners were. Rude. Unlikeable. Matching their gloomy, colourless world.

All the more reason for her to return to the States as soon as possible. She needed sunlight, colour, flowers and birds.

'Forgive me, miss, but I feel inclined to warn you that not everyone you meet is going to be as friendly as you might be used to,' Captain Berland said as they walked forward. 'Nor as trustworthy. Please use caution at all times.'

She couldn't help but glance over her shoulder at the brown-haired man walking towards a black coach with a gold crest on the door and pulled by a pair of fine-looking, matching buckskin horses. Although, like his waistcoat, those flecks in his eyes, the crest on coach door and the hide of the horses was a lovely golden hue, she held no hope that anything in her life here would be bright and shiny. Colourful. 'Be assured that I will heed that advice, Captain. I will indeed.'

As they reached the first stair of the steps leading up to the house, the amount of shouting coming out of the open door was impossible not to hear.

Still holding her elbow, the Captain reached over and patted her arm with his other hand. It was meant to be comforting, but when an aged ship Captain who has seen many things in his lifetime feels the need to offer comfort, even a young woman who has never been more than twenty miles away from home knew it was not good.

Annabelle forced her feet to continue forward, even as more impending doom shrouded her.

An older woman appeared in the doorway. Short, round and as grey as a squirrel. 'Forgive me,' the woman said. 'It's just...just...' With both of her hands pressed against her full bosoms, the woman's sigh was mixed with a rumbling moan sound. 'Oh, Lady Annabelle, I didn't expect you to look so much like your mother. It simply took my breath away. Totally emptied my lungs. I had to shout for the others to come and see.'

The women, three of them, all wore white aprons over their grey dresses and the man wore a black suit coat over his grey shirt and pants. If not for her own blue dress, Annabelle would have thought she'd gone colour blind.

'Come, come,' the woman said, waving a hand. 'Come in out of this dreary weather. The sun was shining yesterday. Shining as bright as ever, but today it's been cloudy and drizzling. I do wish it would make up its mind. Just rain and get it over with or move on and let the sun shine.'

Following the Captain's urging, Annabelle continued walking forward, each step feeling heavier than the last.

'I know you can't remember us. You were just a wee babe the last time any of us saw you. I'm Mrs Quinn,' the woman continued, gesturing to herself and then others. 'This is my husband, Mr Quinn, and that's Mrs Martin, and that's Miss Wayne. We've all been with the household since before your mama was born. Lord, but we've missed her and you. Nearly gave up hope of ever seeing you again.'

Stopping on the top step, Annabelle nodded to each person. 'Hello.' She didn't attempt to re-member their names because she wouldn't be here long enough for that. She wasn't sure how just yet, but she would be leaving, making her way back to the States as soon as possible.

The man and women each returned her greeting with a slight bow and the words, 'My lady.'

Mrs Quinn stepped forward and took a hold of her arm. 'Come inside, His Lordship has been informed of your arrival. We didn't expect you this soon. The letter just arrived yesterday.'

Letter? The shiver that rippled over Annabelle was impossible to hide.

Captain Berland looked down at her. 'Would you like me to escort you inside?'

Although she would rather not be alone, the Captain had fulfilled his duty and she shook her head. 'That's not necessary.'

He gave her arm another pat. 'Then I will oversee the unloading of your trunks.'

'Thank you.'

He began to release her arm, but hesitated. 'It's been my pleasure to oversee your travels and hope you will enjoy your time in London.'

Because he looked so serious, as if he didn't want to leave her, she pulled up a smile and then stretched on her toes and kissed his cheek. Nothing about her situation was his fault. 'Thank you, Captain Berland.' As she settled back on her heels, she couldn't stop herself from making a request. 'If you hear news, any news at all, I would appreciate—' She pinched her lips together, unable to continue. The idea of her country being torn apart by a war that was anything but civil filled her with fear. That's where she should be, back home, working alongside others to save her country.

'I have already made instructions for news to be delivered to you regularly,' he said. 'Goodbye, Miss Smith.'

'Godspeed to you.' She turned, stepped away and allowed herself to be escorted inside the tall brick home by Mrs Quinn.

Anger raged through Andrew Barkly, the Duke of Mansfield, known as Drew to his friends. He threw his hat on the seat, stepped inside and pulled the door of the coach shut with more force than was needed.

'How did that go?'

Drew sat, levelling a glare at Roger Hardgroves, the Fourth Marquess of Clairmount, his best friend who had insisted upon trailing along today, albeit because he wanted the scoop first hand, not filtered through the vines of London gossip that could often be as far from the truth as a six-legged dog. 'Exactly as I expected.' Hell. The Earl of Westerdownes was the devil himself.

'You should have petitioned Albert while you had the chance,' Roger said, peeping behind the heavy curtain covering the window.

'Please do not humour me with your advice.' Drew knew he should have petitioned the Prince to absolve the betrothal, but hadn't felt it was necessary. It had been as if the betrothal had given him a two-headed coin. One that made him safe from the bounds of matrimony—an institution he never wanted to join—by both sides of the coin. Being betrothed saved him from all the young ladies seeking to claim a titled husband and their overzealous mothers who were even more hungry for their daughters to wed a man of the peerage. The flip side of that coin had saved him from marriage as well. The Earl's granddaughter had been gone, missing for almost twenty years, and he'd been ninety-nine per cent sure she'd never return.

The timing of her sudden and imminent arrival couldn't be worse. He couldn't ask the Prince for a favour with the way Albert was ailing. Only family and a few insiders knew of Albert's illness. Just as few knew of the scandal that Queen Victoria and Prince Albert's oldest son was creating by refusing to end his affair with an Irish actress.

'Was that her?' Roger asked.

'Who?'

'Your betrothed.' Roger was still peering out

through the curtains. 'The woman you nearly collided with on the pavement.'

The wheels of the coach started to roll and Drew pulled aside the curtain next to him, staring at the Earl's terraced house as they drove past. He hadn't given the man and woman on the pavement much thought, other than wishing they would get out of his way. And her eyes. He'd noticed them. Like an evening star, they'd shone a with hint of brilliance among an otherwise colourless sky.

'Was that her?' Roger repeated.

Drew let his curtain fall back into place. 'No.' Westerdownes had said his granddaughter would be arriving near the end of the month, and would be sent by carriage to Mansfield within hours of her arrival. Drew didn't want her sent to his country estate and had argued the point.

To no avail.

He had no choice but to comply with the Earl's demands.

'Her arrival will set tongues wagging,' Roger claimed. 'Folklore surrounding the disappearance of the Duchess of Compton and her daughter is still alive and well. Some have claimed their bodies are buried somewhere on the old, dead Duke's estate. Along with the Compton emeralds.'

Drew knew every story that floated around concerning *The Lost Duchess*. From the Duke of Compton murdering his young wife and daughter, to them being kidnapped by gypsies and the one most likely—that the Duchess had run away with a young lover.

Whatever had happened had never been of interest to Drew. The mine, the livelihoods of those working there, had always been his focus and every step to make significant changes had been an uphill battle. Some called his ideas radical, others said they were too costly. Several, including Westerdownes, refused to even consider that empowering workers would benefit everyone.

Drew believed it would and his work in proving those benefits had never left time for him to think about tales of a long-lost duchess and her daughter. Until now. He sat back, set an ankle atop his opposite knee. 'No one is to know of her arrival.'

With surprise showing on his face, Roger asked, 'Why?'

'For the exact reason you mentioned. Tongues will wag.'

'Rightfully so. Everyone wants to know what happened, where she's been all these years.'

Roger's tongue could wag as fast and hard as the best of London's gossipers; to keep it still,

Drew would share all he knew. He trusted his friend, but more than that, Roger had a way of discovering gossip long before it became gossip and that might come in handy. 'America.'

With a dark brow lifted over his piercing green eyes, Roger encouraged, 'Do tell.'

'For a vow of silence.'

Roger feigned a look of aghast. 'You're my best friend.'

'And you are mine, which means I know you well,' Drew replied, with his own brow lifted. 'Hence my request.'

Roger laughed. 'Mums the word, old man, but I must know why.' Blowing on his fingernails, then rubbing them on his lapel while raising a brow, Roger continued, 'A secret of this magnitude could provide a highly sought-after bachelor any number of favours.'

The only thing ever on Roger's mind was his next conquest. Drew, too, enjoyed the companionship of a willing lady in his bed, but he enjoyed his bachelor life more and wasn't prepared to give that up by being too free with his services. He wasn't willing to give up his single status at all. Marriage brought constraints that forced a man to choose between his family and his work, his duties. He'd lived that life as a child and wouldn't repeat it as an adult. 'The Earl of

Westerdownes is suspicious that the woman arriving may not be his granddaughter. The letter he received was from a merchant in Virginia, who stated the Duchess had died several years ago and that he was sending her daughter, Lady Annabelle Fredrickson, to England for her safety while the States are at war with each other.'

'Interesting.' Roger scratched one of his thick, black sideburns. 'Westerdownes claimed he'd searched the world over for them.'

'I don't believe he searched for them at all,' Drew admitted. He had nothing to back his suspicions, other than general knowledge, which to him was enough. 'The Duke of Compton had been old, some say on borrowed time when he married Westerdownes's daughter, not to mention when the Duchess and her daughter disappeared. I believe Westerdownes knew all he had to do was wait. The Duke would die. All his unentailed assets that he'd left to his daughter would go to—'

'The Earl,' Roger interrupted. 'What an enterprising old goat.'

'Cold old goat,' Drew supplied. 'He doesn't *want* this to be his granddaughter.' Westerdownes hadn't said that, but Drew had read between the lines. Furthermore, he knew the Earl of Westerdownes well and the man was a money grubber.

'Because she will inherit her father's holdings.' Roger's eyes grew wide. 'Correct that. Her husband will inherit her father's holdings. You.'

That was the part that left Drew conflicted. Even though her inheritance would add to his wealth and give him full control of the mine, he didn't want any part of the betrothal that had been imposed upon him as a child. But if she turned out to be Annabelle Fredrickson, he also didn't want her cheated out of what was rightfully hers, especially not by her very own grandfather. Injustices, all injustices, infuriated him. He'd made fighting biases and inequalities his covenant and therefore couldn't help but consider her plight in all of this. 'If she's not who she claims to be, she'll be sent back to America.'

'And if she is?' Roger asked.

The weight that settled in Drew's chest was painful. 'Then, I'll have to abide by the betrothal.' There was no other option. The betrothal had been initiated because of the coal mine on his property and the vein of coal that extended into the old Duke's property. The property Westerdownes now oversaw.

Roger's sigh matched Drew's. The two of them had vowed bachelorhood together, years ago, and had both settled into the lives they had. Enjoyable lives that suited them and their friendship. Roger had his own reasonings. For Drew, it came from his childhood. Of being the unchosen one when his father had chosen between family and duty.

Drew popped his knuckles at the tension that was filling every part of his body. 'Westerdownes doesn't want anyone to know of the arrival of this woman, nor does he wish for anyone to discover who she is, or who she is portraying, until it's been determined if she is, or isn't, his granddaughter.'

'How does he plan on determining that?'

'We did not get into specifics, other than he's sending a man to Virginia to interview the merchant. In the interim, once she arrives, he expects me to keep her at Mansfield. Secretively.'

'If she is Lady Annabelle, that will give the two of you time to get to know each other before you wed,' Roger said with a grin.

Drew's nerves stung and his glare let his friend know that he found no humour in the situation.

Roger frowned slightly. 'Do you know exactly when this woman is to arrive?'

'No. Westerdownes said the Captain of the ship bringing her from America will deliver her to his home next month.'

Roger rubbed a hand across his face, then he

leaned forward. 'That was her, Drew. The woman you almost collided with on the pavement was Lady Annabelle Fredrickson. I'd bet my inheritance on it.'

A shiver rippled Drew's spine. 'That's impossible. Why would you think that?'

'Because I've known sea captains my entire life. They have a walk. A stance. I can't explain it, but I know it when I see it and the man who walked up that pavement with that woman was a sea captain.'

Drew wasn't ready and had to deny that possibility. 'No. Westerdownes said next month.'

'There are a number of possibilities for her being here early, a different ship, a change in schedules, but I'd bet my—'

'I heard you the first time,' Drew interrupted. He then cursed under his breath because, whether he was ready or not, that very well could have been her. His betrothed.

Chapter Two

'Don't just stand there snivelling!'

Momentarily stunned, Anabelle stared at the old man. She had never expeirenced such unabashed hatred. It felt as if she was being pelted by hundreds of tiny arrows. Poisoned arrows that made her skin sting beneath her clothing.

Was this how he'd treated her mother? With utmost loathing? With unabashed revulsion?

That possibility, along with his blatant rudeness, fuelled her ire, caused all the indignation she'd kept at bay since leaving America to hit a boiling point. 'I am not snivelling.' She marched into the room where he sat in a huge chair by a roaring fire. 'I was merely waiting to be invited into the room. It's called manners. Something my mother taught me.'

His hawk-like nose curled. 'I see she also taught you how to be rude, insufferable and selfish.'

'Selfish! There was not a selfish bone in my mother's body.' Her anger had her entire being trembling. What she'd read in her mother's diary was flooding her brain. She didn't care if this man was her grandfather or not. With his beady dark eyes, pointed nose and chin, and red jacket, he looked like a buzzard sitting on an old, dead tree branch. 'She was kind and loving. Things she obviously didn't inherit from you.'

'Ah, the reason you are here, to inherit something. I'm glad you got right to the point.'

Her mother's small chest was still in her hands and she clutched it tighter. 'I'm not here to inherit anything. It was not my choice to leave my homeland and, I assure you, I will not be staying.'

'No, you will not.' He waved a hand at the doorway. 'Get the carriage. Get her out of here.'

Mrs Quinn, rubbing her hands together, stepped further into the room. 'Forgive me, my lord, but it is already late in the day. Surely the lady could—'

'No!' He slapped the arm of his chair. 'I can't stand the sound of her foreign voice!'

Annabelle was more than willing to leave. Anywhere would be better than here. Furthermore, it would merely be the first step of her journey home. The fact he didn't like her voice didn't matter a wit. Her American accent was far easier to understand than his snooty English one.

However, she did feel a great sense of empathy for Mrs Quinn, who had tears in her eyes. 'It's all right,' she said softly to the older woman. 'I prefer to leave.'

'Oh, my lady,' Mrs Quinn whispered softly. 'You've only just arrived.'

'It's fine,' Annabelle assured her as she steered the other woman out of the room without a final glance at her grandfather. She didn't want to be anywhere near his wrath. There was no wonder why her mother had left and Annabelle was more than willing to follow in her mother's footsteps.

That happened within the hour. During the interim, she'd been escorted into a dining room and provided with a pot of tea and a plate of small sandwiches while her grandfather had kept the household staff scrambling to meet the needs of his shouts. Sympathy for the life her mother must have lived before escaping to America had grown every second Annabelle had stayed in that house.

Being escorted out through the back door, into a carriage with her luggage stacked on top, had been a great relief.

'Here, my lady,' Miss Wayne said, draping a

lap blanket across Annabelle's knees soon after the carriage began to roll away from the home.

The interior of the coach was damp and dank, musty-smelling, and the worn canvas curtains let in blasts of chilly air with every bump the wheels rolled over. Which was every second. The coach travelled with the same teeth-jarring way as a buck board with no springs.

'Thank you.' Annabelle smoothed the blanket over her knees. 'Surely it won't take long to reach a hotel.'

Miss Wayne, who was as short, plump and as grey as Mrs Quinn, fiddled with her own lap blanket, tucking it beneath her thighs as the carriage bounced along. Annabelle had insisted she did not need a companion, yet the woman was sitting on the opposite bench with her cheeks and nose growing red from the damp and chilly air.

When Miss Wayne didn't reply even after she'd seemed satisfied with her blanket and stopped fiddling with it, Annabelle wasn't sure if the older woman had heard her. 'It won't take us long to reach a hotel, will it?' That's where she'd requested to be taken. The nearest hotel. She would seek out the man on the slip of paper that Captain Berland had given her, and if he couldn't assist her in her return to Virginia, she would seek out the Captain. He might be hard to convince, but right now, those were her only two choices.

Miss Wayne held a smile on her face, but didn't make eye contact.

Annabelle had raised her voice and was sure the woman had heard it over the noise of the carriage. 'I asked you a question.'

Miss Wayne nodded. 'Yes, my lady.'

Annabelle wanted to ask if she meant, yes, it would take them a long time, but another question needed to be asked first. 'Why do you keep calling me that? My lady? My name is Annabelle.' Or Belle. Some people had called her that because her father had called her Belle-girl. Others had called her Miss Smith, which wasn't really her name so she couldn't use it. Could she?

'Because you are a lady,' Miss Wayne replied. 'You are the daughter of a duke and duchess. Therefore, "my lady" is the proper way to address you, my lady.'

She'd been raised as a merchant's daughter and that's who she wanted to continue to be. Furthermore, she had far higher concerns than what was and was not proper in England. 'How long will it take us to reach a hotel?' She would prefer one near the train station, but right now, one with a window that closed and had heat of some sort would be fine.

'We are not going to a hotel, my lady.'

Annabelle sat straighter in her seat. 'That is where I requested to be taken.'

The woman's smile never left her lips, but it was strained. 'His Lordship ordered for you to be delivered to Mansfield.'

'Ordered?'

'Yes, my lady.'

Annabelle sucked in a breath and tried to hold her anger at bay. 'Mansfield? Is that a nearby town?' Hopefully, it was closer to the ocean— that would assist in her overall journey back home.

'No, my lady.'

Flustered by so many things, she chose one she could control. 'Annabelle. My name is Annabelle. No more of "my lady".'

'Forgive me, but it wouldn't be proper for—'

'I don't care if it's proper or not. My name is Annabelle and that is what I want you to call me.' In the overall scope of things, it didn't matter, other than it grated on her nerves because she didn't want to be here and she didn't want to inherit anything, not even a proper address.

'Very well.'

A wave of grief washed over Annabelle at the way the other woman hung her head. She hadn't meant to hurt her feelings. 'I apologise, Miss

Wayne. I'm a long way from my home and don't know all of your customs. Please, could we simply address each other by our given names? I would appreciate it. What is yours?'

Lifting her head, the woman gave a slight nod. 'Effie.'

'What a lovely name.' Holding a smile on her face, she continued on to a subject that did matter. 'Now, Effie, how far is this town of Mansfield?'

'It's not a town, Miss Annabelle.' Effie paused as if saying her name had pained her. 'It is a country estate.'

'A country—' Annabelle wrenched open the curtain. There were no homes, no shops, just countryside, and the horses' hooves were no longer echoing off cobblestones. The road was dirt and the horses were moving along it at a quick pace. It was also raining. Dropping the curtain, she asked, 'How far away is this estate?'

'We will not arrive until after midnight, my lady.'

At that moment Annabelle's concern was not on the address, or herself, it went to the coach driver. 'It's cold and wet outside. The driver can't drive until midnight in these conditions.'

'He dressed warmly.'

'Not warm enough for this weather. We must turn around.'

'He has strict orders not to stop. For anything.'

'Great Scott! Just because he hates me does not give that insufferable old man the right to put others' lives in danger. Has he no mercy?'

Effie grimace. 'He is the Earl of Westerdownes.'

'More like the master of hell.'

Effie's eyes grew wide and she covered her mouth with one hand.

Annabelle huffed out a breath to ease the anger flaring inside her. Her grandfather was attempting to punish her, lock her away, miles from town, probably in some old, abandoned castle, all to prove he had charge over her like he'd had her mother.

He didn't.

He didn't have the right to harm others, either. 'The driver could end up with pneumonia.'

'Grady will be fine,' Effie said softly. 'He's an excellent driver and his heavy cloak will keep him dry.'

Annabelle's anger increased. She was the reason this older woman and the poor driver were travelling across the English countryside in the chilly rain. 'I'm terribly sorry you and the driver are involved in this mess. I should have held my anger at the house.'

Effie pinched her lips, as if trying not to speak, but then whispered, 'The Earl intended upon sending you to Mansfield as soon as you arrived, but your arrival was sooner than expected and that upset him.'

Her spine quivered. 'He—you all—knew of my arrival?'

'Yes, my lady. The letter from the merchant arrived last night, but it stated you would be arriving next month. We were all surprised when you arrived today, instead.'

Annabelle closed her eyes, let the events of the past month float through her mind. Life had been unsettling since war had been declared across the States back in April, but weeks ago, when rumours spread that their wonderful town of Hampton would become quarters for Federal troops, her life had changed considerably. She wasn't allowed to leave the house and her father suggested she needed to move some place safe. Away from Hampton.

She'd refused and had thought he'd accepted it. He hadn't and must have written a letter to her grandfather, planning on sending her to England. Unbeknownst to her.

Word that Union ships had entered the bay

came the same day that Captain Berland's ship had travelled up the river and arrived at port. Two days later, travelling trunks had been delivered to their house and Cecilia, their longstanding household maid, had quickly begun filling them. Annabelle had emptied them just as fast, until her father had physically hauled her to the ship. Captain Berland's ship wasn't equipped for passengers and she'd been put in quarters that had been vacated by the first mate.

Her father had insisted she had to leave now, while ships could still sail out through the river to the harbour. She'd begged, pleaded, cried, but it had all been to no avail.

She hadn't even had the chance to say goodbye to anyone, including her two best friends, Clara and Suzanne. That worried her. Clara had just had a baby in December and was all alone at their small farm, because her husband Mark had joined the army in April and Suzanne often needed help in getting lessons ready for the school children. They both must be wondering what had happened to her. Others had to, too. She'd thought of all of them while on the ship.

Captain Berland must have sent a messenger with her father's letter to London, to her grandfather, in advance of securing travel for the two of them to take the train to London this morning.

Before her father had left her on the ship, he'd given her the treasure box, told her it would explain everything.

It had provided her with many things she hadn't known, but it hadn't explained everything. 'Why had my grandfather planned on sending me to this estate that we're travelling to?'

Effie pinched her lips again and looked down at the floor.

'You might as well tell me, because I won't stop asking until you do and as you said, we are stuck in this coach until after midnight.' She hated the thought of once again being trapped, with no escape, but unless she was willing to open the door and leap out, chancing broken bones or worse, she was stuck in the carriage until it arrived at their destination.

Effie sighed, then quickly said, 'He is having you investigated.'

'For what?'

'Being an imposter.'

For some unfathomable reason, that made Annabelle laugh. Then again, it wasn't that unfathomable. 'Oh, Effie, I wish I was an imposter.'

Effie wrung her hands together. 'Oh, but you aren't, my lady.'

Annabelle glanced at the box the sitting on the seat beside her. She hadn't opened it at the house, hadn't shown anyone the necklace. 'How do you know?'

'Because you look exactly like your mother. You have her thick black hair, her nose, mouth, cheeks and blue eyes. The resemblance is uncanny and undeniable.'

Annabelle had been told she looked like her mother for years and was honoured by that, because she'd thought her mother was the most beautiful woman on earth. The kindest, too. She couldn't remember her mother ever saying a cross word or being sad. She was always smiling. Always happy. Even when she'd grown ill, unable to get out of bed, she'd still had a smile on her face and kind, comforting words for both Annabelle and her father.

She'd been twelve when her mother had died eight years ago and would never forget the last time she'd heard her mother's voice. She'd locked it in her mind.

'Arlo will take good care of you,' her mother had said softly. *'He always has. He loves you as much as I do. And you must take good care of him, for all he's done for us. Promise me you will. He'll need you, just like we needed him.'*

Annabelle had promised and that was what hurt her the most about being sent away. She loved her father and he loved her. They had taken care of each other for years and they should still be doing that. Now more than ever.

'We, the staff, all believe that is why the Earl was so angry. Because you aren't an imposter.'

Drawing her attention back to Effie, Annabelle asked, 'He wants me to be one?'

Effie bowed her head, avoiding eye contact by fiddling with her lap blanket.

Annabelle unfolded the blanket across her knees and pulled the edge up over her arms to ward off the chill that had completely settled into her forearms. 'We are in this coach until midnight, Effie, so take your time answering.'

Effie grimaced.

Annabelle smiled and waited.

As if accepting she might as well share what she knew, Effie said, 'You are a very wealthy woman, my lady. Wealth you inherited from your father.'

Money was the least of her concerns. She had not been sent penniless on this trip. 'My mother didn't want anything from him and neither do I.'

'It's more complicated than that, my lady.'

'Do explain.'

'You were betrothed after your birth to the Duke of Mansfield, a man who will profit greatly by marrying you.'

Annabelle's mouth went dry as her body

began to tremble. 'Marry? The Duke of Mansfield? Our destination?'

It was well after midnight when Drew was informed a coach was coming up the roadway. He and Roger had barely arrived back at his home in London when a messenger had arrived with a note from Westerdownes, stating that a woman posing as Lady Annabelle Fredrickson had arrived and that she and a companion would be leaving for Mansfield immediately.

So, that's exactly what he'd done.

Left for Mansfield immediately, on horseback.

He'd made it to his estate hours ago and the staff had everything ready for his guest.

Guest.

Disgust rose inside him. He hated romantic entanglements, which had been exactly what the betrothal had kept him safe from for years. He'd seen men grovel because of a woman, been at each other's throats because of love triangles and he'd seen them broken. His own father had been broken by the death of his mother. By the loss of love.

He wouldn't grovel, or fight, and he sure as hell wouldn't be broken by love. 'Have them shown to their rooms,' Drew told his man, Donald.

'You do not wish to greet them?' Donald asked.

'No. I'll make introductions in the morning.' He had informed Donald, a man he trusted with his life, who their guest was, but the rest of the household had merely been told they'd be hosting an American for a few weeks—one Miss Annabelle Smith.

'Very well, Your Grace.' Donald stepped out of the study and closed the door.

Drew moved to the window and watched as the coach rolled up next to the house. The rain had stopped a few hours ago, and the golden summer moon provided enough light for him to confirm the woman stepping from the carriage was indeed the same one he'd seen earlier in the day.

Or so it appeared. She was wearing the same clothes. He wouldn't know for sure until he saw her eyes. They'd settled in his mind. Not only the colour, but the sadness he hadn't acknowledged then, but somehow remembered now.

He pushed the heavy air out of his lungs. During his long ride to Mansfield, he'd sought to latch on to anger over his position of being betrothed. Sought hard, but the outcome of that long-ago agreement had benefited him, and others, greatly. His father had entered into the agreement with the Duke of Compton after the birth of the Duke's daughter. The betrothal allowed his father to expand their coal-mining operation on to the Duke's land, which he had left to Annabelle. An act that had grown the operation, increased its success. A success that Drew had continued to build upon after taking over for his father.

Marriage was the price he'd have to pay for that success. Not doing so would be selfish when he thought of all the people the mine employed. All the livelihoods that depended upon him. There were still many changes he wanted to make at the mine, for the people who worked there and at other mines.

The front door opened and he could hear Donald's deep voice and a much softer responding female voice.

Perhaps all of his thoughts were for naught. She might not be Lady Annabelle, but rather an imposter, as the old Earl alleged.

Drew waited until the scuttle of hauling luggage inside the house and up the stairs had long passed before he blew out the light in the study and made his way up the staircase to his own room. The house was silent and still, which was exactly how he liked it. Having grown up an only child because his mother had passed before his first birthday and his father was off serving the

Royal Family, he'd always been alone and knew no other life.

Nor did he want to know another life. He'd spent enough time in boarding schools and other homes of friends that had been full of children and family members to know what that was like and what he wanted. Though the companionship of others was enjoyable at times, there was much to be said about solitude. About quiet, peacefulness. That was why he much preferred Mansfield over London. Always had.

Donald had laid back the covers of his bed and, as Drew stripped and crawled between the crisp sheets, he admitted this was also something he didn't want to give up. He enjoyed the ability to sprawl across the bed, not worrying if anyone else had room to sleep. Perhaps he was simply selfish, but was still not of mind to change that.

He was not of a mind to change many things and fell asleep counting them.

Assuming his company would sleep late considering the hour of their arrival, Drew headed straight to the stables the following morning, to get in an early ride before joining his guest for breakfast. He was avoiding meeting her. In fact, he wished he'd never have to meet her.

Like the house and the wall encircling the garden, the stable was made of red bricks built upon a stone foundation and as Drew ambled along the gravel pathway between the home and stable, he wondered about Champion. He hadn't taken the time last night to look in on the old horse. Once as black as the ace of spades, but now spouting grey around his nuzzle, the horse had belonged to his father and had travelled thousands of miles, escorting and protecting the Royal Family while his father had served in the royal guard. As of late, Champion's feet had been bothering him and the groom couldn't seem to find the issue.

With that on his mind as he entered the building, Drew wasn't sure if he'd seen movement in the loft above the row of stables along the wall or not and paused to listen and watch.

The only sounds filling the area were soft snorts from the horses. He slowly walked the length of the stables, looking above the entire way. It might have been a flash of sunlight that he'd seen, but the sun had barely been up long enough to wake the birds.

At the end of the pavement, he peered over the half door, to where the coaches and carriages were parked. Along with the one that had arrived last night belonging to Westerdownes.

Nothing was out of place and, at this hour of

the morning, the groom would be up at the house, partaking in breakfast before beginning his day.

Too curious to let it go, Drew walked back to the other end of the row of stables, where the ladder led to the loft and made his way up the rungs. The dust motes in the air said something had moved in the area recently and though he wasn't overly pleased about what type of creature might be scurrying about in the loose hay, he did want to know. A badger could have been burrowed in the hay when it was transferred to the loft. Stuck up here, it could die and contaminate the hay.

He poked at the hay with the toe of his boot as he walked, until he heard what sounded like a well-muffled sneeze. Moving to the centre of the loft, where there was an opening between the stacks of hay, he walked to the wall.

There, attempting to hide among the stacks of hay, was a woman, crouched down, covering her mouth and nose with both hands, and looking up at him with the same set of blue eyes he'd seen yesterday.

Today those eyes were startled.

In his hurry to leave the Earl's home, he hadn't got a good look of her and took his time doing so now. Yesterday, her hair had been pinned up beneath a hat. Today it was flowing over her shoulders in soft waves and as black and shiny as coal. Combined with those sparkling blue eyes, she was attractive enough to turn the heads of men and have the women whispering behind lacy folding fans. Her dress was yellow, with tiny white flowers and white lace near her wrists and neckline.

Her fingers were trembling. So were her knees, judging from the way the material covering them fluttered slightly against the floor.

He had to bite back a smile because she was quite an enchanting sight. 'Is there a reason you are in the loft hiding behind a stack of hay?' he asked.

She nodded.

'May I ask what that reason is?'

She nodded again.

He lifted a brow, waiting.

Her slender fingers slipped down her face and she folded them together just below her chin. 'I saw you walking towards the building.'

Her honesty was surprising, but it wasn't her statement as much as it was the sound of her voice that he heard. The way she spoke, slowly, with a distinct drawl. She was definitely American, from the South, and her face, her dainty nose and petal-shaped lips, was as attractive as the rest of her, including the captivating accent.

'You were in London yesterday,' she said, somewhat accusatory.

'Yes, I was,' he admitted. 'At your grandfather's house.'

'Are—are you...?'

'The Duke of Mansfield? Yes, I am.'

Her eyes grew wide. 'You're Andrew Charles Barkly?'

He'd never heard his name sound so charming. 'Yes.'

'*You* are a duke?'

There were days he was as amazed by that as she sounded. 'I am.' He held out a hand, waited until she took it and rose to her feet. 'And you are Lady Annabelle Fredrickson.' Releasing her hand, he bowed slightly before saying, 'Also known as Annabelle Smith.'

Even her sigh was lyrical. 'I much prefer the latter.' She cocked her head to the side as her gaze went from his boots to his shirt, then his face in a long and slow appraisal. 'Does everyone call you "my lord"?'

'No.'

She sighed again, but also offered a hint of a smile as she nodded. 'That is good. We have given names for a reason.'

He gave her a compulsory nod. 'We do.'

'What do they call you? Andrew or Mr Barkly?'

'Some call me Andrew. Others call me Drew, or Mansfield, or Your Grace.'

'Your Grace?'

He nodded. 'It's the proper way to address a duke.'

She shook her head and closed her eyes. Her long lashes, slightly tipped up on the edges, rested near her pinkening cheeks for a long moment before they lifted again. She looked at him and huffed out a breath.

Gladly changing the subject, he asked, 'Why didn't you want me to see you?'

'I didn't want you to think I was sneaking around the barn.'

'Stable,' he corrected. 'The barn is on the other side of the house.'

Her mouth made a perfect O as her shapely brows lifted. 'And the difference would be?'

'The horses are kept here, in the stable, and the other animals—cows, pigs, chickens, goats and sheep—are kept in or near the barn.'

'Thank you; that quite explains it, doesn't it?'

He was fighting hard to not smile. Her innocent charm was as enchanting as her beauty. 'Yes, I believe it does.' A hint of concern rippled through him as a thought formed. 'Are you out here because you were planning on running away?'

'No. I was not planning on that this morning.' She waved a hand, gesturing for him to step back while saying, 'May I?'

'Of course.' He stepped back so she could move out from behind the hay.

The hem of her yellow and white dress swished against the floor as she walked to the edge of the loft and looked towards the open rafters at the far end. 'They are the reason I came into the stable.'

He moved to stand next to her. 'Who?'

'Them,' she whispered.

He scanned the area she pointed at and, seeing two blue birds sitting on the rafter, asked, 'The budgies?'

'We call them parakeets. I saw them out of the window of the bedroom. They were sitting on the rock wall and were still there when I found my way outside, but then they flew in here.'

'They probably have a nest in here somewhere.'

'A nest? Don't they have a cage?'

He began to understand. 'Did you climb into the loft to catch them?'

She shrugged, then nodded. 'I thought they might have gotten loose.'

'Their ancestors might have, but those two are wild. Do you not have wild ones in America?'

'Parakeets? No. They are kept in cages as pets.'

'It started that way here, too. The Queen was given a pair many years ago that she kept in a cage. For years thereafter, nearly every ship that arrived from Australia had budgies in their hulls, but the supply outnumbered the demand to keep them as pets and now we have a large number of them across the countryside.'

'So they are free? They just live here because they want to?'

He was growing used to her accent in some ways; in other ways, it was still captivating him. Along with the delight on her face. Her smile was so bright her eyes were sparkling. 'Yes, they are free and live here because they want to.'

'That is the first delightful thing I've seen, or heard, since arriving in England.'

'Don't let them fool you,' he warned. 'They can be pesky. They like anything that shines and shimmers and they like to mimic sounds, especially whistles.' To prove it, he let out a soft whistle.

Almost instantly the sound was copied by one of the birds.

Her laugh was soft and melodic, as was the whistle she let out.

When no response came from the birds, her smile faded.

'Don't feel bad. It takes them time to learn

a sound before they can mimic it,' he said. 'They've heard me whistle before. That was the first time for you.'

'Excuse me, Your Grace. Is something amiss?'

Drew glanced down to the floor, where the question had come from. 'No, Finnegan, we are just getting a closer look at the budgies,' he informed the groom.

'Very well,' Finnegan replied as if that wasn't odd. 'Do you wish me to saddle Fellow for you?'

Changing his mind about the early morning ride, Drew replied, 'No, thank you. We will return to the house for breakfast shortly. I'll ride after that.'

'Very well, Your Grace.' Finnegan gave a slight bow and walk out of the door.

Drew stepped back, giving her room, and waved a hand towards the ladder. 'After you, Miss Smith.'

Chapter Three

During the walk to the house, Annabelle wondered what she should think about the man walking at her side. She would not refer to him as Your Grace. That grated on her nerves. She did not want to be here and would not partake in any such titled nobility. The original colonies had fought against that almost a hundred years ago, and she was an American. Therefore, she would use names, as she did back home.

Whether Arlo was her father or not, she'd been Annabelle Smith for as long as she could remember and would continue to be. It felt right. Lady Annabelle Fredrickson did not. And she most certainly would not get married just because some old man thought she should. That was ludicrous.

Furthermore, in her diary, her mother had stated that she'd left England for her daughter's sake. Annabelle had thought her mother had been referring to her father and grandfather, but now believed her mother had been more specific than that. She hadn't wanted her daughter married off by an arranged marriage. Therefore, it would not happen.

This was the man she was supposedly betrothed to and, considering her mother's arranged marriage, Annabelle was surprised that he wasn't four decades older than her. He was young and handsome, if she had a mind to think of him that way, which she did not. She did, however, not mind his accent. It was intriguing. At her father's warehouses, she'd heard accents from around the world. Languages, too, and he was easy to understand. Easy to listen to, too.

She couldn't help but wonder why a man like him would agree to marry someone he didn't know. Did the English not believe in love? Was that why it was such a sombre place? Why people were so grumpy?

Still in the midst of wondering about that as they walked around the tall and long rock wall that the parakeets had landed on earlier, she stopped when he did.

'Is there an issue?' he asked.

It was a moment before she realised he was asking that question of the man hurrying around the corner of the wall towards them. Donald—that's how he'd introduced himself last night—was nearly as tall as Andrew—or Drew. She rather liked that name, it was different.

'Your Grace,' Donald said with a slight bow upon arriving in front of them. 'I'm pleased to see the lady is with you. Her maid just came downstairs quite upset that she was missing.'

'As you can see, she is not missing,' Drew replied. 'Merely taking a walk before breakfast.'

'Very good.' Donald stepped aside so they could move forward. 'The meal will be served whenever you are ready.'

Annabelle waited until they were a few steps in front of Donald before asking, 'Am I not allowed to go outside by myself?'

'Of course you may, but you should inform your maid so she doesn't worry about you.'

'Effie isn't my maid. She's...' Annabelle wasn't sure what Effie was to her. 'My prison guard, I guess.'

'Prison guard?'

'Yes. She was ordered to stay with me while I'm here, by my mother's father.'

'The Earl of Westerdownes.'

'Yes.' Then, curious, she asked, 'An earl is beneath a duke, correct?'

'Yes, but they are both ranks of the peerage.'

For some reason, she felt the need to explain. 'I'm aware of that. Studies of countries around the world are provided in American education, including their governments and monarchies, though our government was formed by the people, for the people, and does not allow any titles of nobility.' The fact that the country she loved so much was at war was as sad as it was maddening. Residents of Virginia were torn, with some supporting the North and others supporting the South. She'd read the political propaganda from both sides, and her point of view was that it was all over political gain and money. The very same thing that every war was fought over. 'I'm assuming Westerdownes is also an estate. One my grandfather owns. Is it near here?'

'It is an estate, a small one, and, no, it's not near here.'

'Well, Effie works for him, not me.'

'She is your companion,' Drew said. 'I will assign a maid to you.'

'For what?'

'Do you not have personal maids in America?'

Although she considered Cecilia a family member, she nodded. 'Cecilia has been with us for years and helps with the cooking and cleaning.' She missed Cecilia as much as she missed her father and should be with them, helping them, and others, during this time. She would find a way to get back home, sooner rather than later. Questioning exactly what was expected of her until she left, she asked, 'Is that why you will assign a maid, to help me with the cooking and cleaning?'

'No, I have household staff to see to those duties. A personal maid would assist only you.'

'Assist me with what?'

'Your personal needs. See that your clothes are pressed, assist you with bathing and dressing, and—'

'I don't need any help with those things.' She knew of some women back home who always needed assistance to tie them in their tight corsets to make their waists look thinner. She much preferred the front-lacing corsets with no whale bones. 'If a grown woman can't button her own buttons and tie her own laces, her mother didn't do a very good job of teaching her to take care of herself. My mother taught me to do all those things before I started school.'

'Where was—? Where *is* your home?'

'Hampton, Virginia.' A sense of happiness filled her just saying the name. 'It has a lovely harbour and our house is on the edge of town. It's a fine house. Big, but not a castle like yours.'

'This is not a castle, it's merely a manor house.'

Merely is not the word she would use to describe his house. Made of large bricks and stone, it was three storeys tall and as long and wide as one of her father's warehouses. Certain the birds had escaped from a cage, she'd been afraid the parakeets would be gone by the time she'd finally found her way to the ground floor and a door that had led outside. It had been very late when they'd arrived and she'd been half-asleep when Donald had shown her and Effie to their bedrooms last night. Hers was extremely large for a bedroom, more than three times the size of hers back home.

'I hope you found your room here satisfactory,' he said, as if knowing that was what she was thinking about.

'Yes, thank you. It's very lovely and I was very glad to see the sun rising into a blue sky this morning. I was afraid it never shone here.'

'I was very glad of the sunshine, myself.' He brought their steps to a stop and waited for Donald to hurry around them and open the large door before them.

Effie was right inside the door, wringing her hands as Annabelle walked into the house. Spying Drew, Effie instantly dropped into a curtsy.

'I apologise, Your Grace,' Effie said.

'No need. The lady merely wished for some

fresh air this morning,' Drew said. 'I assure you she was perfectly safe the entire time.'

'Thank you, Your Grace,' Effie said, curtsying again.

He gave Effie a slight nod, then turned to Annabelle, bowing slightly. 'I will see you at breakfast, Miss Smith.'

Annabelle wondered why it sounded as if he was making an excuse for her, but it was the way that Effie was trying to hide how she was looking at her beneath her lashes that she fully understood. It would be proper for her to curtsy, but she wasn't going, to, nor would she call him 'Your Grace'. She was an American, therefore she said, 'Thank you, Drew.' Smiling to herself because she did like how that name sounded, she turned and walked around the other woman.

'Forgive her, Your Grace, she—'

'Has permission to call me by my given name,' he replied.

A hint of satisfaction increased her smile as Annabelle walked down a long hallway. For a moment. Then she thought of Effie and how she was merely doing her job. One that had been assigned to her. Annabelle paused and turned to the older woman following her. 'I apologise, Effie, I didn't mean to worry you by going outside without telling you. I'm just not used to all of these rules and, truthfully, there are some that I just can't abide by because I don't believe in them.'

Effie bowed slightly. 'I have prepared for your morning toilette and found a crinoline in one of your trunks.'

Caged crinolines were the rage beneath the fashionable wide skirts, but she'd only worn one once, to an evening event. It had been cumbersome and had been nearly impossible to sit while wearing the wired contraption. She much preferred a layered petticoat, which she was already wearing, but Annabelle chose to hold her silence on that. Unfortunately, she couldn't help the sigh that escaped.

'I apologise, my lady,' Effie said quietly. 'It was my wish for you to make a good impression.'

'That's all right,' Annabelle said, although she had no worries about making a good impression because she had no plans of staying here. However, considering she was unfamiliar with her location, she would need assistance to leave, get to the sea and on to a ship to sail her home, so perhaps she should attempt to make a good impression to gain an ally. Of course, she'd have to figure out who that ally might be first. She had no doubt that the old Earl had ordered Effie to stay with her to keep her from escaping.

It appeared that Effie had discovered how to

move about the house because they took a different route and a different set of stairs, but managed to end up in the same bedroom that she'd slept in last night. Annabelle made a mental note of every turn by choosing an object that stood out. A beautifully framed painting or intricate sconce or highly polished hall table holding a lovely vase of flowers.

She would need to learn the layout of the house and the grounds, and the horses in the stable. One of the horses would be needed for her escape. Though her grandfather wanted her to be an imposter, it would be profitable for Drew if she wasn't.

Although he was far younger than she'd expected and rather likeable, as well as handsome, none of that would make her marry him. After knowing her mother's experience of marrying a man not of her choosing, she fully understood why her mother didn't want that to happen to her. There could never be love in a marriage like that and love was important to her. She'd known it her entire life and couldn't imagine living without it.

She and Effie had barely entered the room, which truly was luxurious with its canopied bed, thick carpets laid out on the floor, a large brick fireplace and a lovely sitting area with two light blue upholstered chairs near the tall windows filling the room with light, when a young woman entered.

Her long brown hair was neatly plaited and, as she curtsied, she introduced herself as Rosemary and stated she had been assigned to be Annabelle's personal maid.

While Annabelle was preparing her protest, Effie took charge, flying around like a mother duck frantically gathering her ducklings.

Within moments, Annabelle found herself in a chair before the tall, ornate mirror with Rosemary brushing her hair. 'There is no need for me to change my dress,' she told Effie, who was digging through the trunks she'd brought from America. 'The one I'm wearing is perfectly fine.' The wide skirt of the yellow gown was covered with tiny embroidered white flowers, while the solid yellow bodice was decorated with white lace, including the high collar and cuffs at the wrists. The skirt had a white lace overlay in the back that was enhanced by the bustle tied around her waist. It was a lovely dress, one that she'd purchased this spring for bright summer days. She'd chosen it this morning because the sun had been shining and because the chiffon had travelled well and hadn't needed ironing.

Seeing how Effie bowed her head, Annabelle once again felt a wave of guilt at how hard Effie was simply trying to do as she'd been trained. 'Breakfast will be served shortly,' Annabelle said. 'And we don't want to keep anyone waiting.'

'Yes, my lady,' Effie said.

Annabelle's attention returned to the mirror and she watched Rosemary swiftly braid one side of her hair, then coil it with the other side that she'd already braided. With the use of pins and yellow ribbons, the young woman created a plaited chignon that was far more elaborate and becoming than any hairstyle Annabelle had ever created for herself. 'You are very talented, Rosemary.'

'Thank you, my lady. My mother taught me. She was once a lady's maid.'

'Once?'

'Yes, my lady. When she was very young. Before she married my father. She works here now, overseeing the kitchen and household, and my father oversees the stable and grounds.'

'How old are you?'

'Seventeen.' Rosemary stepped back and bowed slightly. 'It will be an honour to be your maid.'

Annabelle twisted left and right to see as much of her hair as possible. The way the yellow ribbon was plaited and twisted into the design was truly lovely. Standing, she smiled brightly. 'If you were to become my maid, there would be one rule.'

'Yes, my lady, whatever you wish.'

'That you do not call me "my lady". My name is Annabelle.' She waved a hand towards the older woman as she continued, 'And this is my companion, Effie.'

Drew drummed the tips of his fingers on the arm of his chair while he sat at the table awaiting the arrival of his guest. Lady Annabelle Fredrickson was an intriguing woman. A beautiful woman and not what he had expected. She had none of her grandfather's superior attitude and that left Drew wondering if she really was an imposter. The only way for him to know for sure was for him to engage in his own investigation. He wasn't about to be trapped, not into a marriage or anything else.

Drew gestured for Donald to approach the table and quietly requested a message be sent to Roger to visit Mansfield this week.

As Donald left the room, Drew found himself staring at the commissioned painting of Champion in his prime, standing on a knoll not far from the house. There had been a time that, as a child, he'd thought his father loved that horse more than he'd loved him, because Champion always went with his father, while he'd been forced to stay here, home alone.

Not fully alone. The house had always been fully staffed, including nursemaids and later tutors, all of whom he'd known better than he'd known his father. Yet, his father had been the one he'd loved. The one he'd ached to see. That ache had eventually turned into a hardness that not even death had softened. He'd learned of his father's death from Prince Albert, who had sent a royal carriage to the school he'd been attending to transport him to Buckingham Palace on a cold winter's day. Drew still remembered the ice on the lashes of the horses when they'd arrived at the Palace after the long, cold ride.

He'd been sixteen and had known such a summons would not bear good news. He'd been right. There had been another assassination attempt. Once again, his father had saved the life of the Queen and the Prince, but in doing so, he'd taken a bullet meant for the royals. A bullet that had ended his life.

Reginald Andrew Barkly had been a childhood friend of Prince Albert's, and that friendship had continued onward, securing a position as a member of the royal guard after Albert had married Victoria. Years later, after singlehandedly saving Albert from an assassination attempt and capturing the shooter, his father had become the Duke of Mansfield, bestowed by the Queen for saving her beloved husband.

Upon his father's death, Drew had been bequeathed the title and holdings, and it was widely expected that he'd carry on the lineage, producing a son who would one day hold the title.

Movement near the doorway caught his attention. Drew stood and forced the air to not lock in his lungs as she entered the room. Her hair had been braided and pinned in an intricate design, which looked lovely on her, but her beauty wasn't within her hair, or even the yellow dress. She had clearly refused to change, despite her companion's likely insistence, and he liked her fortitude. Many women acted helpless, as if that made them more attractive. It didn't. To him, it made them appear weak and that was not a quality that inspired him in any way.

'I hope I did not keep you waiting,' Anabelle said, the hem of her wide skirt swishing as she crossed the room.

'You did not,' he lied, adding only to himself that to most men the wait would have been worth it. She was striking. But he was not most men and, striking or not, he would prefer he was not stuck playing host, or anything else.

Donald followed her to the table and held her chair.

She thanked the servant for his assistance as she took her seat and then said, 'I believe I did keep you waiting and I apologise.'

With a nod to Donald to serve the meal, Drew sat.

'Would you prefer to have our conversation while we eat, or afterwards?' she asked after Donald had poured them each a cup of tea and exited.

'Whichever you prefer,' Drew replied.

'I would like to get it over with as soon as possible.' She laid her napkin on her lap. 'Because I believe it's best for you to know right away that I will not marry you.'

Her bluntness didn't surprise him, nor did the seriousness of her gaze. She wasn't afraid to let her opinions be known and he appreciated that.

'I'm sure you are a fine person,' she continued, 'and will some day make someone a fine husband. I'm just not interested in marriage. To you or to anyone else.'

'I'm sure you'll make someone a fine wife,' he replied, biting the inside of his cheek at her belief that a betrothal could be cancelled so easily. It wasn't humorous and he felt the same way about marriage, but her innocence, or perhaps stubbornness, was entertaining.

'Perhaps some day, but not at this time. I have things I must see to first and, when I do marry, it will be to a common man, not a titled man from the peerage.'

Drew could feel her disgust, but was saved from having to respond as the door opened. He waited until plates of eggs, sausage, devilled kidneys, black pudding and bread placed before them and the servants had left the room, before asking, 'What things must you see to?'

'My family, our home, our livelihood.'

'Here or in America?'

She frowned while chewing and then swallowing. 'America, of course. I shall return as soon as possible.'

'How?'

'By whatever means I must.'

Her confidence hadn't wavered an iota in her response and he wondered if she already had a plan in place. 'What about your family here?'

'An old man who hates me?' She shook her head. 'He hopes I am an imposter.'

Drew hid his surprise and took a sip of tea before asking, 'He told you that?'

'No. He called me rude, insufferable and self-ish, claimed he couldn't stand the sound of my voice and sent me here.' She cut off a slender piece of sausage. 'Effie told me he hopes I'm an imposter and that you most likely hope I'm not, since a marriage would be profitable for you. I can understand that, but I will not abide by some backwoods custom that I do not believe it.'

Her backwoods custom comment made him grin even while he maintained his anger at how the Earl had insulted her. Although he did agree with her, he didn't have the freedom to admit that. 'The custom you speak of has been beneficial for families for centuries.'

'Beneficial for families, but what about individuals? It certainly wasn't beneficial for my mother, or pleasant.'

The stories he'd heard said as much, yet he knew she couldn't remember her father. She'd been a baby when they'd left. 'Your mother told you she wasn't happy with your father?'

'The Duke of Compton? No.' She took a sip of tea. 'I learned about him and her unhappiness from her diary.'

'When did she pass away?'

She sighed softly. 'Eight years ago. I was twelve. She was in bed when I came home from school one day, with a fever, a cough. My fath— My stepfather said she'd get better soon, but within a few days she was gone.'

'I'm sorry for your loss,' he said sincerely.

'Thank you.'

They each ate a few bites in the silence that followed, before he asked, 'Is that when you read her diary?'

'No. I didn't know there was a diary until I'd been...' She sighed heavily. 'Until I was on the ship, on my way here.'

That did surprise him, but he concealed it. 'Was that the first time you learned you were the daughter of a duke?'

'Yes, and that I was being sent to live with a grandfather I'd never known existed.' Her smile was that of mockery. 'Who immediately sent me here, to live with a man he promised I would marry.'

'Your grandfather didn't initiate the betrothal between us. Your father did, along with my father.' He was too young to remember, but had been told the story of how the Duke of Compton had been sorely disappointed by the birth of a daughter and how his father had needed to expand the coal mine to make it profitable.

'How old are you?' she asked.

'Twenty-six. How old are you?'

'Twenty.'

She ate a few more bites of food, then took a sip of tea. As she set her cup on the saucer, she looked at him quizzically. 'Why does the Earl of Westerdownes want me to be an imposter? What does it matter to him?'

He leaned back in his chair. 'When the Duke of Compton died—shortly after your mother left—all of his unentailed holdings went into the care of the Earl of Westerdownes until your mother and you returned.'

'So that's the inheritance he thinks I'm after.' She crossed her arms. 'And that's why you want to marry me.'

It wasn't a question, merely a statement. Though a marriage to her might benefit him, the benefits to others of him not marrying her were greater. 'I don't want to marry you. No more than you want to marry me.'

Chapter Four

Annabelle wondered if she should be insulted. She wasn't. In fact, she was more relieved than anything. However, she was also confused. 'Then why did you agree to let me come here?'

'Because we are betrothed and, because of that, the success of my coal mine is dependent upon your grandfather.'

His expression had grown serious. Very serious. His brows were furrowed and his lips had become a firm line.

'How so?' she asked.

'Our betrothal created a kind of partnership of the coal mine on Mansfield. A major shaft of our mine extends beneath the Compton property you've inherited. The original agreement stated all proceeds of your half of the venture would be put into a trust, to be paid out upon our marriage. However, when the Earl of Westerdownes began overseeing the investments, he demanded and was granted royalty payments in his name. Because of that, I've been able to use his payments in reports to Parliament as to the success of the mine. I must add that although the contract still directed that all of those payments were to be put in the trust, I can't guarantee that happened.'

'You don't believe he has done that, do you?'

The way he pinched his lips said he wasn't willing to answer.

She leaned an elbow on the table and rested her chin on her hand. 'The truth won't hurt my feelings. I'd actually prefer to know the truth, good, bad or indifferent.'

'The truth is, I don't know. I've never looked into it.'

'Why?'

'Because it didn't matter.'

Contemplating that for a moment, she asked, 'Because you never thought I'd return to England.'

A hint of grin curled the edges of his lips and it made her want to smile.

'Truthfully? Yes,' he said.

'But if I did, you would ultimately receive the money my grandfather was supposed to be saving.'

He gave a slight nod.

'Why don't you want to marry me?' she asked. 'Are you in love with someone else?'

'No. I simply enjoy being a bachelor.'

She decided to ponder on that later and asked, 'Do you want me to be an imposter, too?'

'I want you to be who you are, whether that is Lady Annabelle Fredrickson or Annabelle Smith.'

A heavy weight settled inside her and she sat back. 'So do I.'

He lifted a single brow. 'Meaning?'

She sighed. 'Meaning that I don't want to be Lady Annabelle Fredrickson. I've been Annabelle Smith my entire life and that is whom I want to continue to be.' The heaviness inside her grew. 'But how can I when the man I thought was my father isn't my father? He's my stepfather.' The fact that Arlo had sent her away at a point in their lives when they needed each other more than ever still hurt so badly.

'Well, if it well help, during your stay here, everyone is to believe you are Annabelle Smith, from America and simply visiting for a time.'

She stared at him, trying to read his face, but it was rather expressionless. 'They are?'

'Yes.'

'Why?'

A hint of surprise crossed his face before he hid it. 'I thought you knew.'

'You mean about my grandfather trying to prove if I'm an imposter or not?'

'Yes. He doesn't want anyone to know that you're in England until he can prove if you are his granddaughter.'

A flash of happiness filled her so quickly it reached her lips before she could stop them from smiling. 'That's right, he doesn't. Thank you!'

'You're welcome. It appears that has made you happy,' he said.

'Yes, it does. I much prefer being Annabelle Smith. An untitled American.' Pushing her chair back, she said, 'If you will excuse me, I need to speak with my companion.'

He stood at the same time she did and gave a slight nod.

Feeling happier than she had for some time, she nearly floated across the room and out through the door. Being an American trying to get back home would be a lot easier than Lady Annabelle Fredrickson trying to escape to America. She didn't know exactly how she would make it happen, but she would do anything to return home.

Furthermore, now she had a solid reason why Effie should not call her 'my lady' and why the other woman didn't need to worry about her following rules she didn't believe in.

Drew forced himself to not let his mind focus on Annabelle, but once he was on Fellow's back, riding across the knolls covered with the green grass of summer, it was impossible to think of anything else. Most women inspired to become a lady, a titled woman of the peerage, yet she wanted to be nothing more than a southern belle. She was a very fetching one and that accent of hers lived in his mind, making him smile at random moments.

Empathy filled him at times, too. Her discovering that her mother had been a duchess and that the man she'd thought was her father wasn't her father had been shocking. Traumatic. He'd seen that on her face.

He'd told her the truth, that he wanted her to be who she was, but that didn't ease anything inside him. Probably because he knew the truth. She was the long-lost Duchess's daughter and his betrothed.

His gut told him so.

It also told him that Westerdownes would never allow her to be his granddaughter. In his younger years, the Earl had been a rounder and gambler. He had squandered any inherited money and had literally sold his daughter to the highest bidder to maintain his lifestyle.

A new bout of anger at the Earl grew inside Drew. The old man would likely have done the same thing to his granddaughter, but the Duke and his father had made their contract first, beating the Earl to it. However, that had worked in Westerdownes's favour for years.

It had worked in his own favour for years, too. The changes he'd already made at the mine, and those he was intent upon making, were considered radical because they didn't come without expense. However, they were also proving to be good investments and Westerdownes's royalty payments had continued to go up. No one could deny that the changes haven't been profitable.

That would change if it was proven that Annabelle was Westerdownes's granddaughter, Drew's betrothed. He'd be forced to marry her and miners across the country would be the ones to suffer because without profit proof, Parliament wouldn't act as quickly to support his changes nationwide.

There were other worries, too.

Fellow must have felt the shiver that rippled through Drew, because the horse paused in his steps long enough to give himself a good shake.

Drew couldn't do the same. No amount of shaking would clear it away his thoughts.

Annabelle didn't want anything from her grandfather and wanted to return to America. If she did, things would go on as they were, but her not inheriting what was rightfully hers was far from right or fair.

When—and it would be when, not if—she was proven to be his granddaughter, Westerdownes would lose nearly everything he had. The only way he wouldn't would be for the betrothal to be voided. Then Westerdownes could go on overseeing her assets. However, the betrothal couldn't be voided very easily. The only sure way was a death.

His or hers.

Drew urged Fellow into a faster gait, then into a gallop as that thought took a stronger hold in his mind. The old Earl was stubborn and wasn't going to give up the hold he had on her funds and properties easily. If at all. That was disconcerting.

It was all very disturbing and a mess he wished he wasn't caught up in. He was, though—had been for years.

His arrival at the coal mine was noticed as soon as Fellow topped the knoll and by the time they stopped near the main building, Gunner Erickson was standing on the steps, waiting.

'Good day,' the tall, blond man, who was built like the Norse God of Thunder, said while pulling off the thick stocking cap covering his mass of curls. Winter or summer, the man wore the knitted hat.

'Good day to you,' Drew replied while leaving the saddle and then slipped Fellow's reins around the post. 'Has the baby arrived yet?'

Gunner appeared to grow another two inches and his smile was as bright as the sun. 'Naw, my Lena says we have a few weeks yet.'

Drew shook Gunner's hand while slapping his massive shoulder. The couple was anxiously awaiting the arrival of their second child. Their first had been a little girl, who was now about four or so. 'How is Lena doing?'

'Good. Good.' Gunner's cheeks took on a rosy glow. 'She's a good woman, that Lena of mine.'

'That she is,' Drew agreed. He'd also agree that Gunner was a good man. The best overseer he'd ever hope to have working the mine. 'And Caroline? What does she think of having a baby brother or sister soon?'

Gunner chuckled deeply. 'She is tickled pink.'

'Good to hear. If any of you need anything, you just send word to the house.'

'Thank you,' Gunner replied as he turned and opened the door for the mine office.

Drew followed the man inside. Gunner had worked for him for over five years and knew the workings of the coal mine inside and out.

'Last month's report looked good.' As did every month and Drew attributed that success to his overseer.

'Yah, the men are on a good vein.' Gunner poured two cups of coffee.

Drew took one of the cups as he crossed the large room to enter the smaller one that hosted the office he used while visiting the mine. Gunner followed and they both sat in the sturdy wooden chairs.

'Any concerns or needs I should know about?' Drew asked. Gunner would have sent word if there had been, but it was the way they always started their discussions about the overall operation.

'Naw.' Gunner set his cup on the desk and leaned back in his chair. 'Just that we need workers, like always. I hired two men last week and they are working out.'

'I've spread the word,' Drew said. 'Put out some advertisements.' Parliament had passed an act that forbade women and girls, as well as boys under the age of ten, from working underground in the mine shafts. Drew not only completely agreed with the act, he believed a mine was no place for women or children of any age to be working. He'd made sure that Gunner agreed with him before he'd hired him. There were other mine owners and overseers who didn't agree and, just last month, he'd used the reports from his mine to prove to Parliament that mining could be successful while following the act.

He and Gunner spent the better part of an hour going over the operation before Drew took a full tour of the mine, updating himself since he'd been in London the past month. He'd hated it, but due to his status, being in town during at least a portion of the Season was expected.

Hours later, when he took his leave, rather than head back to his home, Drew rode in the opposite direction, on to the Compton land left to Annabelle.

The manor home hadn't been occupied since the old Duke had died and, with the Earl of Westerdownes overseeing its upkeep, it had fallen into disarray. The gardens were non-existent, merely weeds, and the building's bricks were crumbling on the steps, the shutters and doors rotting away. The last time he'd ridden past the place, there had been signs of squatters. Not the human kind, but rodents, birds, other wildlife.

He'd discussed the state of the property with Westerdownes more than once, but as with most other topics, it hadn't done any good, even when he'd pointed out the decline in property value. Westerdownes wasn't one to invest in anything except his own pockets.

Drew scowled as he brought Fellow to a stop near the stone and brick wall that surrounded the manor home. The wall was covered in vines and moss and the double metal gate was swung open, hanging off-kilter due to broken hinges.

He urged Fellow forward, through the opening, where the grass and weeds had been tamped down, whether by man or animal was impossible to tell. Westerdownes had long ago removed anything of value, but that wouldn't stop people from scavenging whatever wasn't nailed down.

Near the massive steps of the front door, he climbed out of the saddle and tethered Fellow to a branch of an overgrown bush. If the door had been locked, it had long ago been picked because it swung open as soon as he touched the knob.

The inside was dark and dank and the air felt oppressive as he pushed the door all the way open. The scurrying of mice echoed in the corners as he walked inside. The same vines that had overtaken the stone fence had climbed high on the house, covering the windows and filtering the amount of sunlight that could enter the home.

Drew had never ventured inside the house before and had no idea why he was here now, other than a deep sense of curiosity. Even while at the mine, his mind had been on Annabelle and the complications that her arrival had caused. There probably wasn't anything here that would prove her identity, yet he would look around.

It was a large home and clearly showing its age and state of decline.

He roamed through the lower floor, finding one picked-clean room after another, then made his way up a set of stairs to the next floor. More sunlight filtered into the rooms there, but again, they were empty.

Making his way up to the final floor, he walked into the attic area, where there were piles of broken furniture and other such rubbish.

There were other areas he could explore, but he'd seen enough. Though they had been neighbours, he'd never met the Duke or the Duchess. He'd been a small child when the Duchess had left, taking her infant daughter with her, and the Duke had died the following year.

Back in the saddle, Drew paused before leaving, staring at the manor home and knowing one thing for certain.

No part of this was going to end well.

Annabelle lifted a finger and shook her head at Effie and how the woman had once again called her my lady. 'Annabelle, simply Annabelle.'

Effie bowed her head.

Annabelle refused to feel guilty, she felt too light inside and that felt good. Effie had to treat her like Annabelle Smith, an American, and that felt like a win. As though she had control of something.

Another reason she felt so light inside was because Drew didn't want to get married, either. No one could force two people to get married if neither of them wanted to, therefore, she could put all of her focus on getting home and now was the perfect time to start. 'I'm merely going outside to get some fresh air,' she told Effie on her way to the door.

She left the bedroom and, like Hansel and Gretel—although she hadn't left breadcrumbs—she followed the trail of clues she'd memorised to find her way back downstairs and to the front door. The entire home was lovelier than any she'd ever seen. From the highly polished floors, covered at times with thick, colourful carpets, to the high, decorative ceilings that hosted twinkling chandeliers, it reminded her of a storybook palace.

It even smelled lovely, due to the huge vases of flowers and the use of lemon oil that made the wood shine in the sunlight.

On her way to the stable, she had to admit that Drew's manor home was in great contrast to the home she'd arrived at in London.

The parakeets were still in the stable, sitting side by side in the rafters, and the happiness inside her grew a bit more. She whistled softly and smiled at how they cocked their heads as if listening. Whistling again, she walked towards the stalls to examine the horses.

The first stall was empty, but the following five held magnificent-looking animals. Well cared for and well bred. She took the time to say hello to each horse and felt an immediate connection to a pretty black and white one but when she moved on to the final stall, her breath caught at the sight of the large black horse.

'I recognise you,' she whispered. 'From the picture in the dining room.' He was still a gorgeous animal, even with his age showing in his eyes and by the grey hair around his nose and lips.

The horse stayed back, out of reach, and there was something off about his stance.

Annabelle rested her arms on the top rail of the stall and set her chin on her hands. 'You're hurting, aren't you, old boy?' she asked the horse.

He shifted his stance slightly while flicking his tail and Annabelle flinched at the pain she knew he was experiencing. Seeing anyone, animal or human, in distress and not helping had never been an option for her. 'I'll be back,' she told the horse. 'With something that will help. I promise.'

She hurried out of the stables and made her way around the large brick wall to where she'd noticed a vegetable garden from her bedroom window. Mint grew wild back home and she was sure she'd seen a patch of it near the garden.

Hopefully, it was a large patch. She would need a lot.

It would take a couple of days to create a penetrating ointment, but a warm mint tea rubbed on his legs could offer the horse some relief until the ointment was cured.

Excitement filled her at the amount of mint she discovered. She picked all she could carry, then found a back door that led directly to the kitchen.

There she met Rosemary's mother, a lovely,

soft spoken woman named Kate, who was more than willing to help gather the additional items Annabelle needed as she explained that she wanted to help a horse.

'That is Champion,' Kate said. 'The first Duke's horse.'

'The first Duke…as in Drew's father?' Annabelle asked.

'Yes. Finnegan, my husband, has been very worried about Champion. He's old, but other than his hooves hurting, he's in good health.'

'It's not his hooves,' Annabelle replied while chopping mint. 'It's his legs, his joints. My best friend's father owns a livery back home and I've helped him with many horses. The mint will give Champion enough relief that he'll be willing to walk, and the more he walks, the less stiff he'll be.'

'He's stubborn. Finnegan has tried making him walk, but Champion refuses.'

Annabelle didn't want to interfere, but knew she could help Champion. 'Where is your husband? I would like to let him know what I plan on doing.'

'Outside somewhere,' Kate replied while stirring the lard she was melting. 'He takes care of all the animals. I'll go find him after this lard is melted.'

'Thank you.' Annabelle dropped several handfuls of the chopped mint into a kettle of steaming water. 'I assure you I wouldn't do anything to hurt Champion.'

'I can tell that. Finnegan and the Duke have been worried about Champion.' Kate's smile was soft and sincere. 'I'm sure they will both appreciate if you can help him.'

'I know I can help him. A week from now, he'll be a different horse.' A wave of something Annabelle couldn't quite define washed over her as she realised that she might not be here a week from now. Not if the plan she was still laying out in her mind worked. She would just have to explain to Finnegan all that needed to be done.

'Your mother allowed you to help this stable man you mentioned?' Kate asked.

A new wave washed over Annabelle. One of happiness. Some people said that she had the run of the town, but that wasn't completely true. 'My mother and father'—whether he was only her stepfather or not, Arlo would always be her father in her mind—'allowed me to be free.' She giggled to herself at a prominent memory. 'As long as I wasn't misbehaving.'

'Did that happen?' Kate asked, raising a brow.

'Not on purpose, but mischief did seem to find me at times.'

Kate removed the pot of melted lard off the stove. 'The smile on your face makes me want to know more.'

'Well,' Annabelle said while dropping handfuls of chopped mint into the melted lard, 'I've always been fond of animals and when I was about five, I found a small black and white animal in our yard. My mother didn't know what it was, but said I could keep it because it was a baby that must have got separated from its mother. When my father came home he informed us that it was a skunk.'

'What is a skunk?'

'It's a rodent that is quite cute and can be friendly, but it also has the ability to spray a very pungent scent that is extremely difficult to get rid of.' Recalling the entire event made her grimace. 'The baby didn't spray, but the mother did when she came looking for her baby. My father had to replace the wood on our front porch because, even after several scrubbings, it still smelled like skunk.'

'The smell was that bad?' Kate asked.

'Yes, it was.' Annabelle stirred the mint into the melted lard. She could go on about all the other wild animals she'd acquired over the years, but Champion was the animal she was focused on now. 'Once this cools a bit, I'll need to pour it in a jar with a tight-fitting lid and every day add more mint to it.'

'I have plenty of jars,' Kate answered, crossing the room to a large cabinet. 'Will you need one for the water, too?'

Annabelle removed that kettle from the stove and set it on the worktable to steep. 'No, the pot it's in is fine. I plan on putting it on Champion as soon as it cools enough. That's what I needed the old sheet for. I need to cut it in strips to wrap around his legs.'

Kate had collected the sheet earlier, while the lard had been melting, and now set a large jar on the worktable. 'I'll get the cutting shears.'

Within a few minutes, the sheet was cut and they both left the kitchen. Kate went to find her husband while Annabelle carried the kettle full of mint tea and several strips of cloth to the stables.

She set the pot of tea on the floor near Champion's stall. 'I'm back,' she told the horse. 'Just like I promised. Within a few days, you are going to feel so much better.'

The horse looked at her as if questioning her statement.

'That's a promise, too, cross my heart,' she said while taking the lid off the kettle. 'Smell that? It's mint.' She continued talking to the horse as she put the strips in the tea to soak, telling him that she had done this many times in the past and it always worked.

Whether it was her talking or interest in what she was doing, Champion stepped closer to the front of the stall. His movements were so stiff and uneven the desire to help him increased.

'Hello, miss,' the groom greeted her while entering the stable. 'Kate says you wanted to see me about Champion.'

Annabelle stood. 'Yes, I do. I couldn't help but notice he's in pain.' She didn't want Finnegan to think she was suggesting that he wasn't taking good care of the horse. 'I helped a livery owner in my home with horses that were stiff and sore from sea voyages by putting mint ointment on their legs. It made them feel better and I believe it will help Champion, too.'

'That's very kind of you, miss, but it's his hooves that are bothering him.'

The groom appeared sympathetic, but his statement was steadfast, as if he was certain of his assessment. 'Please, feel free to call me Annabelle and I could be wrong.' She gestured towards the strips of cloth soaking in the mint tea. 'But I would still like to wrap his legs if you wouldn't mind. I truly believe it will give him some relief.'

Middle aged, with dark hair and kind green eyes surrounded by wrinkles, the groom looked at her as if not sure what to do.

'Please?' she asked, folding her hands beneath her chin. 'It won't hurt him, I promise. It's just mint tea.'

He glanced around and, afraid he was about to say no, she continued with the truth since pleading didn't seem to work. 'I have to be honest. I'm going to wrap his legs, with or without your approval. And I'm going to rub him down with the ointment once it's cured because it will help him. I'm certain of that and can't stand the idea of him being in pain and me not doing something about it.'

Finnegan scratched the side of his head as he grinned. 'All right, miss—Annabelle. I'll help you wrap his legs. The Duke's wish is for Champion to be as comfortable as possible in his old age.'

Happiness filled her and she couldn't stop herself from giving Finnegan a quick hug. 'Thank you. Thank you so very much. The mint ointment that I'm making will help more than this tea, but it will be a few days before it will be ready.'

As Finnegan opened the stall door, she went on to explain how they should wrap Champion's legs from above the knee all the way to the hooves, and do so several times a day.

'It's kind of you to want to help,' Finnegan said, as they each wrapped a front leg. 'I'm sure the Duke will appreciate it.'

She wasn't doing this for Drew, she was doing it for Champion and said so. 'I hope Champion appreciates it. He's the one hurting. How long has he been like this?'

'A few weeks. It started with a stone bruise, but he acts as if it hasn't healed, refusing to walk.'

'He's made himself stiff and sore by not moving,' she surmised. 'And now any movement causes pain.' She tied off a bandage near Champion's hoof and checked that it was secure all the way up to the top of his leg before she collected another rag from the still-warm tea and moved to his back leg. 'We are going to have to make him walk.'

'He's stubborn,' Finnegan said. 'If he doesn't want to move, no one can make him.'

'I can,' she said, full of confidence.

Chapter Five

Drew noticed the wrappings on Champion's legs as soon as he entered the stable and questioned them as Finnegan appeared and took a hold of Fellow's reins.

'It was the young miss, Your Grace,' Finnegan replied, leading Fellow towards his stall. 'She insisted upon wrapping his legs with rags soaked in warm water and chopped mint.'

Mint. That's what he'd smelled upon entering the stable. Drew walked over to Champion's stall. They were both worried about the horse and his sore feet, but allowing someone else to doctor any of his horses was quite out of the ordinary for Finnegan. 'Why?'

'She's convinced it will make him feel better,' Finnegan answered.

'Yes, I am.' Carrying a large kettle by the handle, Annabelle walked into the stable. 'I've seen it before. Many times.'

'Have you?' Drew asked.

'Yes, I have,' she replied. 'It's time to put new wraps on. The others must be completely dry by now.'

'I'll help you, miss—Annabelle, as soon as I've finished taking care of Fellow,' Finnegan offered.

Drew glanced at the groom. The fact Finnegan was going along with whatever was happening made him need to know more. He unlatched the gate on Champion's stall. 'I'll help her.'

Annabelle's brows arched as she walked forward. 'I don't need any help.'

'I want to help.' He pushed open the gate, held it for her to enter.

'Why?'

She'd stepped closer and he reached down, taking hold of the kettle. 'Because I'm curious to know what you've seen and how a kettle of mint tea is the miracle cure.'

Releasing the kettle to his hold, she walked past him into the stable and laid a hand on Champion's back. 'Have you ever had sore muscles? Ones that ache with every step?'

'Yes.'

'And what do you about them?'

Once again enchanted by her accent and wondering if he'd ridden into his stable or entered a strange world where beautiful women took care of horses, Drew didn't have time to answer before she spoke again.

'You take a hot bath to relieve them,' she said. 'Don't you?'

'As a matter of fact, I do,' he replied. A hot bath could do wonders for sore muscles.

'Champion can't soak in a hot tub, so we are wrapping his legs with warm tea instead.'

In some strange way, perhaps her way, that made sense. 'What about the mint?'

She grasped the handle of the pot, took it from him and lifted the lid. 'Mint is refreshing.' Using the lid, she fanned the aroma-filled steam at him.

Drew bit the inside of his cheek to keep a smile at bay. Finnegan hadn't been able to say no to her idea any more than he could. 'It is refreshing,' he agreed.

She knelt, set the pot on the floor and began untying a knot in the strips of cloth near one of Champion's front legs. 'I'm making a mint ointment that will help more than the tea, but it will take a few days to cure.'

He walked around to the other front leg and followed suit, untied the knot and unwound the cloth from Champion's leg.

She slid the pot closer to him and he followed her instructions.

'What will you do with the ointment?' he asked while wrapping.

'The same thing we are doing with the tea, but without the strips.'

'Who taught you about this?'

'The livery stable owner back home.' Done with rewrapping the front leg, she moved to Champion's hind leg. 'Horses getting off the ships were often stiff and sore from their voyage and those who cared about their animals would take my father's advice and have them seen to by Homer.'

'And you.'

'Yes, I helped him often.'

He knew enough about America and knew enough Americans to know a young woman wasn't often hired to work at a livery. Especially not the daughter of a duchess. Perhaps Westerdownes had reason to be suspicious.

He moved to Champion's hind leg and repeated the process. 'Your mother allowed you to work at the livery?'

'I didn't start helping Homer until after my mother had died. Clara, my best friend, is Homer's daughter and I would often go to their house after school.'

'Clara helps her father in the stable, too?'

'No. She never cared much for horses and had household chores to do as her mother passed away before mine. I'd help her father while she did her chores and then we had time to play before I had to go home. Of course, that was years ago, before Clara got married. Homer needed my help even more after that because he was all alone then.'

Her explanation was believable, but it, too, could simply be a made-up story.

'Once I start using the ointment, I'll expect him to walk more,' she said.

He huffed out a chuckle. 'Good luck. Champion is stubborn.'

'I'm aware of that. It's why he's so stiff and sore. The more Finnegan tried to make him move, the less he would.'

'That's true.' Finnegan had been practically pulling his hair out over Champion refusing to move. Done with the wrapping, Drew carried the used wrappings to her side of the horse.

'I'll take those,' she said, holding out a hand for the strips of cloth. 'I'll wash them and use them tomorrow.' Her smile grew. 'You'll be surprised by how well this works.'

He wasn't putting a lot of weight on mint tea, but she certainly was convinced. Since he was a head taller than her, she had her head tilted back, looking up at him, and her eyes were sparkling as brightly as they had been this morning when she'd been looking at the budgies. For her sake—and for Champion's—he hoped the mint did work. Having worked hard for years, the horse had long ago earned a few years of quiet country living.

Rather than handing her the strips of cloth, he took hers and the kettle. 'I'll carry this into the house for you.'

'Thank you. Did you have a nice ride?'

'I did.' He waited for her to exit the stall gate that Finnegan opened for them. 'I visited the mine.'

'What sort of mine?'

'Coal.'

'There is a coal mine near Hampton, back home.'

He considered telling her that she was half-owner in the mine, but the window of opportunity closed when she asked about the mare in the stall next to Champion's.

'That is Millie,' he explained. 'She's a very even-tempered mare that guests often ride.'

'Guests?'

He grinned at the excitement in her voice.

'Yes. You may ride her if you wish. Just let Finnegan know and he'll saddle her for you.'

Annabelle was elated with the permission to ride the mare and took advantage of that after wrapping Champion's legs for the third time later that evening. The most difficult part of the ride had been convincing Finnegan that she wanted a regular saddle, not a side saddle. She'd finally got her way, but even in that, the saddle was far different from the horned saddles she'd grown up using. It had also taken her a fair amount of time to convince Finnegan that he didn't need to accompany her. He'd agreed only after she'd promised to not let the manor house out of her view.

Keeping her promise wasn't difficult. The house was so large she would have had to ride miles before it would slip from her view. Miles was not what she needed. Just a short ride would let her know if Millie would be the horse to start her journey home. The mare's gait was even and smooth, but it was the mare's stamina that was of concern. Like Champion, it appeared as if the mare was in need of exercise to build up the ability to travel the distance that would be needed to get to the ocean and a ship that would take her home.

Annabelle let Millie set the pace while ex-

ploring the lay of the land and memorising land
markers, much like she had done inside the
house. A lone tree, large rock, or softly rolling
hill covered in green clover all gave her markers that she'd be able to use during future rides
to build Millie's strength and stamina.

By the time they passed a particular tree she'd
noted upon leaving the stable, the sun was low
in the sky and Annabelle was contemplating the
day, the people she'd met and the amount of time
it might take before Millie would be up for starting her journey home. Both Kate and Finnegan
could be used to assist her in her journey. She
was sure of that. They'd both been very accom-
modating.

Donald was nice, but he was committed to
Drew, that was evident in his every move, and
for Drew himself, she was genuinely confused.
He made her feel comfortable, but he was a duke
and the person who had the most to lose by her
leaving. Although he claimed to not want marriage, she knew it would greatly benefit him and
men—all men—took advantage of opportunities
like that. Therefore, she wasn't convinced that he
was telling her the truth about not wanting marriage, which meant she couldn't trust him or en-
list him to aid her return home.

That was going to make receiving help from

Kate and Finnegan harder, too, because like Donald they were very committed to Drew.

Fiddlesticks! It was all so frustrating. Being in a foreign country when she was needed at home. So many men had already left Hampton, joining regiments to fight for both sides of the stars and stripes, and that had left many women needing help. Clara had been beside herself when Mark had left. She'd never liked animals and was having to take care of their small farm by herself. Others needed help, too. The Parson and Mrs Carmichael, Homer, of course, and her father. He was most likely running himself ragged with having to take care of the shipping ledgers by himself.

She truly needed to get home as soon as possible.

With that thought, she nudged Millie into a faster gait.

As she rode past the final grove of trees behind the stable, the muted light of the dusky sky made the figure running towards her look ghostly. She blinked to clear her vision and confirmed it wasn't a ghost.

It was Effie, running towards her.

'Oh, my lady, thank goodness nothing dreadful happened to you.'

Annabelle brought Millie to a halt. 'Why would you think that?'

'You went riding alone and—' Effie bit her lips together and bowed her head.

Annabelle huffed out a sigh. She wasn't used to being such a disappointment to someone. Effie hadn't said that, of course, but Annabelle gathered it from the way Effie clammed up all the time and she knew that was because of the strict class system. A servant had to know their place. Annabelle would rather Effie just said something so she could argue her point rather than feeling guilty each time Effie bowed her head. 'I have never ridden using a side saddle and I'm used to riding alone. I enjoy it.'

'Yes, miss,' Effie said, head still bowed.

Annabelle climbed off the horse. 'Oh, Effie. I wish we could be friends. I know you want me to behave like a lady from England would and I don't like upsetting you, but I'm an American—the daughter of a merchant—and I will always be that.'

Effie nodded without lifting her head.

Searching for a way to make things easier on the older woman, Annabelle continued, 'Perhaps you could help me during my time here. Help me to not worry you so. What if I gave you my full permission to tell me what is expected?'

Effie lifted her gaze.

'You can tell me what is expected, and I'll try to abide by the rules that I can, with your help. Could you do that?'

Effie let out the first true smile that Annabelle had seen her make. 'Yes, miss, I'd be honoured.'

'Good.' Annabelle let out a sigh of relief and began walking Millie towards the stable. 'Is there anything I should know right now?'

'His Grace has been waiting dinner on you,' Effie said.

'Dinner? I already ate dinner.' Annabelle was referring to the sandwiches, fruit and cake she'd eaten before going out to wrap Champion's legs again. She had wondered why Drew hadn't eaten with her in the dining room, but considering he hadn't eaten the noon meal there either, assumed he partook of his evening meal somewhere else, too.

'That wasn't dinner, miss. That was afternoon tea.'

'Afternoon tea? It was supper time.'

Effie shrugged and nodded.

'Oh, goodness,' Annabelle muttered.

Finnegan appeared and as he took Millie's reins, Annabelle thanked him, then with Effie at her side, hurried to the house.

Minutes later, after she'd quickly washed her

hands and checked her image in a mirror to assure herself that her hair wasn't too dishevelled from her ride, Annabelle walked into the dining room and instantly wondered if she should have listened to Effie when the other woman had suggested that she might want to change her dress for dinner.

Annabelle had seen no need for that. Back home she wore the same dress all day. Furthermore, it was closer to bedtime than it was dinner time. However, Drew had changed his clothes into a fitted black and brown suit that went beyond all the Sunday best clothes she'd ever seen. To ease the butterflies that had taken flight, she smoothed the material of her dress over her stomach as she moved further into the room. 'It appears that I have kept you waiting for another meal. I do apologise. I was unaware that you were waiting on me.'

'How was your ride?' he asked from where he'd taken to his feet near the head of the table when she'd arrived in the doorway.

'Very nice, thank you,' she replied, hurrying across the room. 'Millie is just as you described. Very even-tempered and well mannered.' Donald was holding a chair for her and she flinched inwardly because both the servant and Drew were probably thinking that the mare had more manners than she did. 'I do apologise.' She included Donald in her apology with a sincere look as she took her seat. 'I'm usually not so rude. I wasn't aware that there would be another meal.'

'Another meal?' Drew asked, frowning slightly as he sat down.

'Yes.' She lifted her napkin off the table and set it on her lap. 'Did you not have sandwiches, fruit and cake earlier? There was far more than I could eat.' In fact, she'd felt guilty at the amount of food left on the table after she'd eaten her fill.

Drew grinned as he nodded to Donald who quietly left the room. 'That would be afternoon tea, not the evening meal.'

'That is what Effie said,' Annabelle admitted. 'I do apologise for keeping you waiting.'

He nodded. 'Apology accepted and I'm glad you enjoyed your ride.'

'Thank you, I did, and I promise it won't happen again.'

'You will not go riding again?'

He had a single brow lifted in question, but it was his grin that told her he was teasing. It was a fine grin, attractive, and made her smile. 'No, I will ride again. I meant I won't keep you waiting for me again.'

The door opened and Donald held it for two serving girls to enter the room, carrying massive trays that they quickly unloaded on the table that was set with a lace tablecloth, decorative white china with blue flowers, sparkling crystal glasses and a wide assortment of silver cutlery.

Annabelle couldn't hide her surprise at the variety of foods that continued to be set before them. After the massive amounts of foods that had been served at breakfast and lunch, she'd been more than satisfied with the sandwiches earlier. The idea of consuming enough food to be polite made her question how long she'd be able to fit in her clothes. Although there were no other place settings at the table, she asked, 'Is this all for just the two of us?'

'Are you not hungry?' he asked, while nodding at Donald.

She scanned the many dishes. 'Not that hungry.'

Donald had picked up a dish and, after placing some food on Drew's plate, carried the platter to her. She nodded at him, as Drew had done, and admitted, 'I'm not used to eating so much, or so often.'

'How many times a day are you used to eating?' he asked as Donald repeated another round with another dish.

'I would eat breakfast with my father before he left for work, lunch with Cecilia, and dinner with my father when he returned home from work.' Meals at home had always been plentiful, but there was normally only one variety of meat, whereas here there were several, along with various vegetables, puddings, breads, as well as a few things she didn't recognise that Donald continued to add to her plate.

'Not so different than here,' Drew said while picking up his knife and fork now that Donald was done serving. 'The habit of eating later in the evening became fashionable many years ago, which brought about the repast of afternoon tea. If you prefer, I can ask the cook to serve the evening meal earlier and bypass tea time.'

Following his lead, she picked up her knife and one of the forks beside her plate. 'No, please don't adjust your schedule on my account.'

'I rarely partake in afternoon tea, so it won't be much of an adjustment on my part.'

Concerned, she asked, 'Are you saying that you didn't eat sandwiches earlier? Why, you must be starving. Eat.' She waved a hand at him. 'Please. Eat. I am truly sorry to have kept you waiting.'

Right then and there she vowed to not be late to another meal.

She not only held to that for the next several days, she also grew to enjoy mealtimes with

Drew. He was an interesting man, intelligent, and their conversations were not only informative, but they were also fun, even silly at times. He told her all about England, and she told him about Hampton and the people there. Talking about her father and Cecilia, Clara and Homer, and many others, made her miss them terribly and worry how they were doing, but even in that, Drew helped. He'd ask her questions and soon they'd be laughing over something funny that had happened at one time or another back home.

He was very helpful when it came to Champion, too, always nearby when it had been time to rewrap the horse's legs and later rub him down with ointment, and he accompanied her in taking the horse for short walks—something both he and Finnegan were amazed about. She wasn't. She'd known she could get Champion to move. It just had taken a little coaxing.

Drew also accompanied her when she took Millie out for rides.

That's what they were doing this morning, her fifth day at his house, taking a slow ride across the countryside because Champion was following them. Although it was only the second day of using the ointment, Champion's gait was not nearly as stiff as it had been.

'I no longer question your methods,' Drew

said. 'Champion is doing better each day. It's remarkable. Thank you, from him and me.'

Happiness filled her. 'You're both welcome, however, I was not aware that you had been questioning my methods.'

A dimple formed in his cheek as he grinned. 'I didn't want to hurt your feelings, but I wasn't convinced that mint tea or ointment would help him.'

She eyed him closely. He was a grown man, tall and as well built as many of the sailors she'd met back home, yet there was such a boyish charm about him that at times while lying in bed at night, she'd giggle to herself over something he'd said. Right now he had her smiling, yet also wondering. 'Then why do you help me every day?'

'I assumed my motive was quite clear.'

She glanced at the black horse following behind Millie.

'He was part of my motive, but you were the larger part of it,' Drew said.

'Me? Why?'

'You are a guest.' He shrugged. 'I want you to enjoy your time.' A seriousness overtook his features. 'I do hope you have been enjoying your time here.'

The fact that she was made her frown because

she shouldn't be enjoying it. She was exercising Millie daily and slowly gathering information that she would need for her escape, mainly from Kate, who graciously answered questions about the location of the Mansfield manor house while helping with the supplies needed to see to Champion every day.

From what she'd learned, her journey to obtain passage on ship would include travelling through London. The positive part of that was she could take the train to the sea from there. The negative part was that her trail would be easy to follow and she had yet to figure out how to get Millie back to Mansfield.

'I'm sorry that you are not,' Drew said.

She shook her head. 'No, it's not that.'

'You are missing your family? Your father. You're worried about him?'

Deep melancholy washed over her. 'Yes. Very much.' If Captain Berland had heard any news from America, he would send it to her grandfather's home and she feared her grandfather would not forward the information on to her. Even more reason to begin her journey home soon.

'I worried about my father, too,' he said, 'once I got old enough. Before that, I'd just wish he'd come home.'

'You had to have been happy when he did.'

'I was, but it wasn't very often.'

She knew his father and Champion had been in the Queen's Army and that his father had died during an assassination attempt. 'How often was it?'

'About four or five times a year.'

'Four or five times a *year*?' she repeated, shocked by his answer.

'Yes. When I young. When I got older and was in school, I saw him once, maybe twice a year.'

'Twice a year?' She sighed at the sadness that filled her. 'How old were you when he died?'

In unison, they steered their horses around the edge of the wooden pen on the back side of the stable. He waited until Champion took the corner as well before answering, 'Sixteen.'

'And your mother died when you were just a baby?'

He nodded.

She shook her head. 'I feel bad for you, Drew. I surely do.'

'There's no need for that. I'm a duke. I can do nearly anything without a single repercussion.'

She pulled on Millie's reins, bringing the horse to a stop. There was something irregular about his tone, as if he wasn't proud of being a duke. 'You don't like being a duke?'

He stopped Fellow and looked at her. 'Some days, yes, some days, no.'

'Why?'

'Perhaps because of the same reasons you don't like titles.'

'I don't like them because my mother didn't like them and I hadn't known why until I read her diary.'

'And learned she was a duchess.'

'Yes.' The mother she remembered and the one who'd written the diary seemed like two different people. Yet, they had been the same person. That was nearly as crushing as knowing Arlo wasn't her father, because it left her not knowing who *she* was. 'My mother may have been a duchess, but I won't ever be one. I will always be Annabelle Smith from Hampton, Virginia.' With that, she nudged Millie forward and trotted her way to the stable.

His large brown horse, with a blaze on its nose and four white socks, was instantly beside her. 'What if it's proven differently?'

She refused to think of that possibility. There was no need. She'd be back in America soon and would never think of England again. Telling him that would be satisfactory, but she couldn't. He might try to stop her from leaving. 'Is that your hope? That the Earl of Westerdownes proclaims that I am his long-lost granddaughter?'

'I have no hopes either way,' he replied as they turned the final corner to arrive at the front of the stable.

Prepared to ask why, she opened her mouth, but closed it when she noticed he was looking towards the road, where a rider was approaching fast and waving an arm.

'Your Grace!' the rider shouted. 'Your Grace! I must speak to you!'

Chapter Six

Drew recognised the rider as Franklin Watts, one of the miners, and was instantly concerned. Urging Fellow into a gallop, he met the man on the road. 'What has happened?'

'It's Gunner, Your Grace. His wife. Something's not right. She went into labour night before last, but still hasn't had the baby. Gunner asked me to fetch you and the doctor from town.'

As he spun Fellow around to face the stable, the horse nearly collided with Millie. 'Finnegan!' he shouted over her head. 'Send a rider to the village to instruct the physician he's needed at the Gunner Erickson residence.'

'I will go to the village,' Franklin said. 'I came here first, because it's on the way.'

'Why wasn't the physician requested before now?' Annabelle asked.

'Because Lena refused to have him summoned, miss,' Franklin said, before addressing him again. 'I will go get him now, Your Grace.'

'Yes, hurry,' Drew replied. 'Tell him I request his attendance immediately.'

'I will, Your Grace. Thank you!' Franklin spun his horse around and galloped down the drive.

'I will hitch a coach for Kate!' Finnegan shouted as he led Champion into the stable.

Drew waved, indicating he'd heard Finnegan, and then nodded to Annabelle. 'If you will excuse me.' He had no idea what he could do to help either Gunner or Lena before the physician or Kate arrived, but turned Fellow about and heeled him into a gallop.

The thud of a horse's hooves close behind had him glancing over his shoulder. 'There is no need for you to accompany me,' he shouted to Annabelle.

'I believe there is!' she replied, gaining ground on his mount. 'Do you know how to deliver a baby?'

'No. Do you?'

'I guarantee I know more than you do!'

He slowed Fellow enough for Millie to gallop at his side. 'You guarantee?'

'Yes. I told you about Clara, my best friend. She gave birth right before Christmas and I was with her the entire time. Helped Dr Wingard bring Abigail into this world.'

That was definitely more experience than he had. 'Very well.'

They paced the horses and arrived at the small house that Gunner and his family lived in near the mine within the hour.

Not wearing his familiar stocking cap, Gunner's blond hair was sticking out in all directions, but it was the man's expression that cut Drew to the core. 'How's Lena?' he asked, as they rode into the yard.

'She says she fine, but she's not,' Gunner said, shaking his head. 'She's not. I wanted to get the doctor last night, but she refused. Kept saying it would be fine, but it's not.'

Drew leaped to the ground. 'The physician is on his way,' he said, rounding Fellow to assist Annabelle down, but she was already out of the saddle.

'Hello. I'm Annabelle Smith,' she said, moving towards Gunner. 'Will you introduce me to your wife? I'd like to help.'

Drew nodded at Gunner's questioning look.

'Ya—ya, I will. Thank you. This way,' Gunner replied, leading them into the house.

It was a small home, made of cobblestones,

which Drew had been inside before, but he hadn't realised just how small the house was until he noticed how Gunner had to duck to lead Annabelle through a doorway into the second room of the cottage.

Drew stayed back, then, spying Caroline sitting at the table, meek and solemn, which was the opposite of how she usually looked, he walked over and picked her up. 'Just whom I was looking for. I need help with the horses. They need a drink of water. You will help me, won't you?'

She looped her arms around his neck and nodded. Then she buried her face in his neck. 'Mummy's crying.'

He kissed the top of her head as he walked to the door. 'Everything is going to be fine.' There was a chance he'd regret it, but at this moment, he had to give Caroline hope. 'I promise.'

'You do?'

He opened the door and walked out into the sunshine. 'I do.'

'Who is that girl?' she asked. 'With Papa?'

'That is my friend. Her name is Annabelle and she is going to help your mummy.' It was a lot to put on Annabelle's shoulders, but she was his only hope. That was odd. He rarely needed anyone.

In an attempt to keep Caroline occupied,

as well as his own mind from focusing on unpleasant outcomes, he took his time watering the horses and then unsaddling them, allowing Caroline to believe she was doing most of the work. He felt a sense of accomplishment when her little face was once again pink and she was chattering about numerous subjects.

He was standing next to her as she sat on Millie's back, brushing the horse with a grooming brush when Kate, along with another household servant girl, arrived.

'I'll take care of the carriage,' he told them as he lifted Caroline off Millie's back. 'Go inside.'

'Thank you, Your Grace,' Kate replied, carrying a large basket. The serving girl was carrying one as well.

He and Caroline had the horse unhitched and were watering the animal when Gunner walked outside.

'I can't thank you enough for coming,' the man said. 'And for bringing along Miss Smith. She had my Lena laughing within minutes. Mrs Finnegan told me to leave, but Miss Smith said that she'd be with Lena the entire time and that I should go check on Caroline as Lena wanted. I see you've taken care of her, too.'

'She's taking care of the horses for us,' Drew

replied, patting Caroline's tiny back. 'And doing a fine job.'

'They were thirsty, Papa.' In the next breath, Caroline asked, 'Is Mummy still crying?'

'No, honey,' Gunner replied, kneeling in front of his daughter. 'Mummy is smiling now. She has Miss Smith and the other women helping her.'

'Everything is going to be fine, Papa. The Duke promised.'

Drew had to swallow against the thickness in his throat as he met the little eyes full of hope beaming up at him. Many people had depended upon him for many things over the years, but this promise, which was in all honesty completely out of his control, was the one he hoped he could uphold among all the others. 'Yes, I did,' he told Caroline and then scooped her off the ground. 'Now that the horses are watered, show me those kittens.'

'They are in the barn!' she exclaimed, once again hugging his neck.

For the next several hours he attempted to keep Caroline's mind, and Gunner's, off what was happening inside the house. It was impossible to keep his own off it. By bringing Annabelle along with him today, he'd put expectations upon her that should never have been put there and that didn't lessen even after the doctor arrived.

She'd come outside once, to let Gunner know that all was fine and that it shouldn't be much longer. Drew had stared at the spot where she had stood in the yard while reassuring Gunner with a soft smile and gentle touch on the arm long after she'd retreated inside the cottage. The image of her, of her light green dress with wide white collar and full skirt, of her long hair pulled back and tied in a matching green ribbon, was imbedded in his mind. Along with the compassion that had filled her face as she'd spoken to Gunner.

The household servant, Julia, had also come outside with food for him, Gunner and Caroline. The child was the only one who ate. His mind and Gunner's were too preoccupied.

What felt like hours, and most likely had been, after the food and dishes had been hauled back into the cottage, Annabelle once again stepped outside. Drew wanted to rush across the yard, but knew it was Gunner she'd come outside to see, so he held on to Caroline's hand as the other man made his way forward.

The whoop that Gunner let out echoed across the land. Drew filled with happiness as Gunner hurried inside the cottage.

'Is the baby here?' Caroline asked him, pulling his hand.

'I believe so,' he replied, lifting her into his arms and crossing the yard.

A wave stronger than pride, stronger than any emotion he'd felt in the past, washed over him as his gaze met Annabelle's. Her blue eyes were bright and her smile nothing short of brilliant.

'You have a baby brother, Caroline,' she said, meeting them in the centre of the yard.

'Yippee!' Caroline then frowned slightly. 'Just one?'

'Yes,' Annabelle replied with a giggle. 'Just one. You can see him in just a few minutes. Your papa will come get you.'

Drew set Caroline on the ground. As she ran towards the cottage, he asked Annabelle, 'The baby and Lena?'

'Are both fine.' Her expression softened and her smile dulled. 'The baby was breech, so it was a difficult delivery. Lena is tired, worn out and will need time to heal.' Laying a hand on his arm, she continued, 'I hope you don't mind, but I suggested that Julia stay with Lena for few days, maybe a week, to help with the baby and Caroline, until Lena is able to manage.'

It was amazing how deeply the entire situation struck him. He would have been at a loss without her today. The desire to hug her was so strong, so very strong. 'Yes.' He shook his head. 'No, I don't mind. That is a very good idea. For Julia to stay here.'

'Thank you.' Her smile had returned. 'I know it wasn't my place to offer one of your servants, but I'm sure Julia will be a great help.'

'Yes, she will. You were right to offer.' He took hold of her hand, held it near his chest, then wrapped his other one around it, too. 'You were right about Champion and right to come here with me today. Thank you.'

She folded her other hand around their clasped ones and closed her eyes for a moment before looking up at him again. 'Thank you for being such a good person.'

He couldn't go as far as to agree with her in that. Ye, he felt as if he'd grown roots and couldn't move, couldn't pull his eyes off her. It was taking all he had to not lean down and brush his lips against hers, or even just press them to her forehead. Needing to break whatever strange hold she had over him, he tried for humour. 'Even though I'm a duke?'

She giggled. 'Yes, even though you are a duke.' Squeezing his hands, she added, 'A title doesn't define a man.'

Her direct honesty did more than his attempt

at humour had done, it brought everything back into prospective. 'You are correct. It does not, but it does define other things.' The thoughts that entered his mind then were not welcome ones. They were making him wonder if he should take the idea of marrying her deeper into consideration. She blazed with beauty and charm and her quiet grace held the true quality of a duchess. So did her compassion and intelligence. If he had to marry, he could do far worse.

It was complicated and complex, yet simple at the same time. She didn't want to be a duchess.

Tearing his gaze off her, he noted Caroline standing near the cottage door. He forced his mind back to the day, to where they were and why. Releasing their clasped hands, he said, 'Caroline's been in the barn all day. We should see she washes her hands before meeting her baby brother.'

The warmth, the utter glow of happiness remained strong inside Annabelle after everything had been settled at the Ericksons' and she and Drew mounted their horses for the ride home. She'd always taken joy in helping others, and today was no different, except that Drew's attendance had somehow changed things. Knowing she'd been helping him, even if not directly, had done that to her. Changed something inside her. From the moment she'd walked into the cottage, she'd vowed to see the best outcome possible for Lena and the baby.

She would have done that no matter who it had been and couldn't quite explain, or understand, what the difference was today, but it was there. Deep inside her she'd wanted things to work out for Drew, too. Perhaps because she'd seen the worry on his face as soon as the rider had stated his mission. Other than doctors, she didn't know a man who was willing to deliver a baby, yet Drew, upon hearing that that's what was needed, hadn't hesitated.

He hadn't hesitated in taking care of Caroline, either.

A lot could be said about how a man treats women, children and animals. Therefore, a lot could be said about Drew. About his compassion and respect. Duke or not, there was nothing pretentious about him. He had a heart. A kind, caring heart.

'It's not much further,' he said.

'I know, I remember this stream from earlier today.' She nodded towards the water trickling along its own path next to their route. 'It certainly was an eventful day.'

'Yes, it was.'

'And a wonderful one.' The warmth inside her was so amazing she drew in a breath and let it out slowly.

He glanced her way.

She smiled. 'Oscar John Erickson, that certainly is a fine name, isn't it?'

'It is.'

Her thoughts were going in all directions, and she snagged upon one of them. 'Don't you find it interesting how a baby is given a name, any name at birth, yet they become that name?'

He frowned slightly.

She went on to say, 'Lena could have named Oscar anything. Roy or Theodore, or even Gunner Junior, and they would have all been a fine name.'

'Yes, that is true.'

'Yet, Oscar fits him, don't you think?'

He laughed. 'Yes, Oscar fits him.'

She liked his laugh. She liked the way he talked, too. Sometimes she found herself listening to how he was talking more than what he was saying because it was like listening to a song. Nodding, to herself and to him, she said, 'Lena said Oscar was Gunner's father's name. That's why she chose it.' Curious, she asked, 'Were you named after someone?'

'Yes. My father and my mother's father.' Her

gaze said she was waiting for more, so he explained, 'My father's middle name was Andrew and my grandfather's name was Charles.'

'That's nice. I don't believe I was named after anyone.'

'Your mother never mentioned her ancestry?'

'No.' She thought for a moment, until a memory formed. 'I did ask her if I had any grandparents one time, because some of my friends did, but she said there wasn't anyone except her, me and my father. She said that was all we needed and I never asked again.' Shrugging, she added, 'Because she was right.' Curious again, she asked, 'Do you have grandparents?'

'No. They died long ago, but I do have a few aunts, uncles and cousins in Scotland. That's where my mother was from.'

She had always been curious about nearly everything, but when it came to him, her interest was stronger than ever. 'Was your mother betrothed to your father?'

'No. My father was injured and she nursed his wounds. A year later, he went back to Scotland, married her and brought her back to London, and then out here, to Mansfield.'

He'd told her how the Queen had titled his father Duke after he'd taken a bullet meant for her husband, Prince Albert. His mother had been the one to nurse him after he'd taken that bullet. Annabelle couldn't help but imagine that his parents had fallen in love and how happy his mother must have been when his father came back for her and married her. It sounded like a true love story.

She sighed at the mere idea, until a tiny shiver rippled over her arms. The story also had a tragic ending. His mother had died before he'd turned a year old. He didn't even remember her, not at all.

'I'll have the evening meal served immediately,' he said.

The manor house had come into view. Julia had said that neither he nor Gunner had eaten much of the food she'd taken out to them. Even if they had, that had been hours ago. Although the meals Annabelle had partaken here were plentiful, breakfast alone was scarcely enough for a man of his size to live on. She had been hoping to put the ointment on Champion's legs before dinner, but she could do that afterwards. She hadn't kept him waiting on her for a meal since she'd promised she wouldn't and wouldn't today, either.

What she would do was change her clothes before joining him in the dining room and she was happy that Effie had a clean dress laid out. One of her best. It was silvery blue with intricate flowers encircling the white skirt made from white silk piping. Her father had ordered the dress for her from New York, after she'd seen one like it in a catalogue.

'Hurry, help me change,' she instructed. 'Drew is hungry and I don't want to keep him waiting.'

Effie stepped forward to assist, but it was the way her lips were pinched that Annabelle noted. 'What have I done now?' she asked. 'Just tell me.'

'Well, miss,' Effie said quietly, 'forgive me, but a proper young lady would not have been gone all day.'

Annabelle shoved her dress down over her layers of petticoats and skirts. 'Some babies take longer than others.' Not convinced that was all of it, she added, 'Please don't tell me that I shouldn't have helped a neighbour. That can't be improper.'

Effie gathered the skirt of the blue dress and held it, ready to drop over Annabelle's head. 'No, miss, but assisting in a birth is most improper for an unmarried woman.'

Annabelle popped her head and arms out of the dress openings and began buttoning the front buttons. 'Assisting in the delivery of a baby is improper?'

Effie nodded as she tugged and smoothed the wide skirt. 'For a young, unmarried woman. It should be left for older, married women.'

That was one rule she didn't mind breaking.

'Oh, well, I've done it before and I'll do it again if the need arises.' Annabelle sat down at the vanity and waved for Effie to pass her a wet cloth to wash her face while Rosemary removed the ribbon and brushed her hair. 'It is nothing shy of witnessing a miracle right before your eyes.'

'Yes, miss.' Effie's face was red.

Annabelle scrubbed her face with the cloth. 'I don't mean to shock you, Effie, but I know where babies come from and how they get there.'

Effie's face was even redder, and one hand was pressed against her chest when Annabelle handed her the washcloth. 'Do mothers here not teach their daughters anything?' Her mother had told her where babies come from and Cecilia had filled in the rest when Annabelle's monthly had begun.

Effie rinsed out the cloth and hung it on the edge of the washstand. 'Yes, miss.'

Annabelle sighed.

Rosemary styled her hair in a loose chignon, decorated with tiny, white flowers, and Annabelle nodded her satisfaction. 'Thank you, Rosemary.' Standing, she nodded to Effie. 'And thank you, Effie.' She fully understood that Effie was not here by choice and could empathise with that. 'I appreciate both of you and your quick and efficient help. Now, I must get downstairs.'

* * *

By the time she arrived at the dining room, she was nearly breathless. Even though she'd learned her way around, the house was very large and a day didn't go by where another elaborate painting or exquisite vase caught her attention and needed a second look. Finding the dining room empty, she leaned against the doorway for a second.

'It will be a short time before the meal is served.'

She spun, smiled at Drew, very glad that he wasn't waiting on her, but then, realising she had a few minutes, she glanced down at her dress. 'How long before it will be served?'

'I'm not sure exactly, but can find out for you.' Frowning slightly, he added, 'Why?'

There might be time to see to Champion's legs, but she would hate to get ointment on her dress. It might cause a permanent stain. 'I was hoping to see to Champion's legs at least one more time today.'

He smiled and held his arm out for her to take. 'You'll be happy to know that Finnegan rubbed the ointment on him twice during our absence. Once this afternoon and again just a short time ago.'

Relief filled her and her heart warmed as she laid a hand on his arm to be escorted down the hall to the drawing room. 'That was so very kind of him. Once a day will still help, even twice, but three is the best. I will thank him for taking care of the task today.'

'Like me, you've made a believer out of him with your mint tea and ointment.' Drew led her into the drawing room. It was one of her favourite rooms in the house with its white and gold curtains, fern plants on spindle-legged stands, vases full of neatly arranged flowers and porcelain figurines positioned on other tables and upon the mantel above the massive fireplace.

It was the room they had a pre-dinner drink together each night and she'd come to look forward to the time.

He stopped near the gold brocade sofa. She released his arm and sat, watched him walk over to a buffet cabinet and pour two drinks from the crystal decanters. Before arriving, she'd never tasted gin, but chilled, with lemon and sugar, it was very refreshing.

He handed her a stemmed glass and sat in the chair across from her, sipping on his own glass of amber-coloured liquid. Her thoughts went to the day and how he'd kept Caroline busy, both before and after Oscar had been born. He was quite a remarkable man and, suddenly, she realised that she would miss him when she left.

It seemed ironic, because she'd only been here a short time. The fact her home was across the ocean meant they couldn't be friends for ever and that was saddening.

'Would you be interested in seeing the estate left to you by Compton?'

His question took her so off guard, she went completely still.

'It's run down and devoid of any furniture or personal possessions,' he said. 'But it is where you were born.'

It was where she'd been born and she wasn't sure whether she wanted to see it or not. 'May I think about it?' she asked. A part of her wanted to know more about her mother's life before she'd arrived in America. The diary had revealed a sad, tragic life, yet she remembered her mother as a loving, happy person and wondered if she'd ever been happy while in England. She wanted to believe that she had and had asked Effie about her, only to be told that she, Effie, was not permitted to talk about her mother.

'Certainly,' Drew replied.

An odd knot had formed in Annabelle's stomach and she wasn't sure what that meant. 'Would you take me?'

'Yes.' He smiled. 'Whenever you want.'

That eased the knot, which felt significant in

some way. 'Thank you. I will think about it and let you know.'

'Very well.' He took a sip off his drink and then eyed her with that mischievous and boyish look she'd seen before.

She sipped her drink and tried to mimic his look, but knew she wasn't as good at it as he was.

He chuckled. 'How do you feel about cats?'

'Cats?'

'Kittens specifically.'

She laughed. 'Have you been given a kitten?' Lena said as much would happen when she'd heard he was in the barn with Caroline. The mother cat, and the kittens, were Caroline's most prized possessions.

'I was told that I could have the pick of the litter.'

'Which one did you choose?'

'I haven't yet.'

She giggled. 'Yet?'

He sighed, shrugged. 'I couldn't say no.'

'Of course you couldn't.' He was too kind, too considerate for that.

'I suppose one more won't hurt.'

There was no reason to hide her grin as she took a sip of her drink. There were a couple of cats that lived in the barn and stable, keeping the mice population down. She'd specifically told the large tabby-coloured one in the stable that mice were fine, but if she found any parakeet feathers, she would not be happy. Every time she walked into the stable, she whistled, but the birds had yet to mimic her. However, they mimicked Drew's whistle, even when he hadn't whistled.

'Will you be able to tell the new one from the ones in residence now?' she asked. 'Caroline may ask for updates and may ask to see it when she comes to visit.'

'That is true.' He rested his elbow on the arm of the chair and his chin on his fist. 'What colour are the cats around here?'

She started to answer, but then realised what he was doing and waved a single finger. 'Uh, uh, you are on your own with this one.'

There was that look again. 'But why?'

'Because it's your cat to pick out.' Knowing she would give in if this conversation continued, she changed the subject. 'Kate, Mrs Finnegan, said she would put together a basket of food and supplies for Lena tomorrow and I offered to deliver it.' She had also offered to help Kate during Julia's stay at the Erickson home, but Kate had assured her that there was no need for that. She had plenty of household help.

'Wonderful idea. I'll escort you,' Drew replied. 'You can help me pick out a kitten.'

She laughed. 'What part of no did you not understand?'

'I didn't hear you say no.'

'It was implied and you know it.'

'They are really cute, about the size of your glass, and one is black and white with a…'

She set down her glass, covered her ears with both hands and shook her head. 'I can't hear you.'

He spoke louder, describing the kittens, until she dropped her hands from her ears. 'Stop!' Laughing, she added, 'You are a brat, do you know that?' There was no doubt in her mind that she would help him pick out a kitten.

They were both laughing when Donald appeared in the doorway. 'Excuse me, Your Grace. A guest has arrived.'

Chapter Seven

Drew had invited Roger, so he should be glad
to see him, but the tightening of his jaw, mainly
over how his friend's tongue was nearly hanging out and his eyes never left Annabelle, let him
know just how unhappy Roger's appearance was
making him.

She'd been full of charm as he'd introduced
them, but throughout the meal the three of them
shared, she'd grown quiet. That was part of the
problem. Roger loved a conquest, especially
those who didn't appear overly interested.

In fact, the less interested, the harder Roger
pursued.

That had never bothered Drew before, but it
did now.

'Your accent is exceptional,' Roger said. 'Like
a melody to my ears. I imagine you must sound
like an angel when you sing.'

She set her cup on its saucer. 'I do hope not, because that would mean I was dead.'

Roger laughed. 'That is not at all what I meant, Miss Smith. I was referring to how you would sound to my ears.'

'You must have remarkable hearing if you can hear angels sing, Mr Hardgroves.' She laid her napkin on the table. 'I would like to see to Champion. If you will excuse me?'

Drew's jaw loosened as he smiled. Roger's charms were not working on her and that pleased him. He also had no intention of informing her that propriety said she should call Roger Lord Clairmount. 'Certainly.' He stood. 'I'll join you.'

'I shall join you as well,' Roger said, leaving his chair to rush around the table. 'I haven't seen the old boy in ages.'

Drew beat him to her chair, but she hadn't waited for either before standing. He offered her his arm and she laid a hand upon it as they left the room and made their way out to the stable. She was quiet, responding only to questions directed solely to her. He was quiet, too. Roger was the one doing all the talking and it was grating on his nerves.

His nerves stung a bit more when she didn't whistle when she entered the stable. He'd withheld his own whistles the past few days, hoping that would entice the budgies to respond to hers.

As if he'd missed her visits, Champion greeted her with a muffled knicker.

'Would you like me to summon Finnegan?' Drew asked.

'No,' she replied, stroking the glossy hair on Champion's neck. 'I'll speak with him in the morning.'

'Concerning what?' Roger asked. 'Champion? He looks as fit as a fiddle to me. He's quite the old war horse. Served the Queen well.'

Having seen the changes gradually, Andrew hadn't recognised just how much Champion had changed since she'd arrived. The horse's stance was no longer strained and he regularly moved around his large stable area. That, too, was due to her. Since she'd started wrapping Champion's legs, she'd instructed Finnegan to put his feed and water in a different area each day, making the horse take a few steps to reach them. 'He does look good,' Drew said, patting the horse on the rump. 'Very good.'

She smiled and dipped her head slightly.

'Ready to return to the house?' Drew asked.

Nodding, she stepped away from Champion and looped a hand around his elbow. Upon entering the house, she bid goodnight to both him and Roger and proceeded to the staircase.

He gestured for Roger to follow him into his office.

'She doesn't say much, does she?' Roger stated, while pouring himself a glass of whisky.

Drew's mind quickly recalled the long conversations the two of them had had since her arrival and he waited until Roger had stepped away from the table before he poured a glass for himself. 'Perhaps because you didn't shut up long enough for her to speak.'

Roger sat in an armchair. 'It's called breaking them down. Once you do that, you'll have them eating out of your hand.' He took a drink, swallowed. 'That is why you summoned me here. To have her eating out of my hand and leave you alone.'

That had been a tactic they'd used more than once when Drew hadn't been able to shake the onslaught of a particularly zealous young woman. 'No, that is not why I summoned you.'

Roger lifted a brow. 'She is an extraordinarily lovely woman. Mayhap the most beautiful woman I've seen in a long time, and...' Roger sighed '...with that southern charm, she could wrap a man around her finger long before he realised it was happening.'

Drew crossed the room, stopped near the window and gazed out at the darkness that had shrouded the earth while they'd been in the stable. 'She has not wrapped me around her finger.'

'But she is beautiful. Extraordinarily so.'

He agreed with Roger's assessment, but found no reason to voice it.

'Have you changed your mind?' Roger asked. 'Think marriage might not be the end of the world as we know it?'

Letting out a sigh slowly, Drew turned and walked to the chair adjacent to the one his friend sat in. What he thought about marriage wasn't the issue. 'I summoned you here because you, my friend, know more gossip than the London rags, otherwise known as newspapers, and I need information.'

'Then I am your man.' Roger set his glass on the table next to his chair. 'In fact, I was delayed in answering your summons because Ryan Westmaster died. In bed. However, it wasn't his bed. It was Lady Fritz's bed. Galen Fritz was not there, because the Marquess was at the Conagher residence, in bed with Lady Conagher. Gerald Conagher was not there, because the Earl was at the Westmaster residence, in bed with Lady Westmaster.'

Drew shook his head.

'A servant of the Fritz household,' Roger continued, 'went to the Viscount's household to get help in moving Westmaster's body home, hoping to cover up exactly where he'd died. Of course, it's all being swept under the rug and people are pouring out sympathy for Leah Westmaster, being widowed at such a young age.'

'Young?'

Roger shrugged. 'Forty-five isn't that old.'

'No, it's not,' Drew agreed before asking, 'Whose servant was in your bed?'

'Not this time, my friend. I obtained the information from Lady Conagher's personal maid, Aurora. I vowed to not tell a soul, but everyone knows you and I share the same soul, so...' Roger shrugged, and changed the subject. 'Tell me about Miss Smith. Is she or is she not?'

They'd been dubbed twins while scholars by the headmaster of their school, because they'd been as close as brothers and had remained so all the years that followed, but when it came to his thoughts about Annabelle, Drew wasn't ready to share them with anyone. Hardly even himself.

He swallowed the last of his drink and set the empty glass on the table. 'If she is or isn't the daughter of the long-lost Duchess is what I want you to discover.' Drew spun the glass beneath his finger in a circle on the table. 'That is, if you don't already know.'

Roger rubbed his palms together. 'You'll be glad to know that I took it upon myself to learn a lot about the Duchess of Compton and her disappearance. As a matter of fact, that is why I became acquainted with Aurora. Her mother is the head of Westerdownes's household staff and Aurora told me that the Earl forbade his staff from mentioning his daughter's name long ago. Doing so would result in termination, or worse.'

'Do tell.'

'It is alleged that two staff members who didn't heed his warning ended up on ships to Australia and are still there. They face imprisonment for theft if they return to England.'

'What of his daughter?' A notion formed and Drew asked, 'Did Westerdownes claim she stole from him, too?'

'I've never heard that.' Roger stood, crossed the room to refill his glass. 'Aurora was a small child when the Duchess went missing, but does recall a time when the Duchess came to the house with her baby. The household staff was elated for they hadn't seen her since her wedding. She wanted to stay, but Westerdownes refused and sent her back to Compton.'

That was all part of the rumours, or stories,

that Drew had heard over the years. 'But?' he asked, knowing Roger knew more.

Roger took a swig off his glass. 'She never arrived back at the estate.'

'How do you know that?'

'According to Aurora, the coach driver who had been assigned to drive her back said the Duchess had knocked on the coach roof, signalling for him to stop. When he'd stopped and opened the coach door, she was nowhere in sight. The inside of the coach was empty. He searched the surrounding area, but couldn't find hide nor hair of her, though he did discover a single baby bootie beneath the box seat.' Roger sat in his chair, took another sip off his drink.

'This sounds like more folklore about the Duchess's disappearance,' Andrew said.

Roger held up a finger. 'That driver was Aroura's father and her mother still has that bootie.'

'A baby's bootie doesn't—'

'I'm not finished. The driver proclaimed that the Duchess must have signalled for him to stop, then climbed in the box beneath the seat with her infant and waited until he'd been searching the roadway to climb out, sneak out of the carriage and disappear into the woods. Not knowing what to do, he continued on to the estate. No one greeted him upon arrival. The only person to acknowledge him was the groom later that morning who asked when he'd arrived. Knowing if he told the truth, either the old Duke or Westerdownes would have his head, he lied. Said he'd arrived in the middle of the night, brought the Duchess back. Her luggage was atop the carriage, so he gave it to the groom, returned to London, to Westerdownes's house, and held true to his story of dropping her off in the wee hours of the morning.'

'Why?'

'Why?' Roger shook his head. 'To save his own neck and that of his wife and daughter.'

'But what of the Duchess? He left her alone, with an infant, in the woods.'

'Where, he felt, she was safer than with either her husband or her father.'

Drew rose to fill his drink, letting the story sink in.

'Want to know the rest?'

He glared at Roger. 'Yes.'

'The Duke had the Earl's house searched, looking for the Duchess. The Earl claimed it was because the Duke had done something to her. He had proof, his driver's testimony that she'd been delivered to Compton, which the groom confirmed, and admitted that he'd carried in the Duchess's luggage. That groom disappeared a short time later.' Roger shrugged. 'Whether he ran off or found the end of his life at someone else's hand is unknown, but rumours were that he was the young lover the Duchess ran away with.'

Back in his chair, Drew scratched the back of his neck. It was an interesting tale and nearly as believable as all the other tales as to what had happened to the Duchess of Compton, but none of it gave him the answer he needed. 'What I need to know is if Miss Annabelle Smith is indeed Annabelle Fredrickson or not.'

'That I do not know,' Roger admitted.

'You need to find out,' Drew replied, 'because that is the reason I summoned you here. I want proof if she is or if she isn't before Westerdownes declares his findings.'

Roger rubbed his chin, scratching both of his thick, black sideburns at the same time. 'Westerdownes doesn't want her to be his granddaughter.'

'I know, that's why I need proof.'

'Before you marry her?'

'I said nothing of marriage.'

'No, you didn't. But you are considering it.'

That was the one thing he wasn't about to admit, not to Roger, or himself. It was a moot point. Annabelle wasn't interested in staying in England. She had told him so, but more than that, he knew that the reason she took Millie out for rides, longer ones each day, was to condition the horse. Get the mare ready for a long journey. He had no idea if she already had a ship in mind— perhaps that of the Captain who had delivered her to England. Either way, she had a plan on getting herself back to America. He knew one other thing. He would not be the second Duke to have a wife suddenly disappear, leaving tongues wagging and rumours flourishing.

'I can't say I blame you,' Roger said. 'Besides her beauty and that southern charm that could wrap a man around her finger in the blink of an eye, your wealth will increase substantially.'

'None of that is why I want to know the truth.'

'Then why?'

'For her sake,' Drew admitted, being fully truthful. 'No matter what the outcome, she deserves to know the truth.'

Roger nodded, then grinned as he looked down at his own hand, at the little finger he held up.

Annabelle truly didn't want to be rude, but she didn't care for Roger Hardgroves, the Fourth Marquess of Clairmount. That was how he'd introduced himself and he'd sounded quite pompous in doing so, and instilled even more determination in her to not use proper titles. He reminded her of a blackguard. That's what her father had called the sailors who got off the boat and were looking for one thing while in port. A woman's favours. She'd seen that in his eyes the moment he'd looked at her.

She hoped he wasn't planning on staying long. Drew was often close at hand, had accompanied her on rides and helped with Champion, but he hadn't watched her every move. Roger Hardgroves would and that would make her escape that much harder.

He was the one who bore watching. That was something she would do, while making sure that he didn't like her. The fastest way to get rid of unwanted attention was dislike. Men were fickle in that sense. They would move on, find someone they did like. Cecilia had taught her that when Jaime Johnson had asked to come calling. He'd been looking for a wife and she had not been interested in him or marriage. She'd only been sixteen at the time.

'How is he this morning?'

Lost in thought, Annabelle startled at the question. The sun was just starting to rise and though she knew Drew was an early riser, she hadn't expected him up this early. Not even the kitchen staff had crawled out of bed when she'd sneaked through there to collect the ointment.

She started to rise from her crouched position next to Champion, to answer Drew's question, but another sound made her heart thud as fast as his voice had. Leaping to her feet, she asked, 'Did you hear that?'

'I did,' Drew answered.

Looking overhead at the pair of parakeets on the rafter, she had to bite her lips at how big her smile had grown. 'They mimicked my whistle. I didn't whistle when I walked in this morning. I thought they might still be sleeping.'

Drew entered Champion's stall. 'They probably thought that you should still be sleeping.'

The smile on his face made her breath catch, but she didn't look away. She never had when it came to him. Perhaps that should surprise her or at least make her question why, but right from the start, she'd met his gaze and held it, as he had hers. As if neither of them cared if the other knew what they were thinking, or perhaps it was the other way around, that they each *wanted* the other to know what they were thinking. As in like minds.

'Perhaps,' she admitted. 'And you. Why are you out here so early?'

'I could ask you the same question, but I know the answer.' He ran a hand along Champion's neck before lowering down behind the horse. 'Pass me the jar.'

She knelt and slid the jar over near the horse's legs on his side. 'I didn't want Finnegan to have to do this again today.'

'His job is to see to the care of the animals.'

'I know, but I started this and I will see it through.'

'Will you see other tasks through as well?'

Tilting her head so she could see him beneath Champion's belly, she asked, 'What tasks?'

'Please don't say you've forgotten.'

'Forgotten what?'

'Picking out a kitten when we take the supplies to the Erickson home.'

She pinched her lips to keep her giggle muted. 'We aren't back to that, are we?'

'Back to what? There was nothing to go back to. You agreed to take the supplies over, did you not?'

Finished with the front leg, she moved to the hind leg. 'Yes, but I did not agree to pick out a kitten.'

'But you will.'

This time she kept her lips pinched, not replying, and put extra pressure on Champion's legs while rubbing on the ointment. Her reward was spontaneous. Champion twisted his long neck, looked at her and closed his eyes as he let out a long breath of air, as if he was enjoying her actions.

'I can see your feet, I know you're still there,' Drew said.

Smothering another giggle, she replied, 'Put extra pressure on while rubbing in the ointment. He likes that.'

A moment later, Champion twisted his head the other way and snorted, then stamped a foot.

'Are you trying to get me kicked?' Drew asked, while toeing the glass jar of ointment further away from Champion's feet.

'No. You must be doing it too hard.'

'Or he just likes the way you do it better.'

'Perhaps,' she said, sounding conceited, because she meant to.

Drew laughed and they continued to rub down the horse's hind legs and then moved back to the front ones, giving them the same treatment. Afterwards, they let Champion out in the corral, so he could walk around at will. She didn't want him in the pasture yet in case he wandered too far and became sore.

Finnegan arrived and she thanked him for taking care of Champion the day before. After their discussion, he asked if they wanted Millie and Fellow saddled for a morning ride.

Annabelle wanted to say yes, but knowing breakfast would soon be served, declined, explaining they'd be riding over to the Erickson cottage later this morning.

'We could have done both,' Drew said as they walk back towards the house.

'I assumed you wouldn't want to keep your guest waiting for breakfast.'

'Roger has been coming here since we were in school and will eat when he's hungry.'

'You've been friends for a long time.'

'Yes, we have.'

'How long will he be staying?' As soon as the words were out, she wished she could withdraw them. It was his house and very imprudent for her to question how long his friend stayed.

'I'm not sure. Does his being here bother you?'

'I have no right to be bothered or not. It is your home. I, too, am merely a guest.' That was true, but it went deeper than that. She had come to enjoy having a large portion of Drew's attention, which was quite unlike her. Monopolising someone's attention wasn't a trait she'd known lived inside her and wasn't overly sure how to respond to it.

'Does he know?' she asked, wondering if that

could be at the base of her unusual behaviour. As of now, Drew and Effie were the only ones who knew about her mother and her grandfather's hope that she was an imposter.

'If you are the daughter of the lost Duchess of Compton?'

She nodded.

He didn't respond until they were walking up the steps to the house. 'He saw you at Westerdownes's house in London and knows the Earl sent you here while he's investigating your legitimacy.'

Legitimacy. She had never considered herself illegitimate, but in the eyes of others, she was, and perhaps in her own eyes because she didn't want any part of the life her mother had experienced as the Duchess of Compton. Yet she was her mother's daughter. She had proof of that in the box in her bedroom and by not being so, she was denouncing her very own mother. The woman who had fled this country to save her.

She searched Drew's face, wishing in this moment that she could read his thoughts, but unlike other times, when they seemed to be in tune with each other, she had no idea what he was thinking. 'Thank you for telling me the truth.'

He frowned slightly. 'Why wouldn't I tell you the truth?'

She shrugged, not completely sure, but then she knew. 'Because you don't want me to be the Duchess of Compton's daughter any more than I want to be her.'

Donald opened the door and, upon stepping inside, they bid each other farewell for now and went their own ways. Her mind was even more of a tangled mess. Getting back home, where she was needed, where she was just her, was still her goal, and she would see that it happened, yet there was this part of her that was opening inside. It wanted to show Drew the contents of the box. She wasn't sure why. She wasn't sure if he'd believe her, either. He hadn't known her mother. Wouldn't recognise the necklace. As for the diary, it could be proclaimed false. That her mother had known the Duchess who had gone missing and taken the story on as her own.

That possibility had never crossed her mind, but it did this morning, to the point she asked Effie, 'Do I really look like my mother?'

Her weathered face, with its button nose and jowls brought on by age, lit up so brightly, Effie appeared years younger. 'Yes, my lady, very much. You startled the entire household when you appeared on the steps that morning. It was like turning back the clock of time.'

'Are there any portraits of her? At the Earl's home? Of when she was young?'

Sadness or something even darker flashed across Effie's face as she shook her head. 'No. There had been, but they've been long gone.'

'Why?'

'I cannot say why they were destroyed.' Effie spun around then and lifted the pale peach dress off the bed. 'We mustn't keep the Duke waiting, especially not with a guest in the house.'

Annabelle let out a sigh. 'No, we mustn't.'

Drew and Roger were in the dining room when she arrived, but the guest only stayed as long as it took to eat his breakfast before he stated that he needed to be off and would see them both later in the day.

A rather large bout of guilt prevented Annabelle from eating more than a few bites, which apparently Drew noticed.

'Are you not hungry this morning?'

She set down her fork. 'I'm sorry. I should have been more pleasant to your guest.'

'As I told you, Roger has been coming here for years. He comes and goes as he pleases. That has nothing to do with anything you did.'

Not convinced of that, she removed her napkin from her lap and laid it beside her plate. 'My being here has disrupted your life, hasn't it?'

'No, not noticeably.'

She wasn't convinced of that, either. 'What would you be doing if I wasn't here?'

'I'd be in London.'

'I have disrupted things.'

'In London, being quite bored.'

'Bored, why?'

'Because I would be attending balls and parties, sporting events and horse races.'

Sitting up straighter, she levelled a clear gaze on him. 'That doesn't sound boring.'

A twinkle in his eyes glimmered brighter. 'I do enjoy the horse racing, but the rest can be quite tedious.'

'Then why attend them?'

'Because as a duke there are certain events that I'm expected, or some may call it required, to attend, especially those hosted by members of the Royal Family.'

She nodded, remembering parties and soirées where a large number of men stood near the punch table, tugging on their ties and looking quite bored. 'Required can take the fun out of things at times.' Planting both elbows on the table—yes, she knew better, but didn't care—she rested her chin on her folded fingers. 'So, tell me, if I wasn't here and you weren't required to be in London, attending an affair, what would you *like* to be doing?'

'Working at the mine.'

'Then why aren't you?'

He placed his elbows on the table and threaded his fingers together. 'Because, like the functions I'm required to attend, not working at the mine is also what is expected.'

'But you own it.'

'Yes, I do. As a duke, I'm expected to merely oversee the workings of it. From a distance. Not get my hands dirty.'

Dissatisfaction was written on his face and in the slight slump of his shoulders. She didn't like that and, while searching her mind for a solution, she snagged on something he'd previously told her. Smiling to herself, she removed her elbows from the table and once again tried to mimic the mischievous grin that he'd mastered so well. 'And as a duke, you can do nearly anything without repercussion.'

He frowned.

'You told me that,' she said.

Leaning back in his chair, he looked at her for some time and then nodded, but it was the

way that he laughed that she liked the most.
'Yes, I did.'

'Then work at the mine. Don't just oversee it.'

Chapter Eight

He had lived his life for twenty-six years, yet it had taken a southern belle, who might or might not be the daughter of a duke, to make Drew see the light he'd been searching for. Rather than work beside the miners, see first-hand what was needed, he'd relied on others to report to him. Why? Because of society.

The same society that demanded he should extract as much profit as possible from the mine rather than invest it back into his workers.

Other owners had recognised his changes and how they were working and were making their own changes as a result, and there was a lot more he wanted to see done.

Like Gunner's house. It needed to be remodelled so he didn't need to duck to walk into his bedroom. Because the home was owned by the mine, Gunner would never ask to change it. As

Drew considered that, he wondered about the impact of miners being able to purchase the homes they rented from the mine and what the miners might think of that.

He'd never know until he asked.

Excitement about making even more radical changes than those he'd already made had filled him, but it became bittersweet when, hours later, he attempted to solve Annabelle's issues as easily as she had his. The amount of food and supplies Mrs Finnegan was sending over to the Ericksons' meant they travelled to the cottage in the carriage rather than by horseback. After they were well settled into their journey, he asked, 'If given any choice in the world, what would you like to be doing right now?'

She grinned at him, fully catching on to what he was doing, but then sighed and cast her gaze out over the countryside. 'Be in Hampton, have supper ready for my father when he returned home from work, fill in the ledger for him afterwards.' The smile she flashed at him was also in her eyes. 'His handwriting is nothing shy of chicken scratches.'

Her smile left and sadness filled her face as she continued, 'I've been filling in his ledgers since my mother died.'

He wanted to promise her everything would be fine, just as he had done for Caroline, but she couldn't be assured as easily as a child. Instead of saying anything, he transferred the reins to one hand, put his arm around her and gave her a gentle, one-armed hug.

She leaned against him. 'I wish I knew what was happening there.'

'Was there fighting near your home?'

'Within the state, yes, but not close to Hampton. I knew many men who left to serve and soldiers passed through town regularly, but it was when ships entered the bay that my father made me leave. He didn't give me a choice. Just put me on a ship.'

Drew rubbed her upper arms. 'He wanted you to be safe.'

'I was safe at home. We had a big cellar, a place to go if the fighting got too close. Everyone said there was too much water to worry about land battles, any attack would come by sea, but there, too, being a distance upriver, were we safe.'

'Not all battles are fought with cannons and calvary charges,' he said. 'One man, executing a thoroughly thought-out plan, can create a ripple effect that can cause entire cities, entire empires to fall.'

She leaned her head back, looked up at him. 'You say that with conviction. Why?'

'My father.' Each time he'd seen his father, he'd been told why it had been so long between visits. At a young age, the tales of trials, tribulations and successes had made him proud. Years later, after his father had died, he wondered if facing combat on the battlefields had been easier for his father than facing the memories at home. That of his wife dying. Of his son being raised by servants.

His aunt had alluded to that, about how in love his parents had been. How his mother had anxiously awaited his return, how she'd vowed to follow him anywhere, and then how devastated his father had been over her death. Drew had concluded the rest himself. How seeing him, the product of their love, was too much of a reminder for his father to see him any more often than he had. 'He was in many battles and executed many plans.'

The sounds of birds, horses' hooves and the carriage's turning wheels filled the silence for a few moments before she asked, 'How old is Champion?'

He wasn't sure if she changed the subject on account of him or her. Either way, he answered, 'Close to thirty.'

'I assumed as much.'

Drew knew he should remove his arm from around her shoulders. He just didn't want to. Not yet. 'What's your favourite colour for a horse?'

'I don't know that I have a favourite colour, it's the horse itself that I take a liking to or not. Some are ornery. Doesn't matter what colour they are or how kind you are to them, they are just down-right ornery.'

There were times when her accent made him smile for no reason than how amazing certain words sounded. It was that way right now, along with the fact he was forming his next question. 'Is the same true for cats?'

'Well, now, I supp—' She twisted, looked at him with that gleam in her eye that tickled every one of his senses. 'Very funny.'

'Was it?'

'No.'

He laughed. 'I thought it was.'

She slapped his leg. 'You almost caught me, but you didn't. I'm not picking out your kitten.'

Her hand was still on his leg and he covered it with one hand. 'Why not?'

'Because it's your kitten.'

'I'll share.'

Shaking her head, she leaned back, but left her hand on his leg. He kept his hand on top of hers and they talked about various other things—but not heavy subjects—the rest of the way to the Ericksons' house.

Gunner was working at the mine today and, feeling like a third leg inside with all the women, Drew retreated outside along with Caroline. As luck would have it, she was content with his answer that the kittens were still too young to leave their mother and that he couldn't choose which one he wanted until they were older. When she returned to the cottage, he busied himself by hauling in coal for the stove and various other chores he knew Gunner would otherwise need to complete once he got home that evening. Drew knew society would look down upon him doing household chores, but he didn't care, just like he didn't care if they looked down upon him taking a more active role at the mine.

It wasn't long after he'd completed the chores that he and Annabelle shared a noon meal with Anna, Caroline and Julia; then they took their leave.

'I'm sorry that took so long,' Annabelle said as they settled into the carriage. 'Oscar is so adorable it's hard to put him down.'

'I'm sure it was.' He didn't really know. He'd never held a baby.

'Thank you for completing the chores. Lena told me to stop you, but I knew you wouldn't listen to me.'

'I listen to you.'

'You wouldn't have stopped, though, would you have?'

He shrugged. 'They needed to be done.'

She let out a long sigh, then twisted, facing him. 'How far away is the estate?'

'Not far. Maybe half an hour or so.' He waited a moment, knowing she was thinking hard, before asking, 'Would you like to drive past it?'

'Yes, I would. If you don't mind.'

'I don't mind.'

He probably should have minded and never suggested it in the first place. It looked worse today than it had the other day. The overall condition wasn't fit to be called an estate. Besides the weed-filled and overgrown yard and gardens, inside the plaster was cracked and falling off in places and it smelled dirty—sour and vinegary.

Despite all that, Annabelle ventured from room to room, floor to floor. So did he, going ahead of her to check for scurrying vermin and broken, warped or loose boards, and knocking down cobwebs. The stairs creaked as they walked up them and he held her hand, keeping her close.

'It appears that a significant amount of up-keep is needed,' she said, carefully stepping from stair to stair. 'Or maybe I should have said flat-out repairs.'

'Yes, I should have seen to that.'

'Are you responsible for it?'

No, he wasn't, legally, but morally he should have seen that her property was better maintained and therefore withheld an answer.

She tightened the hold on his hand. 'My grandfather was responsible. He took what he wanted and left the rest to rot. He must have been awfully certain that I'd never return.'

Drew had been certain she'd never return, too, and could try to defend himself, but there was no justification except selfishness. In that instance, he was no better than Westerdownes. 'Not you, specifically.' That was still a justification. 'No one knew you.'

'They knew of me and that was enough.' She stepped around him, into a room that had to have been a bedroom due to the raised platform where a massive bed must have once sat. 'I keep trying to imagine my mother here and I just can't.'

The place was hardly a shell of what it had been, an empty, crumbling shell. 'It would have been different then, fully furnished, with curtains and carpets.' He knocked away a cobweb that hung over her head. 'Clean.'

'I know. It's just that she was so happy, so carefree and…happy. That's the only word I can use. She was never sad, never mad. She and my father loved each other very much and they loved me. She always said that we had a wonderful life and we did.' Looking around the room, she added with a finality, 'Because we weren't here.'

She was here now, in England, and she didn't want to be. He took hold of her hand and led her out of the room. They explored a few more rooms before making their way back downstairs and outside. The bright sunshine and fresh air felt good, cleansing.

'What's that?'

He turned in the direction she pointed, towards a heavy metal fenced-in area past the rock wall that surrounded the overgrown yard and gardens. 'A graveyard is my guess.'

Hand in hand, they walked to the area, found the gate that was rusted shut. He got it opened and they entered.

'The Duke of Compton,' she said, reading the large prominent headstone.

Drew stepped aside, giving her a moment of privacy and discreetly used his boot to push aside the tall grass covering the smaller, flat grave markers. Five of them: the Duke's two previous wives and three children. All girls and all died as infants or small children. His spine shivered.

'He was over sixty when I was born,' she said, her voice shaky. 'My mother was nineteen.'

Returning to her side, Drew draped an arm around her shoulders, turned her around and escorted her out of the graveyard. She was innocent in all of this, yet was the one being affected the most, hurt the most. That wasn't right and it hooked him deep under his skin. 'I can't help you get back to America, Annabelle. Not right now. We don't know what's happening there, how dangerous going back would be, but I will find out as much information as I can. Find out when it will be safe for you to return.'

She stopped. Looked up at him with wide eyes. 'You will?'

Something foreign washed over him, softening every part of him. 'Yes, I will.'

Her gaze fell to the ground for a moment, then back up at him. 'Will you help me go home, then?'

At that moment, there was only one response he could provide, despite whatever consequences that might cause. 'Yes, if I'm positive that it's safe, I will help you return.'

She bit her lips together, closed her eyes. Her shoulders trembled and she reminded him of a delicate flower, fighting to stand strong against whatever forces and elements were being pressed upon her.

He enveloped her in a hug, wanting to protect her against all forces and sources. Her arms went around his waist and she leaned against him. The emotions inside him flared into those he did recognise and, knowing that if she raised her head and looked at him, he would kiss her, he rested his chin atop her head, keeping her close, yet her lips far from his.

She snuggled in closer. 'Thank you, Drew. Thank you.'

He tightened his hold and they stood there for several moments, with the sounds of the breeze rustling leaves and swishing over the tall grass.

When she shifted, he loosened his hold, lifted his head and watched as she took a step back and looked up at him, once again full of the graceful charm and calm strength that he'd seen in her since their first meeting. He had been fully prepared to dislike her that day, fully prepared to not be taken in by anything she said or did. What he hadn't been prepared for was her undeniable virtue and honesty.

Of all the women he'd met, he'd never found

himself fixated on one and never imagined he would. He was this time. And was smart enough to know he shouldn't be. For both of their sakes.

Despite knowing all that, he wanted to kiss her more than he'd ever wanted anything in his life and had to draw up the strength he'd found as a child. That of never needing anyone, anything.

It took a moment, but he found that strength, at least enough that he gave himself a mental headshake. Then, he asked, 'Ready to leave?'

Annabelle glanced behind her, at the graveyard. 'Do you think I should feel something? Even a modicum of something? He was my real father. Even hatred would be better than nothing, wouldn't it?'

'Your feelings are yours to have,' Drew answered quietly. 'No one can direct how you should feel about anyone.'

That might be true. She wasn't sure. Her life, up until reading the diary, had been a lie, but it had been her life. Nothing would change that. However, if she felt anything, even hatred, that would mean she accepted he was her real father and that would mean she couldn't go on being Annabelle Smith. The only person she'd ever been.

Drew took hold of her hand and his touch

filled her with an amazing warmth all over again. It was unlike anything she'd ever known. He made her feel things she'd never felt. When he'd hugged her earlier, she'd wanted to stay right there, in his arms, for ever. Which of course was foolish, and impossible, but it certainly had filled her with a tremendous sense of well-being.

She folded her fingers around his hand. 'I'm ready to go.' Swallowing a thick lump in her throat, she added, 'Thank you for bringing me here.'

'You're welcome. My goal wasn't to cause you more distress.'

'It was something I needed to see. I'm sure of that.'

He gave her a slight bow of his head and a great longing sprang forth. She wanted to stretch up on her toes and kiss him. Just his cheek. Back home she would have done just that, without a second thought, but with him, things were different. She wasn't worried if it was appropriate or not, she just… Well, she was afraid. Afraid how wonderful kissing him might be.

As they walked to the carriage, she questioned why that scared her. She liked the feeling of friendship that flowed between them, it made her feel warm and comfortable, even while the rest of her was a mixture of complexities she'd never encountered. That frightened her a little bit, too. Maybe her problem was that she liked him too much.

Too much for a simple thank-you kiss.

He had promised to help her get home and that was far more than she'd ever hoped.

Concluding that could be why she liked him so much, she said, 'Captain Berland said he'd send word of any news, but I'm quite certain he doesn't know where I am now.'

'I'll have word sent to the Captain, informing him that you are at Mansfield and that all news should be sent here,' he replied while assisting her into the carriage.

Concern, not just about what news she might eventually hear about her home, washed over her. She waited until he'd untied the reins from the post and climbed up beside her to ask him, 'What will happen when I leave?' Needing to explain further, she added, 'With the betrothal?'

He shrugged. 'If Westerdownes succeeds in claiming you're not his granddaughter, or at least causes enough doubt that you couldn't be, nothing will need to be done.'

There was such conjecture inside her. She didn't want to be the Earl's granddaughter, yet she was, and denying that meant she was denying being her mother's daughter. That wasn't right.

Yet, being her mother's daughter caused many issues. The betrothal was certainly an issue. Neither she nor Drew wanted to abide by it and there should be a way that they didn't need to, without her denying her parentage. Then again, if she accepted her mother's parentage, she had to accept her true father's as well, didn't she?

There was also the issue of her father—stepfather Arlo. If she accepted the Duke of Compton had been her father, she'd be claiming that Arlo wasn't. Yet, he'd been the one to take care of her, love her, raise her on his own after her mother had died. Everyone in Hampton knew him as her father and she would never want to hurt him by claiming differently.

Why didn't there seem to be an answer for any of that? Flustered, she leaned back in the seat and expelled a long sigh.

Drew patted her hand.

That was another issue. She liked him and believed he would help her get back home. It would be cruel for someone to say they would and not mean it, and he wasn't cruel. He'd been nothing but kind. About everything. She didn't want to see him hurt, either. Would people think there was a reason she didn't want to marry him? Not because she had to go home, but because he was mean or evil?

That wasn't true.

Not at all.

An uneasiness washed over her, not because of him, but because of the direction her thoughts attempted to take. Towards marriage. Between them. Marriage was something she'd thought about, especially when Clara had married Mark. Though she had been happy for Clara, she'd thought more about Homer and how he'd been completely alone when Clara had moved to Mark's house. Homer had never said anything, but she'd known he'd been lonely and had made it a point to help him more and stop over daily. She'd also thought about her own father and how lonely Arlo would be if she married and moved away.

That's when she'd decided that she wouldn't get married until she found someone that she loved with all of her heart. Someone she couldn't live without. Someone who needed her. That's how her mother had felt towards Arlo. She'd said so and learning what her life had been before she'd met Arlo made Annabelle believe even more in true love.

A few young men had asked to court her and she'd attended outings and events with them, but she hadn't loved any of them and hadn't been able to imagine that she ever would.

Now, being separated from her father, from

Cecilia and so many people in Hampton, made her heart burn at times. She had to get home. Had to help them, especially during this time when they needed her the most.

As if he knew her thoughts, Drew's fingers wrapped around hers and he held her hand a bit tighter. It made her heart thud, the way it had earlier. A part of her didn't want to leave here. Leave him. A very selfish part, one she'd never really encountered before, yet it was there.

Her thoughts entered yet another avenue. 'Will you ever get married?' She froze, shocked she'd said that aloud. Then again, she wouldn't know the answer unless she asked.

He shrugged. 'I have no need.'

'What about children?' The question made her stomach do an odd flip and she furthered her question with, 'Who will inherit your estate if you don't have any children?'

He stared straight ahead for several moments before replying, 'I have no illusions about bestowing anyone with the pressures I inherited.'

'By being a duke?'

He nodded. 'In that sense, I agree with your country's abolishment of inheriting peerage.'

'Why?'

His expression held nothing but honesty as he looked at her. 'Because we are all, no matter where we live, nothing but men and women and the same rules and laws should apply to all. No one should be looked down upon because of their birth. Or looked up to.'

'No, they shouldn't.' She couldn't help but think about how her country had fought against having a peerage and won, only to be fighting again, this time among itself, for all men to be treated equally. It seemed as if they hadn't learned a lot from their past.

'Privileges and benefits provided to some aren't always used for the common good,' he said. 'I've seen companies run into the ground, employees not given a living wage, because those who owned the business wanted all it could earn for themselves.'

'Not your mine,' she stated. 'Lena is very proud of Gunner working there.'

He nodded slightly. 'The mine is the one thing that I appreciate having inherited. Not in the sense some might assume. It does provide me with an income, but the income it provides others is far more important. It's their means to have food and clothing and a home to live in. If it was up to me, they'd be provided more benefits.'

'It's not up to you?'

His gaze was straight ahead, but it was how his hand was clenched on the reins that she truly noted. She rolled her hand beneath the one he was holding, so their palms met. 'You can tell me, Drew. Whatever it is.'

'Westerdownes receives half of the profits from the veins of coal on the estate. He has accountants on site, in charge of overseeing every penny he's due. I have accountants, too, who would never cheat him out of his funds. They also look for ways to invest profits back into the mine, which we do—'

'But it could be more if the Earl were to invest back into it, too,' she interrupted, fully understanding.

'Yes, but that is his prerogative.'

'Which would be mine if—'

'It's not your problem,' he said.

'You're wrong. It is my problem. If I can help, I should. My mother taught me that years ago.'

'You have been helping since you arrived. You've helped Champion and Lena and I know you've helped with household—'

'That's not the same.'

He gave her hand another squeeze. 'Helping is helping and you are doing that.'

She bit her lips together to keep from insisting that wasn't the same and that the mine was her problem. In fact, she herself was a problem—

attempting to believe that she wasn't wouldn't do anyone any good.

Leaning her head back against the seat, she studied his profile. He was handsome. Very. And noble, in his actions and thoughts. Her heart softened because deep in her core where a unique warmth also resided, she believed she'd seen a part of him that few people ever had. His heart. She highly doubted that others knew how deeply he felt about helping the miners and about being a duke and the unfairness of the peerage. When he'd told her those things, they had come from his heart, a part of him that he kept hidden.

He must trust her as she did him. She would never have asked anyone else if she should feel something for her real father, yet had asked him, because she knew she could. That he wouldn't judge her for just being honest.

Just as they had been about neither of them wanting to get married.

A heavy sigh built inside her. A man who didn't want to be a duke, married to a woman who didn't want anything to do with having a title, would be a disaster from the start.

Chapter Nine

'No.' Drew set his glass on the table beside his chair and glared at Roger. 'What on earth would make you think that was a good idea? Westerdownes doesn't want anyone to know she's here.'

'The Earl doesn't want anyone to know she is his granddaughter,' Roger replied. 'But it's you I'm thinking about you, my friend, and the fact that you're hiding a young woman at Mansfield—a young American woman. That is going to set tongues wagging. You'd be far better off hosting a party, introducing her as a short-term guest in order to quell speculation.'

'What speculation?'

'The speculation that will mount when it's discovered she's here.'

Drew was about to say that no one would discover she was here, but instead narrowed his glare on Roger. 'Who did you tell?'

'No one.'

He glared harder.

Roger held up a hand. 'No one. But word is sure to get out. She helped deliver a baby.'

Drew's stomach sank. He hadn't thought of the consequences of the doctor and others who had already seen her. Knew she was staying here.

'Curiosity alone will bring people out. Some of them might have known her mother. But that can work to your goal. If you want her true identity known, we are going to have let people know she's here. Before you know it, the old Earl won't be able to deny her parentage.'

'I don't want her parentage revealed.'

Roger frowned. 'I thought you wanted her to know the truth. That you wanted the truth. That is why I was summoned here.'

It had been, but that had been before today. 'I've changed my mind.'

'You've—' Roger shook his head, eyed him critically.

'Changed my mind,' Drew repeated. Annabelle didn't want to be the Duke's daughter, she wanted to return to America and he'd offered his assistance. 'I've changed your job, too.'

Still frowning, Roger asked, 'To what?'

'Discovering what is happening in America. Specifically, near Hampton, Virginia. I want to know if there are any battles nearby, any troops whatsoever.'

'That information will be found near the docks.' Roger leaned back in his chair, rested an ankle on his opposite knee. 'Not the sort of district I normally gather intelligence from, nor the type of residents I normally collect information from.'

'You own two shipping companies,' Drew pointed out.

'Technically, I only own one. My grandfather still owns his and I simply assist him in his endeavours while overseeing mine.'

Although he had inherited his father's shipping company, and would one day inherit the other company from his grandfather on his mother's side, Roger hated the sea. 'You know people there.'

'As do you,' Roger said.

'Yes, I do.' Drew lifted his glass, emptied it and returned it to the table. 'Then, I guess your job is done.'

Roger dropped his foot the floor. 'Done?'

'Yes.'

Holding up a single finger, Roger shook his head. 'Not so fast. Why do you want that information?'

'It doesn't matter.'

'Yes, it does, old chap. We've been allies since before we knew the word fidelity.'

That was true and caused a glimmer of a smile to tug on Drew's lips. He did know people, but whether he visited the docks or not, Roger could obtain the information far quicker and was taking the bait he'd laid out.

Roger huffed out a breath and sat back in his chair. 'You know I'll get the information for you, but don't I deserve to know why?'

If it was ever necessary, Roger would bury a body for him, therefore, Drew said, 'When it is safe, I will assist Annabelle in returning to America.'

'Return—' Roger shook his head, offered a blank stare. 'That is what the Earl wants.'

'I know,' Drew said. 'It's also what Annabelle wants.'

Roger rubbed a hand over his upper lip with one hand and held up the little finger on his other hand.

Drew could see why Roger thought that. 'She doesn't want to be the Duchess. Doesn't want anything to do with England. Life in America is all she's ever known.'

'And where does that leave you?'

'Right where I was before she arrived. Betrothed to a woman who will never be found.'

Roger nodded. 'Is that what you want?'

That wasn't something Drew was going to contemplate, not now or ever. 'I have my peerage, a very productive coal mine and the freedom to do as I please. What more could I want?'

'What more indeed?' Roger asked drily.

Drew ignored the question. 'I'd like the information as soon as possible.'

'You do know that things change from the time a ship leaves the American coast until it arrives at an English port?'

'Yes, and I know you won't rely on only one source.'

'No, I won't.' Roger scratched his sideburn before he leaned his head back against the chair. 'How would you feel about a going-away party for your American guest?'

The air on Drew's arms stood. 'You said you hadn't told anyone.'

'I haven't, but under a previous assumption as to why I was being summoned, I took the liberty to let a few people know where I was going and that you might be open to more guests.'

'You did what? Why?'

'Because I assumed my goal was to get her attention off you, and me, for that matter. That is normally the case and the best way to do that is to introduce her to others who would appreciate her attention.'

He and Roger had detoured more than one overly zealous woman away from each other and on to some unsuspecting soul. It was only fair that Roger would have assumed the same would be true this time. It wasn't, though, and a party was the last thing he needed or wanted. 'Cancel your invitations.'

'That would be impossible. Who knows how far and wide word has spread? Even if I took out an ad in the paper, which would cause more harm than good, people would still arrive here. An invitation to Mansfield is more sought after than an audience with the Queen.'

Drew's jaw was clenched tight, mainly because he knew Roger spoke the truth, but also because he'd never wanted to throttle someone as badly as he did right now.

He was still frustrated with trying to figure out what to do an hour later, when he found Annabelle in the stable, nose to nose with Champion.

'You're too late,' she said, with her adorable drawl and even cuter grin, after she'd given the horse a kiss between the eyes. 'Finnegan helped and Champion is as content as can be after his rubdown.'

'I have no doubt he's content.' Any male, of any species, would be content to have her kissing him. The desire to kiss her still lived inside Drew, stronger than it had been this afternoon. He kept trying to forget about it, but that was impossible. Truly impossible.

Her smile faded as she stepped away from the stall. 'You look serious. Is something wrong?'

Wrong?

No.

Disastrous?

Yes.

He moved closer and offered her his arm. 'I have something to show you.'

She laid her hand on his arm, yet still frowned as she asked, 'What is it?'

He didn't know. Just needed an excuse to kill time until he came up with a way to tell her about the party.

Having seen the setting sun on his way to the stable, he hoped there was something spectacular to see about it and led her to a side door where there weren't any trees obstructing their view. Perhaps his luck was changing, because the slanting rays of the sun decorated the horizon with a brilliant orange glow, highlighted with shimmering reds and faint pink streaks that left a single tree on a hill looking colourless, yet beautiful.

Standing at his side, she sighed before softly saying, 'The beauty of a sunrise holds promises of the day to come and the brilliance of the sunset provides the glory of a day well lived.'

Though it had come about by accident, or perhaps luck, he found gratification in having shown her the sunset. 'That's a lovely sentiment.' Nearly as lovely as the soft, golden glow of her skin as she gazed upon the sunset.

'My mother used to say that. She loved walking down to my father's warehouses and watching the sun set over the water.' Her tone was light, carefree. 'She also loved the rain. Said everything needed a good washing now and again.'

'What about you? Do you like sunsets and rain?'

'At times. Do you?'

Grinning at her, he said, 'At times.'

'Why were you frowning earlier?'

He had to tell her and drew in a deep breath in preparation. 'It appears as if we are going to have a party.'

'A party?'

His frustration over the entire ordeal increased at the shock on her face. 'Yes. Roger's visit to

Mansfield led others to believe that it signalled an invitation for an end-of-the-Season ball.'

'But no one is supposed to know I'm here.'

'No one is to know the daughter of the lost Duchess of Compton is here,' he said, hoping to quell some of her concerns. 'Not Annabelle Smith visiting from America. People already know that. The doctor. Lena. Gunner. Others.'

She took a few steps away and gazed at the sunset as if it had lost all its glory. 'Was this party your idea?'

'No. I've never hosted a party for the *ton* and had no intention of ever doing so.'

'Then why are you?'

She'd been lied to her entire life and he didn't want to be a part of that, even though he was deeply embedded in it. That, however, had been beyond his control. This wasn't. 'The truth is, Annabelle, Roger has an aptitude for obtaining information and I invited him here to find out your true identity before Westerdownes did.'

'Why?'

'I was hoping it would give me the upper hand.' He stepped closer. 'At the time, I wasn't sure what your goal was and determined I needed to man a defence. Since then, I've discovered your only true goal is to return home. That's why you were exercising Millie every day, so a long journey wouldn't tax her.'

Her face fell and a pink tinged her cheeks. 'I guess that was somewhat obvious, wasn't it?'

He grinned. 'Yes, it was and I don't blame you for that. Don't blame you for anything. I've told Roger that his job now is to discover what is happening in America and he will. However, he and I have been friends for years and he assumed that my invitation for him to visit was to steer your attention off me and—'

'Off you?' Brighter pink filled her cheeks. 'Steer my attention off you?'

'I'm not saying you did anything improper,' he said hurriedly. 'And I'm certainly not trying to upset you. I'm merely telling you what Roger assumed.'

She folded her arms across her chest, staring at him with little tolerance.

'And to help you understand that—'

'That what?' She tossed her hands in the air. 'Your friend thought I should fall at his feet? Ready and willing to be his next conquest? I've been exposed to sailors my entire life and know a scoundrel when I see one. If that is how your friend and you treat women, it's no wonder you're still single.'

'That has been precisely our goal for years, but that's beside the point.'

'Beside the point?'

This was not going well. 'Yes, besides the point because we are discussing the party that will be hosted here—'

'Where there will be dozens of other men who will attempt to make me fall at their feet instead of yours. Of all the—'

'No.' He grasped her upper arms. 'It's not for men to attempt to make you fall at their feet.' That he would put a stop to immediately.

'Oh? So, it's for women to fall at your feet?'

'No. It's to spread the word of you being here so that when Westerdownes attempts to claim that you aren't his granddaughter, people will question him and seek the truth.'

'You want my true identity revealed?'

'Do you?'

'No. I want to go home.'

'That is what I want, too.' Even before he said the words, he'd questioned the validity of them. He'd agreed to help her and would, despite what he wanted. 'In the meantime, word has spread that there will be a ball here at Mansfield and I wanted you to know so you'd be prepared.'

'Prepared for what?'

'I have no idea who might attend this party,

but some who attend may have known your mother.'

She shook her head and walked away.

He considered following, but had already bumbled things enough.

Annabelle drew in a deep breath and huffed it out as she was about to enter the dining room. There was no one good and solid reason that she could find to be so upset with Drew, but she was. The mere fact that he'd thought she'd throw her attention at him made her blood boil. She had never thrown her attention at anyone, although she'd had ample opportunities. Long before coming here. Or perhaps it was the fact he'd called in a friend to divert her attention that made her so mad. Or maybe it was thinking of women throwing themselves at him.

All in all, she was mad.

Just mad.

Let them have their party. She didn't give two hoots. She'd simply stay in her room. Stay there until word came that she could return home.

Home. Where life was normal.

'I can see you're still upset with me,' Drew said as he appeared in the doorway. 'But it is sincere when I say I do apologise. I did not mean to upset you and I do wish I'd handled our conversation differently.'

She was still mad at him, but also at herself, leastwise her heart for the way it flipped and fluttered due to that charming, boyish grin that he was momentarily settling upon her. 'I have never thrown my attention at anyone,' she said, even though making that clear didn't change anything, either.

He gave his head a slight bow. 'I believe you.'

She had to close her eyes to gather her wits because he was still smiling and her heart was still pounding. 'You can do what you like. I don't care. I will remain in my room.'

'I wouldn't blame you if you did, but that would defeat the purpose of the party.'

'What if someone in attendance remembers my mother, thinks I look like her?'

'That is an issue,' he said as at the same time hurried footsteps sounded behind her.

'By Jove, I've got it!' Roger exclaimed as he rushed towards them. 'I'm a genius!'

She glanced at Drew, and he appeared to have the same thoughts as her—that Roger was not a genius.

Arriving at the doorway, Roger dropped one of his arms around her shoulder and the other around Drew's. 'Wait until you hear!'

'When will that be?' Drew asked drily.

'Let's sit down,' Roger said. 'I'm starving.'

Annabelle wasn't, but she walked along with them, with Roger's arms still around her and Drew, to the table and took her seat.

Once both men were seated, Drew waved a hand at Roger. 'Go ahead, genius.'

Holding up both hands as if was a preacher praising the Lord, Roger said, 'A masquerade ball!'

They each took turns looking at one another, her at Drew, Drew at her, both of them at Roger and him at both of them.

He was the only one smiling. 'No one will know who she is.'

'Until she says something,' Drew said. 'Everyone will recognise her American accent.'

Roger shrugged. 'No one knows that's where the Duchess of Compton went and will believe she is a guest, nothing more.'

Donald appeared, followed by serving girls, and within moments their plates and glasses were full and the room was empty except the three of them.

Annabelle kept her thoughts to herself. She'd always wanted to attend a masquerade ball, but couldn't admit that now. Not after she'd already said she'd stay in her room the entire time.

'That could work,' Drew said. 'As long as she doesn't remove her mask.'

'There would be no need for her to,' Roger replied.

They were both looking at her. She had to say something, so went with logic. 'What about before the ball and afterwards? Mansfield is a distance from London. Won't the guests need to spend the night?'

Drew nodded as he used his knife and fork to slice his meat. 'Yes, they will.' He looked directly at her. Grinned. 'That's when you can remain in your room.'

'You are mocking me,' she stated.

'Simply repeating what you said.'

'With a grin. A mocking one.' She cut the meat on her plate, trying not to smile. It wasn't a laughing matter. He simply affected her in ways he shouldn't. No other man ever had.

'I owe you an apology, Miss Smith,' Roger said. 'I was assuming more than I should have and while doing so, I attempted to get on your good side more forcefully than I should have. You see, I thought—'

'Roger—' Drew started.

Roger held up the hand holding his fork. 'No, let me finish. I didn't know if you were here to ruin my best friend or not. I've always had his

back and he's always had mine, so I felt my interference was needed. Now, I realise that my interference is needed, for you. Whether you are Lady
Annabelle Fredrickson or Annabelle Smith, you
have the right to live the life you choose and I'm
honoured to help you make that happen.'

Annabelle wasn't sure if he was attempting
to woo her again, or if the was telling the truth.
His green eyes were twinkling with merriment.

'You see, my plan is for Drew to host this party
so the most influential people in all of London
will have the opportunity to meet you as Miss
Smith from America. Your accent alone will assure they remember you and when your… When
the Earl of Westerdownes attempts to claim that
you either are or are not his granddaughter, people will have met you and either way question
the age-old betrothal. If the Earl claims you are
not his granddaughter, then they'll insist he re-
leases Drew from the betrothal so he can marry
you and if he insists you are his granddaughter,
then they will insist the betrothal hold true and
you marry, which of course is not what the Earl
wants.'

She could see the method to his madness, but
there was one important detail she needed to
point out. 'But Drew and I do not wish to marry.'

'I know. You want to return to America.'

Roger pointed his fork at Drew. 'And he's vowed to help you. I'll help, too. And that is the best part.' He poked a potato with his fork and popped it in his mouth.

She waited at he chewed, looked at Drew, who shrugged and turned his waiting gaze on Roger.

'Once you've left for America, Drew can claim you refused to remain in England and no one would expect him to uphold the betrothal, even the Earl, so either way you both win. You get to go home, Drew gets to stay in England and the betrothal is null and void.'

'You've really thought this out,' Drew said.

Roger picked up his glass. 'That's what I'm here for. To solve all your woes.'

A shiver tickled her spine at the frown that filled Drew's face.

'You've offered to buy the estate in the past,' Roger said. 'Westerdownes had to refuse because her whereabouts were unsettled. However, once she returns to America, I bet he'll gladly sell to you. She'll have denounced her heritage, which will allow him to keep the money all to himself.'

Annabelle felt her brows tighten as she looked down at her plate. She knew her grandfather didn't want her to be his granddaughter, yet it was oddly disheartening to be so unwanted. Contemplating that, she asked, 'Why can't I just do that? Denounce my heritage?'

'Do you have proof that you're Annabelle Fredrickson?' Roger asked.

She thought of the diary, the necklace, the box that was hidden in her room. Drew was the only person she'd told about the diary. He believed she'd come by it honestly, but others might not. Effie said she looked like her mother, but that wasn't proof, either.

'The proof doesn't lie on her shoulders,' Drew said. 'It lies on Westerdownes's. He's the one that doesn't want her to be, because he's the one to gain the most.'

Annabelle sensed Drew was trying to make her feel better. She didn't. Because she knew he was the one to gain the most by her being Annabelle Fredrickson. He would own the estate without having to pay her grandfather a penny. He could then make all the changes he wanted to at the mine, make life better for a large number of people. She would be home, in Virginia, and never see it happen, but it would. Drew would make it happen. Whereas, if nothing changed, her grandfather would continue to claim every penny he could for himself.

'When will this ball take place?' she asked.

'This weekend,' Drew replied. 'Saturday evening.'

Three days—perhaps even two because people most likely would arrive on Friday due to the distance to London. The ball didn't frighten her, it sounded fun—what did was something that hadn't been said, merely implied. 'Why would people think Drew wants to marry me?'

'Because the two of you will act as if you're smitten with each other,' Roger said with a laugh. 'Everyone loves a good love story. Especially members of the *ton*. It's right up there next to a good scandal.' He wiggled his brows. 'Either way, we win.'

Chapter Ten

Word of the ball had spread through London like wildfire, including into her grandfather's home, because by Thursday afternoon, Mrs Quinn arrived, full of direct orders from the Earl of Westerdownes to cancel the party.

Mrs Quinn didn't display any of the kind, welcoming and excited attitude she'd used when Annabelle had first arrived in London. 'I have been ordered to request that you use whatever influence you have on the Duke to convince him to cancel this event and send everyone home before they get a glimpse of you,' Mrs Quinn stated, having sequestered Annabelle in her bedroom shortly upon arrival.

Annabelle had taken the time to think long and hard about many things and there was one that she sincerely wanted an answer for. 'Why did no one have the level of commitment to the

Duchess of Compton that you all seem to have for the Earl of Westerdownes? Did no one like her? No one feel it was unfair for her to marry a man three times her age? A man who was neither kind nor generous, but in fact, just like her father?'

Mrs Quinn's neck nearly snapped as she turned to level a stare at Effie.

'Effie didn't tell me anything,' Annabelle insisted, having grown fond of her companion despite all of her fussing. 'Nobody has told me anything. What I know, I learned from my mother.'

Effie quickly crossed the room, stood next to her. 'We were all very fond of the Duchess, miss, and very sad when she married the Duke.'

'Yet you remained committed to the Earl,' Annabelle said. 'You still are and I can't help but wonder why.'

Mrs Quinn wrung her hands together. 'It is our duty. He is our employer.'

Annabelle nodded. 'And now it is your duty to help him prove I am not his relative, by whatever means necessary.'

The look that the other two women shared made the hair on Annabelle's arms rise.

Mrs Quinn's face grew soft, sad. 'The fewer

people who know you're here, the better,' she said quietly.

The air inside her chest grew so heavy, Annabelle couldn't push it all out with a sigh.

There was more happening inside her than her continued worrying about her country, her family and getting back home. She was worrying about Drew as well. She'd come to care about him. Care what happened to him. The Earl had a grip on Drew's life, Drew's future, as strongly as the one he had on her and, at one time, on her mother.

It made her feel conflicted inside. She didn't want to care as deeply as she did about Drew. By doing so, it felt as if she was going against the very reason her mother had escaped, taking her to America. To escape an arranged marriage.

She hadn't changed her mind about marriage, nor did she have any reason to think that Drew had, either. It was just all so confusing, and scary when she thought of the Earl and what he could do.

Squaring her shoulders, she said, 'I am not my mother. The Earl will not control what I do. I will be attending the ball and would sincerely appreciate help in creating my costume. I've never attended a masquerade ball and have no idea what that entails.'

* * *

Drew felt as if there was an imposter living inside his body. The things he was feeling, thinking, were as far from normal as any could be. One thing all of him could agree upon was that having Westerdownes out of Annabelle's life for ever was a very desirable outcome.

Though a bit unorthodox, Roger had come up with a way for that to happen. Other than being absolved by the Queen, or because of known infidelity, betrothals were rarely voided.

Roger had also sent word to his companies in Southampton. His employees had connections with ships from countries around the world and could obtain information about every ship that had been anywhere near the American coast.

Drew urged Fellow into a faster gait, having let the horse set their speed since leaving the stable. The one downfall of Roger's plan was that without Westerdownes overseeing her shares of the mine, the truth that his changes were profitable would lie directly on his shoulders. It already had, but he'd had Westerdownes's income as proof. With only his own numbers, Parliament might not be so willing to hear his testaments. Some of his peers considered him irrational, criticising his changes, and that would increase. He didn't mind that and, with Westerdownes out of the picture, he'd have more capital, more freedom to reinvest profits back into the workers.

What he minded was that Annabelle got nothing, except a trip home. He couldn't guarantee that would happen, not until he knew it would be completely safe for her to return to America.

Maybe he should change his stance. Consider going along with the betrothal.

His stomach recoiled and he urged Fellow into a full gallop. There was just no simple way out of any of this and most certainly no perfect outcome.

As the mine came into view, he shoved everything else to the back of his mind. He had the ability to change some things as they stood and that is what he would focus on for the next few hours.

He was actually at the mine for several hours. His conversation with Gunner led him to converse with several other miners about a variety of topics. The insight he'd gained had given him plenty of avenues to explore.

However, all of them slipped his mind when he got close to home and noticed the coach near the stable. Instantly disturbed, he rode past it and didn't stop Fellow until they reached the front door. There, he dismounted, left Fellow near the steps and hurried inside.

'Where's Annabelle?' he asked the approaching Donald.

'Upstairs, in her room.'

'With whom?' Drew's blood was pounding. 'That's Westerdownes's coach.'

'Yes, it is. A Mrs Quinn arrived earlier.'

Drew had been at Westerdownes's town house enough to know that Mrs Quinn was the old man's housekeeper. 'Why is she here?'

'She did not say, Your Grace. Just said she needed to speak with the young miss and they retreated up to Miss Smith's room.'

Drew paced the floor, glancing beyond the hall to the staircase. He couldn't go barging in her room like a lunatic. 'How long has she been here?'

'A couple of hours.'

He stopped. 'And they are still up there?'

'Yes.'

Were they packing her clothes? Westerdownes undoubtably had heard about the ball and sent his housekeeper to retrieve Annabelle. Should he let her go?

Drew raked a hand through his hair. That wasn't the question. *Could* he let her go was the question and the answer to that was no. There was no telling what Westerdownes might have in store for her. 'Send a maid to her room, inform Miss Smith I need to see her in my study post-haste.'

'Yes, Your Grace.' Donald gave a slight bow before he turned about, then exited.

Drew wasn't sure if he saw or imagined a slight grin on Donald's face. Concluding it didn't matter, he made his way to his study. He'd never held this deep of concern over someone. Then again, he'd never met anyone like Annabelle before. He'd never wanted anyone the way he wanted her, either.

The air seeped out of his lungs.

He'd done it. Admitted the one thing he'd been refusing to admit, to even think about, yet it had been there since the moment he'd seen her in the loft of the stable. In the days since then, that want had grown deeper and it had expanded. He didn't just want her body like he had others in the past. He wanted her. All of her. And not just sexually.

She was different. Not only innocent in one particular aspect, but thoughtful, intelligent, trustworthy, dedicated and committed. Determined. He liked her companionship. Liked having her in his home, at his table, in his stable, in his life.

Above all, she needed him. He'd never been

needed before. Never wanted to be needed, but she needed his protection. By damned, she'd have it. From Westerdownes and anyone else.

'Is something the matter? Had you been at the mine? Did something happen there?'

He'd turned to face the open doorway upon hearing her first question and once again his heart pounded inside his chest at the sight of her. She was wearing the same olive-green and cream-coloured dress as she had at the breakfast table, yet, perhaps because of his silent admission, she looked more beautiful than ever. 'Yes, I was at the mine and, no, nothing of concern has happened there.'

She pressed a hand to her breastbone as she fully entered the room and let out a small sigh. 'I was worried when the maid said you needed to speak to me immediately.'

Donald appeared in the doorway and Drew nodded for the man to close the door. 'I apologise for causing concern.'

Her gaze lingered on his face as a gentle smile curved her lips upwards. 'You learned of Mrs Quinn's arrival upon your return home.'

'Yes, I did.'

She crossed the room to the window, gazed out, looking at the coach that was visible. 'She was instructed to either cancel the party or take me to London.'

He forced himself to keep from saying more than asking, 'Which will it be?'

Turning to face him, she crossed her arms. 'It's your party, only you can cancel it, and I will never be *taken* some place I don't want to go ever again.'

Drew bit the inside of his cheek to keep from grinning at her bravado. 'Mrs Quinn is still here.' That was simply his way of saying the other woman wouldn't give in that easily. Westerdownes would have her head if she did.

She smiled. 'I know. She's helping me.'

'Helping you? With what?'

'My costume for the ball. Effie is helping, too, as well as Rosemary and Kate. There were things we needed.' Her smile faded as she walked towards him. 'We have to do this, Drew. For the people who work at the mine, for you, for me. Roger's plan didn't make sense to me at first, but it does now. Even more after Mrs Quinn arrived. My grandfather doesn't deserve –' She shook her head and placed two fingers over her lips for a moment. 'Does he have any money besides—?'

'Yours?' he finished for her. 'No. He was broke when your mother married the Duke.' Along with the tales of how the Duchess had disappeared were those about how the Earl had auctioned his daughter off to the highest bidder. Drew had no way of knowing if that had been true, but knew the Earl had a large, steady income now.

'He won't relinquish it easily,' she said.

She was standing within touching distance and he wanted to do just that, but kept his hands at his sides. 'No, he won't.'

'Then we can't, either. We can't let him win again.' She laid a hand on his chest, grinned. 'What are you wearing to the ball?'

He wondered if she could feel how fast his heart was beating beneath her hand. 'I haven't thought about it.' Between his pounding heart and her touch, he was becoming so lightheaded he wasn't sure he could remember his name right now.

'You haven't?' She lifted her hand, but only to give his chest a playful pat, before resting it there again. 'You have to decide. You can either wear a mask or dress up as someone famous and paint your face, but I'm sure everyone will know who are if you only paint your face. I think you should wear a mask.'

He curled his fingers around the hand she had on his chest to keep it there and worked hard at convincing himself that he could not kiss her. Could not. 'I don't have a mask.'

'Have you ever attended a masquerade ball before?'

'No.' Her eyes were shimmering, making it hard to keep his concentration on the subject. 'Have you?'

'No. I'm excited. I'll have Effie and Mrs Quinn help me make you a costume, too. One with a mask. And Donald. I'm sure he can find things we can use in your wardrobe.'

'I'm sure he can.'

'Did you invite the miners while at the mine today?'

Momentarily confused, he asked, 'Invite them to what?'

She giggled. 'The ball.'

'No.'

'Why not? I'm sure Lena won't be up to coming, not this soon after giving birth to Oscar, but other workers and their families would like to attend, wouldn't they?'

'The mine workers can't be invited to the ball.'

'Why not?'

'Because the ball is only for those of the peerage.'

She took a step back, her face aghast. 'Well, that's not very kind.'

He felt her disappointment. 'It's the way it is,' was the only justification he could think of.

'Back home, everyone is invited. As long as they are breathing, they are welcome to attend.' She shrugged. 'Who knows, we might have even had a few ghosts at some parties. Can't say for sure.'

He chuckled at that, but what she was saying touched him. He'd spent hours talking with miners about ways to support them and this could be a way to show them that he was serious about those discussions. 'We can have another party. One where we can invite the miners and their families. An outdoor party, with games for the children.'

Her smile returned with a brilliance that lit up her entire face. 'That would be wonderful! We could have all sorts of games and events. Three-legged races and—'

He held up a hand. 'Let's get through one party before planning the second one.'

She laughed. 'You're right, but I will talk to Lena about it when I go visit her tomorrow. I'm sure she'll have ideas for the party.'

Drew questioned if he should point out that as a lady of the peerage, she could provide assistance to those in need, but not actually become friends with them. He chose not to, because she wouldn't care and, truthfully, neither did he. When he'd been young, the only friends he'd had had been the servants' children and he'd missed them when he'd left for school.

Memory lane then took him down another path, to that of school, when other parents would arrive to pick up their children for the holidays. How mothers would rush forward, hugging their sons after not seeing them for so long, and how the boys would tell their mothers to not hug them, not kiss them in front of others. He'd been jealous, wished he'd had a mother. That's when he'd started separating himself more and more. Staying in his room until a driver had arrived to bring him home. Home to an empty house. Where there had been no mother to kiss him, no father to ruffle his hair.

He'd sworn he didn't need those things and never would. That he would never need anyone.

'Drew?'

Giving his head a clearing shake, he said, 'Sorry, just wondering what's in my wardrobe for a costume.' That hadn't been in his thoughts, but now that he'd said it it had been, something else surfaced. 'There's no reason for you to have to make something. I'll figure it out.'

'I like my plan better. It will keep Mrs Quinn and Effie busy.' She lifted one shoulder in a tiny shrug. 'Mrs Quinn said she couldn't return without me, so I told her she could stay until after the party. Kate said she could use the extra help.'

'I'm sure she can.'

'So you don't mind?'

'No, I don't mind.'

Her relief was revealed by how her smile grew again. 'Thank you.'

They were still standing in the centre of the room, facing each other, holding hands, and he wasn't ready to release his hold. 'What sort of costume are you making for yourself?'

'I can't tell you.'

'Do you think I won't recognise you?'

'We'll see. Won't we?'

Her eyes were sparkling, her lips glistening, and he wanted to pull her close, kiss her, so badly he had to tighten his muscles, willing every part of him to not move. She smelled fresh, like sunshine and flowers, along with a hint of mint. That made him smile. Her smile increased and she tilted her head, as if aligning it with his so their lips could meet.

Damn it to hell! He drew in a breath, dipped his head and felt the air rush out of his body at the sound of Roger shouting his name while throwing open the door.

'Oh,' Roger said and closed the door just as fast as he'd opened it.

But the moment was gone.

Annabelle had bowed her head and Drew held silent several select words he had for his best friend right now.

It took every ounce of willpower that Annabelle possessed to keep from lifting her face, stretching on to her toes, and kissing Drew. She'd been sure he'd been about to kiss her when Roger had opened the door. The desire for that to happen was tenfold stronger than it had been before. There was more, too. Her belly was all a-flutter and her heart was beating so fast, it was hard to catch her breath.

She tried hard to ignore all those things. 'I… um…'

'I'll see you at dinner,' he said, releasing her hand.

She had no choice but to let her hand drop to her side and walk to the door. There, she managed to say, 'Yes, I'll see you at dinner.'

The hallway was empty. Grateful for that, she hurried to the staircase and up it, not slowing until she reached the hallway that led to her room. She stopped then and leaned against the wall, needing a moment for all the commotion inside her to settle.

There was a painting hanging on the wall across from her. It was of a large ship, sails full of wind as it sailed into a majestically glowing sunset. The painting was one of the landmarks she'd noted when learning her way around the house.

What was wrong with her? Her entire future was at stake. One wrong move and everything would be for naught. Drew wouldn't have full control of the mine and she wouldn't be on her way back to America.

The air seeped out of her lungs. Oh, how she wished she knew what was happening back at home. She tried not to think about it, and when she did, she tried to convince herself that the war had stopped. That the politicians had figured out a way for everyone to be treated equally, just like Drew had said. It had been that way in her hometown of Hampton. People of all nationalities and walks of life had been welcomed into the community, but it hadn't been that way in other places where the rich had focused on getting richer upon the backs of others.

It shouldn't be that way, but in her mind, war wasn't the answer. There should be a more civilised way to make changes. She understood it would take time, because changing minds and habits was never easy, and sincerely hoped the politicians back home had learned that by now. They had been the ones set on war rather than trying to settle things peacefully. Her father claimed politicians usually always got their way and they certainly had this time. He'd also said it wouldn't take the Union long to let the Confederates know they were fighting a losing battle.

She wished she was there, helping to defend her country, yet, as oddly as it seemed, she was glad she was here. Glad she'd met Drew.

It was also comforting knowing that she wasn't in this alone. That she and Drew were working together. They would win, too.

She just had to learn to control these wild thoughts about kissing him that kept popping up.

Annabelle pushed off the wall to make her way to her room, but was stopped after only a few steps.

'Excuse me, miss,' Donald said. 'His Grace is requesting your attendance in his study.'

'Again?' she asked.

Standing stiff and tall, Donald always looked serious, but it was how he smiled with his eyes that she noticed and that's what he was doing now. 'Yes, miss.'

Smiling at him in return, she turned to make

her way back downstairs. This time she wasn't fearful something was wrong. However, she sincerely hoped she wouldn't become overwhelmed with any unusual desires, including kissing.

Drew was waiting for her near the doorway and escorted her into the room, where Roger was standing near the large fireplace. This room was very masculine, with dark wood and large leather furniture, and another favourite of hers because it smelled so nice, like fresh air and spice. Like Drew.

Upon closing the door, he gently touched her elbow, guided her towards the sofa that was flanked by two matching high-backed chairs.

The sombreness in the air caused her concern and she lifted her gaze in silent question to Drew as she took a seat on the sofa.

'Roger discovered something at your estate today,' he said.

What she'd seen there had been nothing but a mess. She shifted her gaze to Roger. 'What?'

He reached behind the chair next to him and lifted out a canvas painting. It wasn't framed and the backside was facing her. Drew sat down next to her and her stomach hiccupped as he took a hold of her hand.

'It was hidden in the rafters of the stable at the estate,' Drew said.

Her breath caught as Roger slowly turned the canvas about. It was her mother. Though it had been years since she'd seen her mother, it wasn't an image she'd ever forget. Dressed in an emerald-green dress, her mother was younger than she remembered, but it was the sadness in the blue eyes that she'd only seen full of happiness that made her press a hand to her breastbone.

The portrait was large, at least two feet wide and three feet tall. Roger set it on the chair and Annabelle rose, walking closer to examine the painting. Her mother's long dark hair was piled high and she wore the very emerald and pearl necklace that was in the box along with the diary.

'It's my mother,' Annabelle said quietly.

'It was wrapped in feed sacks,' Roger said. 'That made me think a member of the stable staff must have hidden it.'

'Effie said my grandfather had all pictures of her destroyed. Perhaps my father issued the same order.' She glanced up at Drew who had stood and walked beside her to the portrait. 'Or my grandfather had once he took over the estate.'

He rubbed her shoulder. 'She was a beautiful woman. The likeness between the two of you is unmistakable.'

She'd been told that throughout her life, but had never seen it because she'd been young when her mother had died. Now, though, she felt as if she was looking in a mirror. This was the proof that her grandfather didn't want her to find. Didn't want anyone to find.

It was a strange reality, knowing that someone wanted her true identity erased. She pressed a fingertip to her forehead, as if that could stop her from thinking, but nothing would do that. Her mother looked so sad in the portrait. There was no light in her eyes. No smile on her lips. Yet there was also a sense of strength in the portrait. The lift of her chin, the squareness of her shoulders, as if she was silently saying that, despite all, she wasn't giving up.

Annabelle couldn't help but wonder about that. The strength it had taken for her mother to leave, to find a better life. She had done that. The life she'd found in America had been full of a happiness that wasn't evident in the portrait in any way.

Had she inherited any of that strength from her mother?

'I will have it cleaned and framed for you,' Drew said.

She nodded. 'Thank you. You know what this means, don't you?'

Drew and Roger exchanged a wary glance.

She knew. This meant she could no longer

deny her heritage. It wasn't the identity she'd always claimed, but it was her identity. She was her mother's daughter.

'It doesn't change our plan,' Drew said. 'It simply means we have proof, no matter which path Westerdownes takes.'

That was true, but it didn't solve the dilemma inside her. She had to decide if she wanted to defend her heritage or return to America and forget all about it. That also meant forgetting all about Drew.

Chapter Eleven

Drew pushed the heavy air from his lungs and shifted his stance, trying to ease the tension from every muscle. He'd never liked parties and hosting one had been the last thing he'd ever wanted.

His house was overflowing with men and women wearing outlandish outfits and acting like fools. They'd begun arriving yesterday and, not wanting Annabelle's identity revealed, he'd escorted her to Lena's to spend the better part of the day, returning last night after dark where she took her meal in her room. She had remained there today. He didn't like the idea of her having to hide, not from anything. She should be free. As free as her spirit. It felt as if he was holding her prisoner and it was for him, not her. That shouldn't be.

Furthermore, his household staff shouldn't have to put up with all the extra work of meeting the demands of people they'd never met before and would never have to encounter again.

The disgusting truth was this was all happening because he didn't want to fulfil his commitments. Yes, those commitments had been imposed upon him as a child, but, none the less, they were his to honour. To fulfil.

Long ago he'd determined to never be in a position where he'd have to make a choice between duty and family, but wasn't he doing that now? And choosing duty?

Annabelle deserved to find and marry a man who would love her, choose her over duty. That was also why he was disturbed. He could never be that man, yet a dark part of him didn't want another man to be that man, either. That didn't make sense. He'd never cared one way or another about a woman like that. Ever. Why now?

Perhaps because he'd got to know her better than any other woman. That was just as unusual—the fact he'd wanted to get to know her right from the start. Which in the end wouldn't make any difference. No matter how well he knew her, he could never love her. A person who had never experienced love didn't know how to give or receive it.

He'd been raised by servants who had been good to him, but they'd never loved him. Neither had his father. His occasional visits hadn't been out of love, they'd been out of commitment. Duty.

His father had fulfilled that commitment and now it was his turn. But he had to fulfil the commitment of not fulfilling a commitment.

No wonder he was so confused. None of it made sense.

An annoying twitter of giggles penetrated his thoughts as a trio of women, holding sticks that their jewelled and feathered eye masks were attached to and wearing dresses that were so frilly and brightly coloured it hurt his eyes, made their way towards him. Drew took a step back, elbowed Roger in the ribs and nodded towards the trio.

He then skirted around Roger and headed towards the doorway, hoping another room would be less crowded and damning the mask over his face the entire way. He could barely see through the eye slits of the purple hood that covered the upper half of his face. The only reason he hadn't removed it was because he'd yet to find Annabelle.

Nearly an hour ago, he'd questioned venturing up to her room. The only reason he hadn't was because he knew she wouldn't skip the event. Upon seeing the portrait of her mother, she'd insisted the ball go ahead as planned, but he'd also sensed a new hesitancy upon her part. There was a new hesitancy towards him, too. It wasn't just because of the influx of guests. During their ride to and from the Ericksons' home she'd been quiet and distant, barely answering his questions about Oscar and Caroline, and the party they'd host next weekend. Two subjects that in the past had made her face light up.

He entered the hallway and turned left, to walk towards the ballroom. The one room he'd been avoiding. Never had he put his name on a lady's dance card when it hadn't been specifically required of him and he had no intention of changing that tonight. As host, it was his job to make sure there were no wallflowers and he'd told Roger that job had been transferred to him. It was only fair since this entire event was Roger's idea.

However, the ballroom was the only room in which he'd yet to look for Annabelle. Despite her insisting it wasn't necessary, he should have had Donald tell him when she was ready and escorted her downstairs.

A tingling sensation tickled his spine and he paused his footsteps, looking over his shoulder. The sight had him pivoting on one heel as a smile voluntarily tugged at his lips. Her ball gown was an affair of blue and white silk and lace. As was the mask covering the upper half of her face, but to him, she was completely recognisable. Her glistening dark hair had been curled and pinned up in a way that left spirals of hair framing her face and neckline.

The square neckline of her dress enhanced the gracefulness of her neck, the gentle slope of her shoulders, but those were things he'd admired long before this evening.

He strode towards her, faster than normal because he didn't want someone stepping out of one of the rooms and encountering her before he reached her.

Arriving at her side, he was a both breathless and tongue-tied.

Both were unusual for him.

'Rosemary was having a difficult time making my mask stay put,' Annabelle said as if apologising. 'The pins wouldn't hold it, so she had to braid the ties into my hair.'

She tilted her head for him to see the ties that held the lacy mask over her eyes and the action made his grin grow. 'They look lovely. You look lovely.'

'Thank you,' she said with a graceful curtsy. 'You look quite dashing yourself. Do you like your mask?'

'As much as a person can like a mask.'

She giggled. 'They are cumbersome.'

'Yes, they are, but yours is very lovely.'

'I'll let Effie know you approve. She shortened my dress sleeves and used that material to make it. I'm not sure where she found the material to make yours, but it matches your waistcoat and frock coat perfectly.'

He had no idea where the material came from. Just as he had no idea where many of the thoughts flowing through his mind had come from. They were all about her, including how he would do anything to help her. To see her happy. And how badly he wanted her. In an attempt to push that thought aside, he gave her a slight bow because it was the only way he could think to pull his eyes off her. 'I'll let her know I appreciate her efforts and talent.'

She sighed and glanced down the hallway. 'I wasn't sure where I'd find you. Effie said not to worry, that at a masquerade ball, no one is introduced to one another, but I've never gone to a party alone.'

He read more into her words and once again wished he had gone upstairs to escort her down. 'You are not alone, nor will I abandon you.'

'I didn't expect to be this nervous.'

'There is no need to be nervous.'

'I can't help it. All the rules Effie kept mentioning made me nervous.'

'What rules?'

'How you can only dance with those who sign your dance card, how you can't talk to someone while dancing with them, how you can't talk to someone you haven't been formally introduced to and how—'

'Forget the rules,' he interrupted.

'All of them?'

He nodded.

'But what do I do with this?' She pulled out the miniature fan-shaped paper dance card from a small lace pouch attached to the waistline of her dress.

He took the dance card and, using the pencil that was attached to it with a gold thread and the palm of his opposite hand as a desk pad, wrote his name on each line. 'There. Now your card is full.'

She giggled while returning the dance card to the pouch. 'Well, that does solve that issue.'

Although he'd much rather stand here, he held out his arm to her. 'Shall we?'

With a tiny, one-shoulder shrug, she said, 'I guess so.'

He'd avoided affairs like this his entire life. When he did attend them out of pure necessity, he preferred positioning himself in the men's drawing room with a drink and male conversation whenever possible.

That wasn't possible tonight and he hated the idea of her being exposed to the flaunting of his peers in attendance. They were all related to titles in some form or another and felt that made them exceptional. It didn't and, even hidden behind her mask, she was far more beautiful than any other here or elsewhere.

Roger entered the hallway just as they approached the door to the room.

'There you are, I thought you'd both abandoned me,' he said.

Drew had no idea where Roger had obtained his gold and black mask, but it did little to hide his identity. The thick black sideburns were a dead giveaway.

'I can see I shouldn't have worried,' Roger whispered before raising his voice to say, 'You look extremely lovely, Miss Smith.'

Others both exiting and entering the room paused to take long looks at Annabelle, which had been Roger's intent.

Once again, Drew wondered if he'd been momentarily insane when he agreed to go along with this plan. Wanting to reiterate that he would not abandon her, he slid an arm around Annabelle, rested his hand on the small of her back and smiled down at her when her eyes lifted to him.

Her return smile was one that allowed him to read her mind, telling him she was ready. He gave her a nod and, together, they crossed the hall.

As soon as they entered the room, people collected around them and soon he and Annabelle had drinks in hand and were conversing about numerous subjects with a variety of masked men and women. Her charm and intelligence filled him with a great sense of pride.

Soon the buzz filling every room in the house was all about the American.

Several men asked if she'd care to accompany them to the ballroom and Drew attempted to keep his eyes averted while she graciously explained each time that she would visit the ballroom later and that her card was already full.

Though she was kind and amiable, her responses weren't easily accepted, and before long Drew escorted her into the ballroom and on to the dance floor.

She danced the waltz as smooth and elegantly as a bird flies and, for the first time since he'd been forced to attend dances in school, he truly enjoyed guiding a woman across the floor.

'Why are men and women not supposed to speak while dancing?' she asked while covertly glancing at couples around them.

'I'm not the one to ask about society rules,' he responded. 'Especially those young women are meant to abide by.'

'Why?'

'Because I'm not a young woman.'

The blue of her mask made her eyes all the brighter. 'I know that.' She leaned a bit closer. 'And I know we are stirring up gossip.'

He increased the pressure of his hand on her back, holding her as close as her wide skirt would allow. 'That was the plan.'

'I know, but now everyone knows you are the only name on my dance card.'

'Do you want to dance with others?'

'No.'

He didn't either. 'Then what is the problem?'

Annabelle knew what the problem was, but couldn't voice it. He looked so handsome, even with his head and face partially covered with the purple, hooded mask that was hemmed with thick gold cording. His tailed jacket and high boots were similar to those others wore, but he stood out. He smelled good, too, a mixture of fresh air and spice, and dancing with him made her feet so light it was as though she was floating. It made her head light, too.

She had to keep telling herself to breathe and, when the next dance was done, she was overly grateful when he suggested they leave the room. Anywhere had to be cooler than the crowded room. Her entire being felt overheated. What she'd assumed was feelings of friendship for him felt deeper tonight. Perhaps because he'd been so attentive. He had a way of making her feel comfortable no matter the situation. He'd had a way of doing that since her arrival, but tonight it was different. She felt as if they were a pair. Like the parakeets in the stable.

'Would you care for something to eat or drink?' he asked as they entered the hallway.

The couple walking towards them held her attention for a moment. Their costumes were quite outrageous. The woman had a gigantic teacup and saucer atop her head—the size of a wash tub—and the man wore a white mask with a nose at least a foot long. Drew nodded at the couple as they continued on their way and then glanced at her. Once again, she felt the connection between them and they both laughed, reading each other's thoughts about the other couples' costumes.

As her giggle subsided, she responded to his question, 'No, thank you. I ate in my room.'

'Why?'

'Have you ever tried to sit down while wearing a caged crinoline?'

'No, I can't say I have.'

'Let me assure you that it's rather impossible.' She thrust a hip sideways, making the wired cage swing against his leg. 'Feel that? It's metal.'

His laugh was louder.

'It's rather impossible to walk up and down stairs when you can't see your feet, too.'

'Why do you wear it if it's so uncomfortable, cumbersome, and potentially dangerous?'

'It's called fashion.'

He nodded, then whispered, 'Teacups must be, too.'

'Hush!' she whispered and slapped a hand over her mouth to muffle her laugh because the teacup lady had changed her route and was now only a few feet behind them.

'Would you care for some fresh air?' he whispered.

Excitement filled her. 'Do you mean it?'

'Yes.'

Keeping her voice low, she asked, 'Could we walk to the stables? I haven't seen Champion since yesterday morning. I know Finnegan has rubbed him down with ointment, but I'd like to say hello.' A hint of chagrin rose up inside her as she thought of another rule Effie had mentioned—one that had been true back home, too, of never being alone with a man. 'That would be highly improper, wouldn't it?'

'Not in my eyes,' he said. 'This way.'

More than happy to comply, she followed him down the hallway and then through a closed doorway. She thought she'd learned the layout of the house completely, but Drew led her through that room and then down a corridor she didn't recognise and out a door that was also unfamiliar. 'Where are we?'

'The north side of the house. We'll have to walk around the gardens and the backside of the wall to get to the stable.'

Contentment filled her. 'That sounds wonderful.'

'I do think we are more alike than either of us realised.'

Yes, they were and she didn't mind that in the least.

Champion didn't mind the visit either. His stance had changed greatly since she'd arrived. He no longer looked pained and moved about in his stall with ease and at will. Tonight, he eagerly walked over and stuck his head over the wood, expecting a pat. She'd barely had time to stroke his nose and scratch him behind the ears before Drew grasped her arm.

'Someone's coming.' Tugging her towards the area where the carriages were stored, he said, 'This way.'

They'd no sooner entered that room when she heard the stable door open and laughter ring out. Drew kept tugging her in his wake, to the door that he'd led her out to see the sunset the other evening.

Once outside, she whispered, 'Who was it?'

'I don't know.'

'What are they doing in the stable?' As soon as she said it, she knew what she should have realised right away. Her cheeks stung. Not for what the couple was doing, but for her own thoughts about kissing Drew, which were stronger than ever. 'Are you going to stop them?'

'No.' He led her along the side of the stable, but stopped at the corner and, after peeking around it, turned about. 'We'll go back this way.'

'Why?' Curious, she didn't wait for an answer and instead stepped forward, peering around the corner. A man and woman were sneaking into one of the many coaches parked along the side of the stable. Her cheeks flushed even hotter and she spun back around and nearly collided against him. Her heart thudded harder, so did her mind.

Was everyone having the same thoughts as her tonight?

He laughed quietly.

'Hush,' she whispered, pressing her hands against his chest. 'They might hear you.'

'I doubt it.'

The moon was shining brightly, making the gold on his mask shimmer and sparkle, almost as brightly as his eyes, and his smile. 'Have you ever done that?' she asked.

'What?'

'Sneaked out of a party to kiss a girl.'

'Not that I can remember.' He touched her shoulders with both hands. 'Have you sneaked out to kiss a boy?'

She hadn't, but had thought about those who had and why they would do that. She was thinking about that now, too. Stronger and harder than ever. Maybe this was her chance to see what that was like. She'd never wanted to kiss someone before and... Before she gave herself more time to think it through, she stretched on to her toes and closed the distance between his lips and hers quickly. So quickly their noses bumped.

Then, before she could react and pull back, his hold on her shoulders tightened and his lips met hers. Soft and warm.

'Kissing is best when it starts out slow,' he whispered against her lips. 'Like this.'

He tilted his head sideways and his lips moved along hers so gently her entire being felt as if it was melting. The contact was so enticing, her lips began to move, meeting his with a perfection she couldn't explain. She couldn't explain the happiness inside her, either.

'Then, it grows faster,' he whispered, never taking his lips off hers.

His lips moved faster then, coaxing hers into a speed that was fascinating and heated. The melting of her body turned in a swirling heat deep inside as the pressure of his mouth became firmer and his lips caught, held and released hers with swiftness she had no difficult keeping up with. Not at all.

When his lips parted and his tongue slid over her bottom lip, she opened her mouth, and arched to become even closer to him. His hands cupped the sides of her face as the kiss continued.

It was unlike anything she'd ever known. Her hands had slid up around his neck. She wanted to hold on to him for ever, continue kissing with their lips and tongues, feeling the amazing sensations within every ounce of her body.

She wasn't prepared for the kiss to end and, when he pulled his mouth away from hers, she was breathing hard and had to blink several times to focus her vision.

'Now we both have sneaked out of a party to steal a kiss,' he whispered. 'And I promise not to tell, but we need to leave before we are the ones who get caught.'

A faint giggle reached her ears and the reality of them being seen cleared the fog from her mind, but nothing would slow the wild beating of her heart or the burning heat inside her.

He took hold of her hand and held it as they slowly made their way back around the garden wall. The glances they shared upon hearing rustling or giggles while snaking their way through the garden filled her with joy. So much so that when they re-entered the house the ball seemed brighter, more fun.

From the security of her room, she'd assisted with the party decorations, folding tiny paper fans for the dance cards, arranging flowers in vases from the garden and tying silk bows on to gold ropes that were draped from the ceilings, and took pride in how festive everything looked in the flickering light from the overhead chandeliers.

That festiveness lived inside her, too, and she found herself laughing more, enjoying the conversation she and Drew had with others and in dancing with him. They danced several times and when they needed a reprieve from the heat, they'd stepped outside on to the patio off the ball-room. Many others stepped outside there, too, making the area nearly as crowded as the rooms inside the house.

She and Drew also shared secretive glances and grins over outlandish costumes, but other times, the glances they shared were just because and it was those ones that stole her breath away. Held her captive as the memory of their time outside filled her thoughts.

'It's almost midnight,' he said close to her ear when they were once again sashaying across the dance floor.

A flash of disappointment washed over her. She truly didn't want the night to end, but the evening had filled her with such happiness, she knew it would live for ever in her mind. 'Will you remove your mask?' she asked.

'Yes. It's expected.'

It was expected of all the guests to reveal their identity, even though several people had long ago discarded their masks. She wouldn't. After this dance, she would go upstairs and hide away until the guests had all left tomorrow.

Although she had met some nice people tonight and would be interested to learn who they were, she wasn't overly upset about leaving. The ball had been fun and would leave her with memories that would last a lifetime, but she was more excited about the party they would have next weekend. Drew had confirmed it with Lena when he'd stopped to escort her home yesterday. Lena had proclaimed she was now as fit as a fiddle and had insisted upon sending Julia home yesterday as well.

'Meet me at the door we used tonight tomorrow morning at sunrise,' Drew said as the song came to an end.

She stepped back as they separated and gave him a curtsy before asking, 'Why?'

'We'll take a ride, a long one, until the guests depart.'

Laying her hand upon his arm as they exited the floor, she nodded. 'I like that idea.'

'I do, too.'

Drew escorted her to the stairs where they had met earlier in the evening. He bid her goodnight and, once she'd reached the top of the stairs after carefully holding her wide skirt out of the way for each step, she chanced a glance over her shoulder, to see him still standing there, watching her. She waved and then hurried along the long hallway that led to her bedroom. The heat of a blush was on her face, her heart was beating as fast as when they'd been dancing and she couldn't remember ever feeling so wonderful.

Effie was in her room, with a nightgown laid out on the bed. 'Were you up here the entire time?' Annabelle asked as she lifted her skirt so the wired crinoline could be untied from her waist.

'No, miss. I helped in the kitchen,' Effie replied.

Annabelle had seen Mrs Quinn several times throughout the evening, always looking as if she was doing a task of one kind or another, whereas the woman had been keeping a watchful eye on her the entire time. Expectedly. That was why Mrs Quinn hadn't returned to London.

The crinoline landed on the floor and Annabelle stepped over it to cross the soft carpet to the dressing table. 'I'm sorry that you couldn't enjoy the evening, too. You will be able to at the party next weekend.'

'That wouldn't be my place,' Effie said while releasing the braids holding the mask ties in her hair.

'Yes, it will be. Everyone will be invited to that party, including you.' Annabelle met Effie's gaze in the mirror for a moment, before the other woman bowed her head and focused on the braids. There were some rules she'd never get used to and treating others as if they were inferior was one of them.

Once the mask was free, Annabelle reached up and removed it. 'My mother taught me to be kind to everyone, to consider their feelings no matter who they were.' Of their own accord, her eyes turned to the portrait of her mother that had been cleaned, framed and hung on the wall near the window. 'Is that how you remember her? How she looks in that picture?'

'Yes, miss. She was very beautiful, and kind-hearted. The necklace she's wearing belonged to the Duke's mother,' Effie said. 'It was known as the Compton emeralds.'

Compton emeralds. As if she needed more proof of her heritage. 'Did my mother attend balls before she married?'

'Yes, miss.'

'How many?'

Effie sighed. 'Not many. The Earl only approved a few.'

'She didn't have a very happy life, did she?'

A long moment of silence echoed in the room before Effie asked, 'Would you like to remove your dress before I brush your hair?'

Annabelle had grown used to how Effie would answer some questions, but not others, and though it drove her crazy at times, she already knew the answer. Her mother's life before she'd gone to America had not been a happy one.

'Yes.' She stood and, though she'd told Rosemary and Effie that they both could assist others tonight, Effie had insisted she could not relinquish her duties.

A short time later, as she blew out the light and climbed into bed after Effie had left the room, a smile tugged at Annabelle's lips.

The window was open and the music that was still playing down below drifted in, just loud enough to lull her to sleep while remembering the kiss she and Drew had shared and wondering if they would share another one tomorrow.

She sincerely hoped so.

Or did she?

Better yet, should she?

Chapter Twelve

The sun was just peeking over the horizon when Annabelle arrived at the door and Drew appeared a mere moment later, riding Fellow and leading Millie already saddled, with Champion following.

'I thought he could use the exercise as well,' Drew said while dismounting. 'Finnegan already rubbed him down.'

'Goodness, this early?'

'Yes, he's getting the horses and coaches ready so people can leave right after breakfast.'

'Are people awake all ready?'

'Some haven't gone to bed yet.'

She'd sneaked down through the back hallway and heard people in the kitchen, but assumed the guests were still asleep. 'They haven't?'

'No.' He helped her on to Millie and then swung into the saddle on Fellow's back. 'I have our breakfast right here.' He gestured towards the basket tied to the back of his saddle. 'We can eat when we get to where we are going.'

'Where is that?'

'A place I want to show you. It's not far.'

Content to ride anywhere he wanted to go, she steered Millie alongside Fellow.

'People were wondering where you were at midnight,' he said.

She had been curious about that. 'Were they surprised when you took your mask off?'

'No, but they wanted to know who you were.'

'What did you tell them?'

'That you are Miss Annabelle Smith, visiting from America, and that you turn into a pumpkin at midnight.'

'You didn't!'

He laughed. 'No, I didn't.' Humour glimmered in his eyes as he continued, 'I told them that the ties of your mask had been braided into your hair and you needed the help of a maid to remove it.'

'You did?'

'Yes, and then I sat back and watched as they searched for you for a good half-hour before I retired.'

He was wearing a simple white shirt this morning and brown pants tucked in his high boots, but it was the smile on his face that made him so appealing. She shook her head at him. 'I'm not sure if I should laugh or reprehend your behaviour.'

'Laugh,' he said.

She laughed and enjoyed the ride and conversation as they rode over the rolling hills in a direction she hadn't yet ventured. The grass-laden hills were larger on this side of the property and they traversed to the top of one.

It was the tallest hill and that alone made her say, 'This is the hill where Champion is standing in the painting.'

'It is,' Drew answered.

'You can see your house from here,' she said as they turned to travel along the ridge.

'We can watch the guests leave,' he said. 'That's what I used to do when my father would leave. Come up here and watch until he disappeared.'

Hearing that made her sad. 'You didn't want to say goodbye to him?'

'He'd say goodbye to me the night before and ride out at sunrise.' He stopped the horse near a small cluster of trees and dismounted.

She'd been getting off a horse by herself for as long as she could remember, yet waited for him to assist her. His touch made her entire being feel as if it was singing a sweet, fun song. An impulse struck, but this time she controlled it and didn't kiss him as he lowered her to the ground. She'd be going home before long and that had been the reality she'd thought about late into the night. Her father needed her. Her community needed her. Her country needed her. Drew didn't and growing more attached to him would only make her sad when she left. Kissing definitely made her feel more attached to him. She'd never had to fight her feelings like this before and it was unbearably frustrating.

Stepping away as soon as her feet touched the ground, she asked, 'Did you ever wish you had a brother or sister?'

'No, did you?'

He was removing Fellow's bridle and she did the same for Millie, so the animals could munch on the grass without the interference of the bits in their mouths. 'Yes, I did,' she answered. 'I used to pretend I had a sister. Sometimes it was an older one named Patty and sometimes it was a younger one named Sally.'

'No brothers?' he asked.

'No.' She walked over to help him spread a blanket on the ground. 'I must have figured girls would be more fun.'

'Why would you think that?'

'From school,' she replied instantly. 'There

were two boys, brothers, Jeb and Joe, who chased the girls with frogs and snakes all the time.' Sitting down on the blanket, she helped unload the basket holding a variety of foods. 'Did you ever do that?'

'No. The school I went to didn't have any girls. It was all boys.'

'Where did girls go to school?'

'At an all-girls school.'

He handed her a plate and they continued to discuss schools, childhoods and numerous other subjects while eating and, afterwards, while watching the coaches departing his home down the hill. He pointed out specific coaches and told her who owned them and what costumes they'd been wearing last night.

She had never imagined what a duke would be like until reading her mother's diary. Drew didn't fit the image she'd imagined then. He wasn't formidable, or mean, or old. Instead, he was fun and the most likeable man she'd ever met.

'Who was your best friend before you met Roger?' she asked after the food had been packed away.

'Didn't have one.' He laid down on his back and clasped his hands behind his head. 'Didn't want one, but Roger didn't have anyone to go home to one Christmas, either. His father had died and his mother had remarried and was on a trip. I felt bad for him and told him he could come home with me. When Donald arrived to bring me home, Roger came with me and we've been best friends ever since.'

'How old were you?'

'Ten.'

She laid down on her side and propped her head on one hand. 'Donald's been with you that long?'

'Longer. Most of the staff have been here since I was born. Their children were my first playmates, but as I got older, they always had chores and I had studies; I had tutors until I went off to school.' He flipped over on to his side, facing her. 'I asked my father during one of his visits why my tutors couldn't teach the other children, too, and that's when I was sent off to boarding school.'

It was a sad tale, yet it made her smile because it made her understand him more. There was no wonder why he'd let her stay and offered to help her—he'd been helping people since he'd been a small child.

'What are you smiling about?' he asked.

'Because this is nice.'

He touched her cheek and her heart skipped several beats because she knew what was going to happen and was very excited about it. This kiss was soft, just a gentle brush across her lips, and ended far sooner than she'd have like. However, the way he stretched his arm out beneath her neck as he laid down on his back again, was nearly as wonderful as kissing him.

'Look at that cloud, it looks like a horse's head. See the head, ears and mane?'

Using his arm as a pillow, she snuggled against his side and found the cloud. 'It does. That one looks like a dragon.'

'Have you seen a dragon?'

'Only in books, how about you?'

'Only in books.'

Later, after they'd left the blanket to walk through a cluster of wild heather that had drawn her attention, Drew knew he'd never spent a more enjoyable morning, but the desire to kiss her long and hard was eating him alive. If she'd been any other woman, he would have already kissed her more than that one small peck. He would have done more than that, being out here all alone. That was what he wanted. More. But with Annabelle, he held back. He wasn't exactly sure why, other than she made him feel things he'd never thought he'd feel. She'd been doing that to him since her arrival, and that had shifted something inside him. Opened a part of him he hadn't known existed.

Would he feel all these things if she was less beautiful? If her blue eyes didn't sparkle like stars at midnight? If her smile didn't light up her entire face? If she wasn't thoughtful and kind and genuine?

If they weren't betrothed? That was at the root of it all. He could have her. For ever. All he had to do was abide by the long-ago agreement between their families.

She didn't want that. He hadn't, either, but now…

'It looks like you have company arriving,' she said.

Drew's attention quickly focused on the two riders approaching the house and a knot formed in his stomach. They weren't company. 'We need to return to the house.'

A short time later, as he escorted Annabelle into the drawing room, he questioned if he should have lied to her. Told her he didn't know who the visitors were, then he could have met with the men and been prepared for what she was about to hear. But he hadn't. He'd been honest. The men were there to report about the war in America.

One of them was the Captain who had delivered her to the Earl's house, and she quickly crossed the room. 'Captain Berland, do you have news? Has my father requested my return home?'

The hope in her voice nearly gutted Drew, especially when his gaze met the Captain's. The news was not good. Moving forward, he touched Annabelle's shoulder. 'Let's sit down.'

He felt her shoulders drop.

Drew pulled her gently backwards to the sofa and remained standing at her side when she sat.

'My father doesn't want me to return yet?' she asked.

The Captain lowered on to the chair across from her, leaning forward as he said, 'I'm afraid there is no home for you to return to.'

'What do you mean?' she asked.

'I'm sorry to inform you that entire town of Hampton was burned,' the Captain replied softly.

'Burned?' Her voice quivered. 'How could the entire town burn? What about the people? My father? And Cecilia? Where are they?'

Drew sat and wrapped a hand around her clasped and shaking hands, once again wishing he'd spoken to the men alone. Wishing he could protect her.

'This is First Mate Burrows.' Captain Berland pointed to the other man dressed in sailor garb. 'His ship arrived from America a short time ago.

I asked him to accompany me, to share what he witnessed. But, miss, I'm—'

'No, I want to hear,' she interrupted. 'Please, Mr Burrows, tell me.' She clung to Drew's hands and looking at him, said, 'Drew, tell him to tell me. Please.'

The unshed tears in her eyes tore at Drew's heart. He could feel her pain, her hurt, and wished he could make it better. 'Mr Burrows, do you know where her father is?'

'No, Your Grace,' the man replied. 'I've heard he boarded a ship, but I didn't witness that.'

'Why would he board a ship?' she asked, her voice cracking.

'The people had nowhere to go,' Mr Burrows said, twisting the hat in his hands. 'Other than the water. They were in boats, barrels, anything that would float. Confederate soldiers hit the town after midnight, with torches, and lit every building afire. We took dozens of people aboard, as many as we could find, hauled them north of the blockade. Every ship nearby did the same.'

'Where was my father taken?'

'I don't know that; I'm sorry. All the ships sailed north, to open ports. We sailed to New York. The people we'd picked up disembarked there.'

Although the man answered her questions, it

was what he wasn't saying that Drew wanted the answers to. Not in front of her, though. She was trembling, her breathing shaky. 'Gentlemen, if you will excuse us,' he said. 'Miss Smith needs a moment.'

'Of course.' Captain Berland stood.

Drew squeezed her hand before rising and walking the men to the door, where he instructed Donald to see them to his study and to find Annabelle's companion. He then returned to the sofa, sat and put his arm around her.

'The whole town can't be gone,' she said, leaning her head against his chest. 'It can't be. People live there. They have homes and businesses. The school and church. The children. It just can't be, Drew. It just can't.'

She didn't need to hear that's what happened during wars, so he just held her. Offered whatever comfort he could as she cried. He kissed the top of her head, whispered that everything would be all right and gently rocked her back and forth.

After a time, she lifted her head. 'I'm sorry. Crying like this.' She wiped the tears off her cheek. 'I have to figure out what to do. For my father and Cecilia, and Clara and baby Abigail. She's just a baby. A baby.'

He kissed her forehead. 'We'll do everything we can.'

'I just can't imagine… Just can't.'

'Shh,' he whispered. 'Don't try to imagine.'

A knock sounded on the door and before either of them moved, the door opened and her companion rushed in, followed by Mrs Quinn. 'Forgive me, Your Grace,' the companion said nervously as she skidded to a stop and performed a quick curtsy.

'Miss Smith has had some disturbing news,' he said.

'Oh, dear. Oh, my. Thank you, Your Grace,' the companion said, rushing to Annabelle.

He stood and assisted Annabelle to her feet. 'She may need to rest for a while,' Drew said to the companion.

'No.' Annabelle shook her head 'I just need to freshen up. Wash my face. I'll hurry.'

Before he could say there was no need to hurry, she was leading the servants out of the room. Drew was amazed at how she did that. Went from being clearly upset, to being staunchly determined. Truly like no woman he'd ever known.

Roger stuck his head in the doorway. 'What's the news?' he asked. 'I've been ushering people back to London as fast as possible, but a few are lingering, hoping to meet Miss Smith.'

'Get them out of here,' Drew growled as he

crossed the room. 'Soldiers burnt her home town to the ground.'

Roger let out a muffled curse. 'What are you going to do? She can't go home, now.'

'I know.' Drew headed down the hall towards his office. 'Just get rid of any lingering guests.'

Both the Captain and Mr Burrows stood when he entered the room. Drew waved for them to sit. 'Miss Smith will be along shortly and I need to know all you know before she arrives.' He looked directly at Mr Burrows. 'Is her father alive?'

'I honestly don't know, Your Grace. The ship that picked him up said Arlo—Mr Smith—had been burned fighting the fire. I don't know how badly. I didn't speak to anyone. Just heard from others.' Burrows bowed his head slightly. 'Many didn't make it.'

Drew's gut churned. He hated the idea of her losing her father under such tragic circumstances, while she was halfway around the world. 'I want to know what ship picked him up, where it is now, who captains it and who owns it.' He pointed towards both men. 'Miss Smith doesn't need to know about her father's injuries right now. She's had enough bad news for one day.'

Annabelle felt as if the bottom had dropped out of her world, but couldn't take the time to dwell on it. Dwell on the fact her home was gone. The entire town. It seemed impossible. What she had to focus on was finding her father. And Cecelia, and, oh, there were so many others. So, so many. Homer and Clara and baby Abigail and Suzanne, and… Just so many.

'You'll feel better after you lie down for a few minutes,' Effie said.

'I don't need to lie down,' Annabelle insisted. 'I just need to wash my face and—' The tears hit again. Every time she thought they were done, they struck again like a storm, pouring from her eyes, down her face. She wished she was back downstairs, with Drew's arms around her and him telling her everything would be all right.

But it wouldn't. Nothing would ever be all right again. She swiped the tears trickling down her cheeks. 'I need a cloth, please.'

It took longer than she wanted, but she finally managed to keep the tears at bay long enough that her eyes dried out. They felt hot and puffy, but so be it. She kept her head up as she walked down the staircase and focused on what she could do. Number one being find her father.

Drew was in his study. Alone.

'Captain Berland and Mr Burrows will join us in the dining room for the noon meal.' He walked towards her. 'They'll need to leave afterwards. It's a long journey back to Southampton, but they will send word of any updates as soon as they hear.'

She wasn't hungry, but understood the men would be and that they needed to leave soon. 'Did they say if they knew anything else? If they are sure it was Hampton and not some other town?'

'Mr Burrows claims it was Hampton.' He cupped her face, rubbed her cheek with his thumb. 'But they'll question every ship that arrives in Southampton, and elsewhere, for information.'

'It's just so unbelievable. So unbelievable.'

He tugged her closer, hugged her. 'I know it is.'

She rested her head on his chest and wrapped her arms around his waist, drawing invisible strength from him. Despite the sadness and worry inside her, when he kissed the top of her head, she felt the warmth of it clear to her toes and lifted her face, wanting to feel more of that warmth, more of that comfort.

What happened next was as natural as the sun rising in the east. His lips brushed against hers with feather-lightness at first, then grew firmer, making her think of nothing else.

The kiss ended as soft and tenderly as it had

started. She kept her eyes closed, focused on the wonderful sensations filling her. There was a hopefulness that hadn't been there before and she latched on to it, sealing it in her memory so she could recall it.

Drew held her close for a few moments before taking a step back and smiling down at her. 'It's time to eat.'

She nodded and wrapped her arm around his as they left the room.

The meal didn't take long, and though they answered all of her questions, neither Mr Burrows nor Captain Berland had any additional information other than what they'd said earlier.

After the men took their leave, she turned to Drew, having concluded one thing. Neither Captain Berland nor Mr Burrows would assist her in getting back to America. They'd made a point of emphasising that there was nothing left of Hampton and that Virginia and nearby Tennessee were the main battlegrounds. Though it was hard to believe, she didn't question what they'd seen or heard. It just made one thing clear. She wouldn't be going to Hampton.

They were in the hall, having walked the Captain and first mate to the door, and she told Drew, 'I need to go to New York.'

He looked at her, frowning.

'That's where Mr Burrows's ship took the people they picked up,' she explained. 'It's logical that that is where my father was taken as well.'

'That might be logical, but it's not logical for you to go to New York.'

'Yes, it is. My father doesn't know anyone in New York. No one he can stay with.'

'Do you? Do you know people you can stay with?'

Frustration grew inside her. 'No, but I have money. My father may not. If the town was torched in the middle of the night, he may have left with nothing beyond his life.' The image of that was torturous. 'I have to find him.'

Drew ran a hand through his hair and sighed heavily. 'I understand your desire to find him, but we don't know where he was taken, if it was anywhere close to New York. Furthermore, he sent you here so you would be safe, I cannot believe he would want you to return to America now. Cannot believe he would be happy that you returned to America, no matter what had happened to him.'

That might be true, but what was also true was that she hadn't left because she'd wanted to. 'There is no fighting near New York.'

'None that the Captain or Mr Burrows knew

of, but there could be now. We have no way of knowing.'

Flustered by his arguments, she said, 'You said you'd help me.'

'I will.'

'Then help me get to New York.'

'I can't.'

She didn't believe that and felt as if a storm was building inside her. A storm of anger and frustration, and hopelessness. 'You're a duke, you could if you wanted to. You just don't want to.'

He touched her arm. 'That's not true, Annabelle.'

She took a step back.

He dropped his hand to his side. 'I will help you. We just need to wait to hear more. As soon—'

'What if we don't hear more? What if no one knows more? Am I just supposed to sit here, not doing anything?'

'You can do exactly what you have been doing since you arrived, nothing has changed.'

'Yes, it has! Everything has changed. I didn't know what had happened and now I do. I can't not do something!'

'You are doing something. Captain—'

'Waiting on more news is not doing something!' It was clear he wasn't going to help her and that made the frustration inside her to boiling over. 'My mother didn't need any help getting to America and I don't either.'

He grasped her arm firmly. 'You are not going anywhere.'

She met his stare eyeball for eyeball. Saw his determination, but felt her own just as strongly. 'You can't stop me.'

'Yes, I can.'

She shouldn't have said that aloud about her mother and wouldn't say any more. Wrenching her arm from his hold, she marched down the hall to the stairway and then up to her room. Her mother had taken her to America for a reason and her father had raised her as his own daughter. She wouldn't let either of them down by now allowing herself to become ruled by a man. Not her grandfather or anyone else.

Chapter Thirteen

Drew had known the ball would send the gossips into a frenzy, but what he'd never have guessed was just how stubborn Annabelle had become. Riders arrived every day with invitations and letters for her, and the ones addressed to him were asking for permission to visit his estate with the precise intention of calling on her.

She declined the invitations, but not via him. She did that through her companion. Which was also how she responded to him about everything. Through Effie. The woman had met him in the dining room the evening after the seamen had left, after their argument in the hall over her going to New York, and informed him that Annabelle would be dining in her room.

He'd accepted that readily enough, but when it had happened during each meal the following day, and the one following, he'd requested her presence that evening, with the ultimatum that she either join him in the dining room or he'd join her in her room.

Mrs Quinn had returned to London and Effie had seemed to be a loss when he'd given her the ultimatum to relay to Annabelle. The companion had sputtered during her nervous reply of, 'Very well, Your Grace, I will tell her.'

He'd half expected Annabelle to ignore his request, but she had joined him in the dining room that evening, with a silence that he hadn't been able to break. He'd then taken her approach and remained as silent as her during each and every meal since then, which was now proving to be utterly stupid.

His only saving grace was that no one, other than the servants, was observing it. Roger had gone to Southampton to gather any bits of information that could be found. Not trusting Annabelle not to take off for parts unknown, he'd denied her access to the stables, other than to see to Champion. The horse was doing much better, but was too old to embark on a long journey.

She hadn't even broken her silence to object to his actions and that had him worried. Her stay here had already endeared her to the servants and he was certain that more than one of them wouldn't think twice about assisting her if she requested it, even though he'd let it be known she was not to leave the grounds.

Damn it, he felt as if he was walking on thin ice in his own home, and that had never happened.

Forcing her to be in his presence hadn't worked, neither had apologising or silence, but he had one thing left. Hopefully it would get her mind off the reason she was so angry, so set on leaving, and eventually see that he was right, that nothing could be done to help her father until they knew more.

He truly wanted to help her and he truly wanted things between them to be as they had been. He missed her. Missed talking with her, spending time with her. Missed the companionship that with her was so different from any others in his life.

The clock on the mantel that he'd been watching for the last half-hour clicked to the moment he'd been waiting for and he crossed his study to open the door. Donald was there as requested. 'Please inform Miss Smith I'd like to see her immediately.'

Donald stood still for a moment before nodding. 'Yes, Your Grace.'

Drew held in his sigh. Even his most trusted

man seemed to be at odds with him. He re-entered his study and positioned himself near the window, where the carriage should arrive within minutes, and waited for what seemed to be an eternity.

When the door opened, he turned to face it.

Annabelle entered without a word, wearing a pale orange dress with a row of bows near the hem that held up the material in a looping pattern and showed a layer of white beneath the orange. It made him think of the ball and the wired crinoline that had rubbed against his legs as they'd danced.

He nodded to Donald to close the door and wondered how long they both could just stand there, not saying a word. Days? Probably. He could be stubborn, too. However, he was ending this silent standoff today.

She stood near the door, arms crossed and giving him a dull stare.

Resting his palms on the windowsill behind him, he leaned his backside against the sill as well. 'Lena, as well as Caroline and Oscar, will be arriving shortly. I've invited them to join us for the noon meal and to stay afterwards for the two of you to make the arrangements for the party this weekend. It's only two days away and the staff need to be informed of the tasks you need them to perform.'

A flash of emotion crossed her face before she managed to hide it, other than the shimmer that had appeared in her eyes. It remained as she gave a slight bow of her head.

That was it, he'd ended his silence, now it was up to her to end hers. He wouldn't say any more. If Lena thought it odd that the two of them were not speaking to each other, Annabelle could explain.

He turned and faced the window, relieved to see the carriage coming up the driveway. His timing had been perfect.

Pivoting on one heel, he crossed the room, opened the door and waved for her to precede him out of the room. Normally, he would have taken her elbow or held out his arm to escort her to the front door, and though there was the want inside him to touch her, he knew that wasn't what she wanted, so merely walked beside her to the front door.

Caroline let out an excited squeal as he and Annabelle walked out of the house, on to the steps.

'We are going to eat lunch with you!' the child shouted. 'Ma said so.'

'That is correct,' he said, moving to the bottom of the steps. 'We are happy to have you join us.'

'Ma said we are going to have a party, too.' Caroline ran to cover the distance between them. 'Not today. Another day.'

'That, too, is correct.' He picked her up. 'Do you like parties?'

She shrugged. 'Never been to one.' Her train of thought quickly changed. 'Have you decided which kitty you want?'

The giggle that emitted beside him was muffled and snubbed out quickly, but it was more of a response than he'd received from Annabelle to anything he'd said or done the past several days.

'I've told Annabelle she can decide,' he told Caroline.

Annabelle was walking towards Lena and, though Annabelle didn't directly respond to his answer, she was shaking her head.

'She'll pick the black and white one,' Caroline said quietly. 'It's the prettiest and has blue eyes just like her.'

He nodded. 'And just like you. You have blue eyes.'

Caroline stared at his face. 'Your eyes are brown. Like Papa's horse.'

'They are,' he answered, chuckling.

'Forgive her, Your Grace,' Lena said, arriving at the steps with red cheeks.

'There is nothing to forgive,' he assured.

'No, there isn't,' Annabelle said to Lena. 'I've compared him to a horse myself.' The smile on her face was to hide the glare in her eyes. 'The opposite end from where the eyes are located, though.'

Lena gasped slightly.

Drew laughed.

Caroline frowned, telling him, 'Your hair doesn't look like a horse's tail.'

He laughed harder at how red Annabelle's cheeks grew. With a nod at her, he let her know that he accepted her insult.

She curled her nose at him, but that didn't hide the shine in her eyes that had grown immensely since she'd walked into his study a short time ago.

The meal had been far from the silent affairs they'd been lately, thanks to Caroline, despite her mother's attempts to quell her chatter. After eating, Drew excused himself to ride over to the mine.

His arrival found Gunner and a new employee named Jim Banks leaning over a table and studying the map of the mine, specifically the offshoots of the main vein on the estate land that ran miles underground.

He spoke with them, listened to the expansion they were planning and, in full agreement with their thoughts, he entered the office to see to the ledgers of receipts and expenditures for the month that was about to end.

However, his focus wouldn't stay on the numbers; it wandered to Annabelle. It had been good to see her smile, to hear her voice and soft laugh. It would be odd, lonely, when she returned to America.

If she had her choice, she'd be there already. That wasn't possible because it wasn't safe for her to go there. It might not be for months.

He leaned his head back and closed his eyes, knowing one solid truth. He couldn't live this way for months.

The happiness filling her was undeniable and Annabelle wondered how that could be when her father was somewhere unknown to her—alone, most likely penniless—while she was here planning a festive party.

Furthermore, how could she be happy when Drew was not only refusing to help her, he was also practically holding her captive, like some prisoner who had performed some awful act of lawlessness? She wasn't even allowed to ride Millie.

All because he thought she might attempt escape.

Not attempt. She would escape, find her way back to America, just like her mother had. Except she was a coward.

Her mother must have had so much courage to leave everything—especially with an infant—and strike out to an unknown world. Unlike her. She was petrified at the idea of travelling to New York.

She would do it, get back to America, it's just that planning to do so, and actually acting on that plan, would be a whole lot easier if Drew wasn't right.

That was why she was so mad at him, too, because he was right. She didn't know anyone in New York. Didn't know if that was where her father had been taken. Didn't know if there was fighting there now. She did know that her father would be happy to see her, but he'd also be upset that she'd returned. Especially in the middle of a war zone.

She looked down at the baby in her arms. Oscar was so precious, so perfect, and holding him made her wonder if some day she would have a child of her own. To snuggle and care for and love unconditionally. That would be so amazing.

She would only have been a few weeks older than Oscar was right now when her mother had left England. She must have been so worried, so fearful that something might happen to one of them as she embarked upon that journey.

That was another reason she was mad at Drew. She knew she was safer here than anywhere else in the world.

'There, all done,' Lena said, arriving with Caroline. 'Thank you. I knew if she didn't go now, she'd have to go halfway home.'

'Oscar and I enjoyed our time together.' Annabelle smiled down at the baby. 'Although he probably won't remember it because he slept the entire time.'

'Excuse me, miss,' Donald said from the doorway of the sitting room. 'The carriage has been brought around to the front door.'

'Thank you, Donald,' Annabelle replied. 'We'll be right there.'

'Are you sure you don't need me to come back tomorrow to help with anything?' Lena asked.

Annabelle stood. 'I know you have things to do at home and I believe we've covered everything for the party.' Since they weren't talking, she had wondered if Drew had either forgotten about the party, or cancelled it, and was glad he was still willing to host it. 'Thank you for all of your help today.'

Lena picked up the basket that held things for Oscar and a doll for Caroline. 'Here, I can take him.'

'I'll carry him to the carriage,' Annabelle said. 'If you don't mind.'

'No, I don't mind. It's been such a fun afternoon. I was so excited when His Grace stopped at the house yesterday and invited us over. He's been very good to our family—very good—and as I said, all of the families are excited to come to the party.'

'I'm excited, too,' Annabelle replied as they walked towards the door.

'Me, too,' Caroline said. 'And I'll bring the Duke his kitty, just like you said.'

An entirely new sense of happiness filled Annabelle. 'Perfect.'

That happiness lingered after Lena and the children left and Annabelle visited Champion.

He was in the paddock and trotted over to greet her as soon as she arrived at the fence. 'Look at you. Trotting about like a youngster.' She stroked his long nose and sighed at the sadness working its way back into her. 'When I leave, I'll make Finnegan promise to rub you down with ointment every so often. Kate knows how to make it and Finnegan will do that. He loves you.'

Champion snorted and nuzzled her shoulder. 'I love you, too.' She smiled despite the heavy sigh that escaped as the pair of budgies landed on the rail and whistled. 'I love you two, too. I've come to love a lot of things about this place and I shouldn't have, because I don't belong here.'

The birds whistled again and Champion gave her shoulder another nuzzle. She blinked back tears as she wrapped both arms around the horse's neck. If she could belong here, she would, because she'd fallen in love with more than just a few animals. One charmingly handsome duke had stolen her heart. She'd figured that out the last few days—that she'd fallen in love—and knew that was the reason she couldn't stay.

She couldn't love him. This was not the life her mother had wanted for her. Her father had given her and her mother the life her mother had wanted for both of them. If he was still in Hampton, if all was still well there, she might have had another option. That choice, if it ever had been there, had been taken away. She had to find her father. Help him rebuild, be there for him as he'd always been for her and her mother.

She owed that to her mother, for risking her own life in order to save hers. Save her from marrying a man because someone else had promised that she would. Even if that man wasn't mean and nasty and old.

Even if she'd fallen in love with that man. It didn't seem fair, but life wasn't always fair.

Releasing her hold on Champion, she kissed the horse between the eyes and slowly made her way back to the house. With each step, she focused on renewing her ability to not speak to Drew. It would be extremely difficult. The only thing that might make it possible was to remember that he didn't want to marry her. He'd been honest about that right from the start and she'd respected that. Had to continue to respect that.

As it turned out, not talking to him at the evening meal was rather easy. She'd expected him to ask about the party, about Lena, Caroline, and Oscar, but he didn't. He remained silent.

The following day was much the same, though she discovered Drew had questioned Donald and therefore knew everything there was to know about the party that would happen the following day. They would have to speak while others were here and the idea of that was nearly as exciting as the party itself. She missed talking with him, missed spending time with him. Most of all, she missed his smile. It had the ability to make her feel as if all was right in the world, even when she knew it wasn't.

First thing she noticed the next morning was the bright blue sky and sunshine. It made her recall the day she'd arrived in London, when she wondered if the sun ever shone. It had been the opposite since she'd arrived at Mansfield. The sun had shone every day.

She quickly bathed and dressed in a bright yellow dress with tiny red flowers, red lace around the square neckline, sleeves and hem, and added two red petticoats beneath the dress. Rosemary fashioned her hair by pulling back the sides and clipping it up with a single barrette, leaving several wispy hanging around her face, then covered it with a floppy yellow hat with a long red ribbon tied around the brim.

'Thank you, Rosemary, that's perfect,' Annabelle said, examining herself in the mirror as she stood. It was one of her favourite outfits. She'd worn it to the spring social at church in May. The heaviness that was never far away threatened to fill her chest.

'You look very lovely today, miss,' Rosemary said. 'Truly lovely.'

Telling herself to focus on the day and not the unknown, Annabelle turned about. Rosemary had already tied a bright blue ribbon in her own hair and was wearing a colourful red, blue and green dress, in preparation for the day. Annabelle hooked their arms together. 'You look lovely, too. It's going to be a wonderful party.'

'Mother says we've never hosted a party like this before,' Rosemary said as they walked to the door. 'One that includes everyone.'

'This is the kind of parties we had while I was growing up. You'll have fun, I promise.'

By noon, dozens of wagons were parked near the stables and people of all ages filled the grounds. Among the neatly trimmed hedges and beautiful flower beds were tables heaped with various foods, benches and chairs holding guests as they gathered to eat and visit, games of horseshoes and croquet being played by young and old, and laughter filling the air with the merriment.

Annabelle was full of merriment, too, in part due to the gaiety of the party, but more because of the adorable black and white kitten that Drew had been gifted as soon as the Ericksons had arrived. The looked he'd graced upon her had made her insides tingle. She had smiled back at him and quickly offered to hold Oscar so Lena could direct the unloading of their wagon.

Her heart skipped a beat when Drew stepped up beside her a short time after he and Caroline had entered the house together with the kitten.

'I'll have you know the kitten has adjusted to its new home,' he said.

Their silence had not been officially broken, but there was too much joy in the air for her to be concerned about that. 'Oh, and where is its new home?' she asked, keeping her eyes on a group of children playing a game of tag. In part because she knew how handsome he looked today. He was dressed like many of the other men, in a simple white shirt and black pants, tucked into his high black boots. It was the red silk ascot and black waistcoat that made him stand out. Then again, no matter what he wore, he stood out. Not because he was a duke, or even how he carried himself straight and tall, but because of his handsomeness alone.

'The small parlour off the back hall,' he said. 'Belle has been given food, water, a basket to sleep in and a small pan of sand for her other business.'

Surprised, she turned, looking up at him. 'Belle?'

He nodded. 'Caroline and I decided on the name, because the kitten has blue eyes.'

'I see—and Belle is in the house?'

'Yes. I didn't want the barn cats to think she's a mouse. She's not much bigger than one.'

His kindness towards all things, large and small, was just one of the many things she admired about him.

Smiling down at her, he continued, 'Nor did I want her in the stable where she might decide that one of your budgies might make a tasty meal.'

'They aren't my budgies.'

He glanced behind her, towards the garden trellis that arched high in the air and was covered with blooming and fragrant honeysuckle. 'Do they know that?'

She knew the pair of budgies were perched atop the trellis. They'd whistled at her earlier. 'How do you know that's the pair from the stable?'

He whistled.

The birds whistled back.

He looked at her with brows raised.

Searching for a response, all she could come up with was, 'I'd say they are your budgies.'

'I'll share.' He took a hold of her hand. 'And I challenge you in a game of croquet.'

* * *

Drew hadn't been sure if she would accept his challenge, but was glad she had. He was also glad that their silent treatment appeared to be on hold for the day. Or disappear completely. He was tired of not talking to her.

Her joy and laughter as they played the game not only echoed in his ears, it reverberated throughout his body, reinforcing all the things he felt for her over and over again.

After their game ended—with her winning—they wandered through the yard, talking with the guests. He introduced her to those he knew and they were both introduced to family members of the men who worked at the mine. Drew felt a unique sense of pride at having Annabelle at his side. Men and women alike were awestruck by her charm and beauty. 'This party was a wonderful idea,' he told her. 'Thank you.'

'It was a wonderful idea,' she agreed, 'but it was your idea, not mine.'

'Perhaps it was a mutual idea, but you planned and executed a wonderful event that I think should be repeated every year. The miners deserve a day of fun with their families.'

'Everyone does seem to be enjoying themselves.' She nudged his upper arm with her shoulder. 'Including you.'

He tightened the hold he had on her hand. 'And you.'

'I am. I love watching the children have so much fun.' She increased her speed and pulled him along. 'It's time for the horse race.'

'Are you riding in it?' Although it would be highly unusual for a woman to participate, it wouldn't surprise him if she did. Her unorthodox ways were just one of the many things he admired about her. He was still guilt ridden about not allowing her to ride Millie, even though it was for her own safety.

She tugged harder on his hand as they rounded the brick garden wall. 'No. You are.'

Sure enough, Fellow was saddled, lined up among the other horses. 'It looks as if I am.'

Her face was aglow with excitement. 'There are ribbons draped over the branches of that big tree way out there. The first man to cross the finish line with a ribbon in his hand wins.'

'Ah, you added a bit of a challenge to the race,' he said.

'Just a bit more fun.'

Her smile was so kissable he had to press his heels into the ground to stop himself. 'What does the winner win?'

She shrugged. 'Same as every other game. Bragging rights.'

He wanted to ask that his prize be a kiss. Instead, he gave her a nod and walked to where Fellow was waiting on the starting line.

This wasn't Fellow's first race. As soon as the shot was fired, he bolted forward and was quickly a full body length ahead of the other horses. Among the cheering, Drew heard Annabelle's voice, rooting for him. That, along with the sound of her laughter, was music to his ears and heart. He held Fellow back, let other horses thunder past him, then urged the horse forward, giving the spectators and riders a playful race. When Fellow shot past the other horses, Jim Banks, on a big palomino, was doing his best to hold the lead.

Drew rode past him, then let Jim catch up and pass him, before he urged Fellow forward again, all the while knowing the real competition would come on the return, when the riders each held a ribbon from the tree.

Closing in on the tree, he set his sight on a red one. To match the one on Annabelle's hat. He could go for a blue one, to match her eyes, but today, it was the red one because he would tie it on her wrist. That was an odd thing to be thinking about when he should be concentrating on the riders behind him, but she was on his mind day and night. Hour after hour. Today wasn't any different.

He slowed Fellow enough to grab a red ribbon and make a smooth turn around the tree, then leaned over the horse's neck, letting Fellow know it was up to him now. There were two other horses that were good contenders: Banks on the palomino and another rider on a big grey. Drew lessened his hold on the reins, giving Fellow full control as the race became a serious endeavour.

Drew's chest was filling with triumph as Fellow pulled ahead by several yards, his mind imagining the sweet victory of handing Annabelle the ribbon and possibly asking her for a kiss when his attention was snagged by dust on the road. As he recognised the carriage approaching, his thoughts instantly changed.

At that moment, the race became more than a competition. It became a battlefield. That of getting to Annabelle before the occupants of that carriage did. It was Westcrdownes's carriage and the sinking in Drew's gut told him that it wasn't carrying Mrs Quinn this time.

Fellow crossed the finish line and Drew was out of the saddle before the horse came to a complete stop. There was no need to search the cheering crowd for her, Annabelle was front and centre, clapping and jumping up and down. He

hurried to where she stood near the sidelines, a
safe distance from the other horses barrelling
across the finish line at full speed.

'You won! You won! I knew you would,' she
said, clasping his arm with both hands.

He rubbed her hand as he looked over her
head, to where the dust swirled upon the arrival
of the coach on the other side of the stable. Holding a smile on his face was difficult. 'Here.' He
slipped the ribbon around one of her wrists and
tied a fast bow. 'Hold on to this for me.'

'It's your—'

'I have to go see about something.'

The smile slipped from her face. 'What?' Her
fingers dug into his arm. 'What's wrong? Don't
tell me nothing. I can tell it's something.'

She would learn soon enough and it would
be better coming from him. 'We have another
guest.'

'Who?'

'The Earl of Westerdownes.'

Her entire being seemed to slump. He glanced
around, looking for her companion, a servant, or
Lena. Someone he could turn her over to while
he met with Westerdownes.

She stiffened and her chin rose as she squared
her shoulders. 'Let's go see what he wants.'

There was determination in her eyes, as well

as trepidation. He shook his head. 'No, it's me he wants to see. I knew he'd be upset to learn I closed down the mine for the day.'

She opened her mouth to respond, but the crowd, as well as the other riders, descended upon them with congratulations and back slaps for him winning the race.

Drew pasted on a smile and hooked an arm around Annabelle's waist to keep her at his side as he congratulated Banks and others on the speed of their horses and a fun race. They were still in the midst of that when Donald arrived at his side.

'Excuse me, Your Grace,' Donald said. 'A visitor would like to see you and Miss Smith.'

Drew hated the idea of subjecting her to Westerdownes. The old man was bitter and hateful to everyone and her previous encounter with her grandfather had not been pleasant. Drew's teeth clenched as he asked, 'Where is he?'

'In the drawing room,' Donald replied.

Chapter Fourteen

Annabelle had experienced anger before, but had never known it could make a room that was so beautifully decorated—with its creamy white curtains, gold brocade furniture and pale green and gold rugs—feel ugly. The anger emanating from her grandfather did that to the drawing room. The same room she'd sat in and held Oscar in her arms as he'd slept just the other day. The same room where she and Drew had shared before-dinner drinks and conversed, laughing over silly things. That of course had been before their silent period, which was over, thankfully.

The shiver that zipped up her spine made her quiver and she drew in a deep breath to fortify herself as Drew's hold on her elbow grew firmer. There was comfort in that and she kept her eyes on her grandfather, as he scowled from where he stood near the fireplace.

The one and only time she'd seen him, he'd been sitting down. Today she noticed he was a tall man, not as tall as Drew, but taller than she'd imagined and had a thick, barrel chest.

'Look at the two of you. Dressed like commoners.' His gnarled finger pointed at her as he continued, 'I'd expect that from her, but you are a duke. Have a pedigree! I've never been so disgusted.'

'Then you've never looked in the mirror,' Drew replied as they stepped into the room.

'What did you say?' her grandfather shouted.

'State why you are here,' Drew said, much louder.

'Why I'm here! I'm here to send those men out there out to the mine! Where they should be!'

Drew urged her forward, towards the chair furthest away from her grandfather. 'Those men are exactly where they should be.'

'Like hell they are! Every hour they aren't working is money lost!'

Drew nodded for her be seated.

Annabelle lowered on to the chair and watched as Drew lowered himself on to the matching chair. His actions increased the scowl on her grandfather's face and she understood why. By sitting, Drew was demonstrating that her grandfather was not the one in charge.

'I do hope you will refrain from any further use of vulgar language in front of a lady,' Drew said, drumming his fingers on the arm of his chair.

Her grandfather's face turned red and he dug inside his long burgundy frock coat. Retrieving an envelope, he threw it on the table. 'That's for her. She can take it and leave.'

Drew didn't move a muscle.

Annabelle didn't move, either. However, she had a voice and couldn't stop herself from using it. 'I don't want anything from you.'

'You better take it.' Her grandfather's eyes felt as if they were trying to burn into her very soul as he grabbed the envelope and walked close enough to toss it on her lap. 'It's all you're going to get.'

The envelope was too light for her to actually feel it through her dress and petticoats, yet it felt as if it weighed a hundred pound and was red hot. Her first instinct was to shove it off her lap and it was hard to not do that, even though she knew no response was her best defence.

'Go on! Take it!' he shouted, with spittle flying from his lips. 'You'll need it to get back to where you came from.' Something akin to joy flashed in his eyes. 'Or near there. Your little town was burned to the ground.'

Annabelle told herself to be strong, to block the hatred. Her mother had taught her how to do that, how to bring up good memories to block out bad ones. That must have been what her mother had done until she'd left for America.

'And the merchant's dead,' he continued his onslaught of shouts.

Annabelle's heart felt as if it stopped mid-beat.

'That's enough, Westerdownes,' Drew stated firmly. 'There is no report that Arlo Smith has perished.'

'There's no report that he hasn't either,' her grandfather snapped.

The air she sucked in was shaky.

'Which is what you hope.' Drew stood slowly. 'Then there wouldn't be anyone to prove her identity.'

'I don't need to prove anything. Anyone can see she's an imposter, looking for money. That's all she wants.'

The hatred in her grandfather's eyes became too strong to block and, for the first time in her life, she was fearful, truly fearful of another human being.

Drew stepped between her chair and her grandfather. 'No, Westerdownes, that is all *you* want. That's all you've ever wanted. Take your leave, now. Whether you are a shrivelled old man or not, I will not tolerate any more of your hatred.'

Her grandfather took several steps backwards, as if seeing something in Drew's face that frightened him, yet he was too used to getting his way to take heed. 'I'm not leaving until every one of those miners return to work!'

'Those miners aren't going anywhere,' Drew said. 'You are.'

'How stupid are you? You can't treat employees as equals! The more you give them the more they'll want! The more they'll take! They'll rob you blind before the day is out! So will she! I always knew it was only a matter of time before that merchant sent her here! For money!'

Drew had grabbed his arm, was forcefully marching him towards the door.

'She's out to ruin me! Ruin what I have built! I won't let her! Won't let you, either! I want my royalties that would have been earned today! You hear me?'

The shouts continued as Drew removed him from the room and they echoed down the hall. Annabelle wasn't listening. One thing he'd said had resonated with her. He'd said he knew. He'd known. He'd known where her mother was all along.

Her gaze locked on the envelope on her lap. It

no longer felt hot and heavy. It felt dirty. Tainted. Yet she couldn't deny she wanted to know how much she was worth to him. That's what was in the envelope. Money.

She picked up the envelope, lifted the flap and then, despite all the anger, hatred and ugliness she'd just witnessed, she laughed. Along with that unbelievable response came a new bout of empathy that she'd felt for her mother since reading the diary. How could a woman who had been so mistreated, so clearly unloved in her younger years, have become the loving, caring woman that she remembered raising her? It didn't make sense, except for the fact that her mother had wanted something completely different for her daughter than what she'd experienced.

Completely different.

And her life *had* been completely different. Even her time in England had been completely different from how her mother's had been. That she owed to Drew. Was there any wonder why she'd fallen in love with him? No. It would have been impossible not to.

The familiar sting of tears burnt her eyes as she held them back. What was also impossible was the fact she could ever admit her love for Drew. Her grandfather had made that clear. Even if Drew would ever change his mind, want to be married, her grandfather would make it impossible.

He'd never wanted her mother to return and wouldn't stop until he got rid of her, too.

Drew entered the room and, as he walked towards her, she held out the envelope.

He took it, pulled open the flap and lifted out the paper. 'A bank draft. For a hundred pounds.'

She nodded. Her father had given her ten times that amount upon leaving America.

'Are you going to cash it?'

She leaned back, stared at the fireplace while her thoughts danced in several directions. 'I don't know what I'll do with it yet. Tear it up. Burn it. Keep it as a reminder. I won't cash it; he's probably told the bank to decline to honour it.' Glancing at him, she said, 'I think he knew where my mother had gone. Knew she was in America, in Hampton, the entire time.'

He set the envelope down on the table. 'Do you think he helped her escape to there?'

'No. But I think he found her or had someone find her for him. And I think he rejoiced when she died, thinking it was all over, that he'd won.' Her thoughts were indecisive, yet she voiced one. 'I'm afraid of what he would do if I proclaimed that I am his granddaughter.'

'Is that what you want to do?'

She sighed. 'I don't know, but I do know it's not what you want.'

Shaking his head, he sat, pulled the chair up next to hers and took a hold of her hand. 'I want what's best for you and only you can decide what that is.'

She believed him because he'd always wanted what was best for people since he'd been a small boy. But what about him? Who wanted the best for him? He'd been caught up in her grandfather's tight fist far longer than she had and that wasn't right. It was all so frustrating. 'I can't decide what to do until I know where my father is. I promised my mother to take care of him, just like he'd taken care of us. I have to do that for her. She took me away so I wouldn't be subjected to my grandfather's hatred and gave me a very good life.' Shaking her head, she swallowed the lump in her throat. 'I have to find him, Drew. I have to.'

He leaned closer, cupped her face. 'I know you do. People are looking. If I knew where to look, I'd take you there, help you. But we can't just start sailing the ocean.'

Her heart melted at the honesty in his voice and on his face. She leaned forward, pressed her forehead against his. 'I know that. You've been right about that from the beginning. I'm sorry for being so stubborn.'

'I'm sorry, too. I just want you to be safe.'

She lifted her head enough to look at him, which might have been a mistake, because like the other night, she didn't take time to think before leaning forward and pressing her lips against his.

The thrill of how the first touch ignited the kiss into a fast, heated coming together of lips, mouths, tongues, was amazing. He tasted so good, smelled so good. She wasn't sure when or how they both came to be standing, arms wrapped around each other and bodies pressed hard together, but it was the most exciting moment of her life.

The kissing, tasting, teasing, had her entire body humming, her heart pounding, and as it continued, a fascinating ache swirled deep inside her.

When the kissing ended, by a mutual need for air, he held her close. 'I've missed you.'

She smiled, because despite all, he made her happy, yet sad at the same time. Burying her face in his neck, she whispered, 'I've been nothing but trouble for you.'

'A good sort of trouble.'

'I didn't know there was a good sort of trouble.'

He took a step back, ran a thumb over her cheek. 'I hadn't either, until I met you.'

'What are we going to do?' she asked, still reeling from his kisses.

'Right now, we are going to go back outside and rejoin the party.' He kissed her forehead. 'When we discover where your father is, we'll decide what to do about that.'

'What about my grandfather?'

He tilted his head to one side, looking at her. 'Let's wait until we hear more about your father before addressing that.'

'Why?'

Drew contemplated his own reasons. He knew what they were—what it was. His heart was far more involved in this than it should be and he needed time to figure out what to do about that. His saving grace was knowing that she was safe here at his house while he took the time to decide on a what was best for all involved. 'Your grandfather is scared,' he said. 'He's afraid others will discover what he knows to be true. That you are your mother's daughter. His granddaughter. It won't hurt him to wallow in that fear for a while.'

She nodded, slowly at first, but then with more purpose. 'Perhaps, once again, you're right.'

He chuckled. 'Perhaps?'

Smiling, she dipped her head, then looked up at him with eyes shimmering with happiness. 'Yes, perhaps.'

He took her hand. 'Come, we have a garden full of guests and games we haven't yet played.'

She folded her fingers around his. 'Yes, we do.'

As they walked to the door, and through the house, Drew wondered what he was going to do when she left. If he was so sure that marriage would ruin his life, why did he not want her to leave? Because she didn't want marriage any more than he did. At least not to him. When she did marry, it would be to a common man. She'd said so herself and, considering all that her mother had experienced and she herself via her grandfather, there was no hoping that she'd change her mind about marrying a duke.

He shouldn't want her to change her mind. Shouldn't want to change his own mind.

The happy shouts of children playing games filled the air as he opened the back door for Annabelle to step outside. Women were fussing around the tables, but it was the men that Drew noticed. They were gathered in a large cluster near the edge of the yard.

'I told Caroline she could check on the kitten,' he said. 'Would you mind finding her?'

'No, I wouldn't mind, nor would I mind checking on the kitten with her.' She squeezed his hand. 'And I wouldn't have minded if you'd have just said you wanted to talk to the men. I'm sure they noticed the Earl's coach and are concerned.'

He nodded at her honesty. 'I'm sure they are, too.' Suppressing the desire to kiss her, even just a fast peck, was difficult. He sufficed by saying, 'Thank you.'

'You're welcome.' She still had hold of his hand and held on a bit tighter. 'It's not your responsibility to save the world by yourself.'

'I didn't know that I was saving the world.'

She giggled softly. 'You have been for years.' With a nod, she released his hand. 'Go. I'll find Caroline.'

He stopped shy of telling her that he wasn't trying to save the world. Hell, he didn't even know how to save himself. Turning, he walked towards the men.

Gunner separated from the group and walked to meet him.

'The men don't need to worry about their jobs,' Drew said.

Instead of his normal stocking cap, Gunner had on a flat-brimmed hat and he removed it, scratching his mop of blond hair. 'Westerdownes wasn't happy about shutting down for the day?'

'No, he's not. I'll pay him his average daily royalty, just like I'll pay the men for the work they missed.' He'd already told Gunner that, but the reassurance couldn't hurt. Slapping the other man on the shoulder, he suggested, 'Let's play a game of horseshoes. Get the fun rolling again.'

Before long the day was as festive as it had been before Westerdownes's arrival and, most importantly, per Caroline, the kitten liked its new home. She'd told him that before insisting that he and Annabelle pair up for a three-legged race.

They had lost to a pair of youngsters who had practically flown from the start to the finish line. They also lost an egg race when he dropped the egg out of his spoon.

'I think you need a new partner,' he said while wiping egg yolk off the toe of his boot in the grass.

'No, I like the one I have.' She took hold of his hand. 'We just need to find something we're good at together.'

He could think of a few things to try, but none was appropriate.

'Look, they are jumping rope over there.'

He tugged her in the opposite direction. 'I'm not jumping rope. Let's visit the food tables. We both know how to eat.'

* * *

The games and festivities lasted until nearly sunset, then, family by family, wagons were loaded and driven off, and it was nearly dark by the time the last of the tables and chairs had been put away. Drew had never assisted in cleaning up after an event, but with Annabelle busy helping with the food and dishes, he'd set in helping the men, which did draw curious looks from the servants. So be it.

He'd attended parties and balls his entire life, yet the one today had been the first one where he'd truly enjoyed himself. He felt as if he'd belonged.

Why was that? Because of Annabelle. Why else. She was changing him. The question was, did he want to be changed?

He was still pondering that the following morning, after enjoying her company at the breakfast table. Just that made the day brighter. His soul lighter. That, too, stuck with him when he arrived at the mine and was met by Westerdownes's accountant, demanding payment for the loss of mining the previous day.

The amount requested was far more than the Earl would have earned had the mine been opened. Throughout a long, drawn-out meeting,

Drew held his ground on the amount and when the payment would be applied to Westerdownes's royalty account. As the other man left, clearly distraught over the task of informing the Earl that his demands would not be met, Drew heard shouting outside.

That wasn't unusual. The mine was a busy place and men often needed to shout to be heard over the noise of carts being pulled by the pit ponies, the conveyers moving the ore, the hammers crushing it and the washing stations. This, however, sounded different.

Drew exited the building and discovered men running past all of the buildings and work stations, towards the entrance of the mine. He joined the rush, questioning the cause.

'There's been a cave in,' a man shouted. 'The new shaft!'

Drew ran through the crowd, to where Gunner and Jim Banks were holding the men back from the entrance.

'Stay back!' Gunner was shouting. 'Give room for the men to exit!'

Drew ordered a dozen men to form a barrier, keeping the others back. 'We'll organise a search as soon as we know more! Just stay where you are! We're going to need each of you in a few minutes. Just stay back! Give those exiting room!'

The crowd became more orderly and he said to Gunner, 'Tell me what you know.'

'Not much. A miner came upon a pile of ore in the new shaft. Don't know if it's the start of a cave in or cart spillage. I ordered everyone out and to be accounted for so we can send a crew in to investigate.'

'Who reported it?'

'I don't know his name,' Jim Banks replied. 'I'm the one he told about it. Said it was in the new section, the main tunnel.'

Men continued to file out of the entrance, one after the other, claiming they hadn't seen or heard anything until there was only one tag left hanging on the board where the miners each hung their metal identifying tag upon entering the mine. A miner rarely, if ever, forgot to hang or collect his tag.

Men quickly stepped forward, volunteering to enter the mine and look for the miner. They were quickly paired up, given an underground area to search and others were positioned to relay messages.

'I'll take the new section,' Drew said.

'No, sir,' Gunner replied. 'Banks and I will. You stay out here.'

'I'm not sending men into a mine that I wouldn't enter myself,' Drew said, collecting a candle and pickaxe. He'd been in the mine before, for several reasons, including rescue missions. 'Join me if you want.'

Both Gunner and Jim joined him. Their way was lit by candles in the holders nailed to the brace beams until they entered the downward slope of the tunnel that would take them to the new section, then they only had the flickering candlelight from the lamps they carried. During the mile-long, down-sloping journey to the new section, they scanned the areas, shouted and listened for responses. There were none and Drew questioned the exact whereabouts of the debris pile.

The mine had been labelled and mapped, and when Jim replied with a number Drew questioned it. 'We aren't mining that section yet.'

'It must have been one of the shaft diggers who told me about it,' Jim replied. 'I don't know the men as well as Erickson.'

His hope was that the last tag had belonged to a man who had still been finding his way out when they'd started their journey inwards. That had happened before. In a panic to get out, a man could easily get turned around, lose his light, get lost in the dark and find his way out after searchers had entered to look for him.

'He said it was just past the last trapdoor,' Jim said.

Trapdoors were installed along all of the shafts and were monitored, opened and closed as needed for carts of ore or men to pass through. Their main function was to prevent gasses from building up and causing an explosion.

For years, children had been hired to man those doors, opening them when they heard the rattle of a mine cart being moved through the tunnel. Following Gunner through one of the doors and then holding it until Jim grabbed the door behind him, Drew couldn't imagine a child sitting in the dank, dark tunnel for up to ten hours each and every day. Unfortunately, that was still happening. Although the law had been passed that women and children couldn't work in mines, the increase in demand for coal was reason enough for plenty of mine owners to ignore the law completely.

He had hope that wouldn't be the case much longer as he had proven mines could still be profitable without hiring women and children.

'The end of the digging isn't too far ahead,' Gunner said, leading the way. 'Ahoy! Anyone about?'

They all grew still and silent, listening for a response. None sounded and they moved forward, came upon the final trapdoor. Gunner shouted again as he opened the door. After no response, he moved forward.

Drew followed, but stopped and spun around when the door slammed shut behind him.

Chapter Fifteen

Annabelle stared at the man sitting across from her, trying to make sense of what he was saying and why. Yesterday he'd said her father was dead, today he was saying her father was alive and in New Jersey. And that he would help her get there.

She knew her grandfather was lying. That it was just another ploy to get rid of her. She just couldn't figure out why his attitude had changed so much. He hadn't raised his voice once since she'd entered the room. The very one he'd shouted in while leaving yesterday.

It would have been a lot of travelling for him to have returned to London yesterday, and then back to Mansfield today, so he must have spent the night somewhere close. She wished Drew was here. He was calm, steadfast. She could be too impulsive at times and was trying hard not to be.

'I've hired a coach that will take you straight

to Southampton,' her grandfather said. 'There's a ship willing to take you to America leaving tomorrow. I've already paid your way.'

She'd yet to say more than the formal greeting she'd given him upon entering the room and not even that appeared to be irritating him.

'You can keep the bank draft and have this.' He laid another envelope on the table.

It was thicker than the one up in her room. Not that it mattered. She wouldn't get in a coach that he'd hired for all the money on earth. Wouldn't do anything he asked of her. Drew had been right. Her grandfather was scared. He knew that if she and Drew worked together, he'd lose all of the money and holdings that he was supposedly overseeing on her behalf.

'I've asked the butler to have Effie pack your bags.'

That seemed to be the straw that broke the camel's back, or at least her silence. 'No.' She sat straighter in her chair. 'There's no need for anyone to pack my bags. I'm not going anywhere.'

The anger she'd seen in him yesterday flashed in his eyes, but he quickly tried to hide it by smiling. 'Passenger travel to America is difficult to obtain right now and your father needs you. He was burned when his warehouses were set aflame.'

She forced herself to not react to that. It was just another lie.

'A ship picked him up in the bay, along with a servant woman. She insisted they find a doctor and the ship sailed to the closest port, which happened to be New Jersey.'

That all sounded plausible, but that just proved how good of a liar he was.

'You have to believe me,' he said, showing a portion of the anger she'd seen before.

'No, I don't have to believe you. In fact, I have more reason to not believe you.' She stood.

'Well, believe this. Mansfield will never marry you!'

She refused to respond to anything he said and walked towards the door. 'Donald will show you out.'

'You're just like your mother! Selfish! She never cared about anyone but herself!'

Annabelle kept walking to the door that Donald had opened. Finnegan was standing next to him and she was glad to see both of them, knowing the two of them would indeed see that the Earl left.

'You won't be so smug tomorrow,' he shouted from behind her. 'Mark my word!'

Donald bowed as she walked out of the door. 'We'll see to him, miss.'

'Thank you.' She walked to the staircase and climbed the steps, refusing to let anything her grandfather had said affect her. She already knew Drew didn't want to marry her and, if what her grandfather said about her father was true, Roger would have already returned and told her.

Effie was standing outside her bedroom door, arms crossed. 'I didn't pack your clothes.' She lifted her chin to make her tiny stature look taller. 'I don't think you should do as your grandfather asked.'

Annabelle pinched her lips together to squelch a smile that formed at the woman's refusal to follow an order by the Earl. It had to have been a first. 'Thank you, Effie. I appreciate that.'

Effie's sigh echoed off the walls as she opened the door.

Annabelle let her smile form and walked into the room.

'He's up to no good,' Effie said, following her into the bedroom. 'He hasn't left London in years.'

'He's scared,' Annabelle said. 'Afraid that I'll reveal my true identity.'

'I don't know if it will help, but Elanor— Mrs Quinn—left this with me to give to you if needed.'

Annabelle frowned as the other woman dug

into the pocket of her white apron covering her grey dress and gasped when Effie pulled out a tiny baby's bootie. A twin to the one in the small chest with the diary and necklace.

'It's yours, my lady, from the last time you came to London with your mum. It must have slipped off your foot in the carriage when she escaped and Elanor has kept it hidden all these years.'

Annabelle took the bootie, examined it closely, even though she already knew it matched the other one.

'I wish I knew how it could prove who you are,' Effie said.

Annabelle shook her head. 'Proving who I am isn't going to change anything, Effie.'

'Yes, it will. You can marry the Duke. Stay here for ever.'

Annabelle heart softened, even as she shook her head. 'I can't marry Drew, Effie. Not even if I wanted to.'

'Why not?'

'For one, he doesn't wish to marry me.' Annabelle huffed out a breath and held up the bootie. 'And for two, my mother took me away from here so I wouldn't be forced to marry a man for wealth or peerage. She wanted me to marry for love.

Like she did the second time, to the man who raised me. The one I still consider my father.'

'My lady,' Effie whispered, 'that's not why your mother left.'

A tiny shiver made the hair on Annabelle's arms stand. 'Why do you say that?'

'Because your mother never knew about the betrothal.' Effie took hold of her hands. 'Your mother knew that your father, the Duke of Compton, had only married her to produce an heir. A son. She was afraid he would hurt you because you were a girl and so she came to London. The Earl refused to let her stay. He said that she was not do anything to keep him from inheriting the Duke's wealth. That's why she ran away before the carriage arrived back at the estate.'

'Why didn't you tell me this before?'

Effie bowed her head as if shamed. 'I couldn't.'

'Because you'd lose your job.'

'The Earl threatened to send anyone who mentioned your mum's name to Australia and he did just that to two servants.' Effie squeezed her hands. 'The Duke came to London, looking for you and your mum. His men tore the house apart and he and the Earl had a terrible row. It was weeks after that when the Duke came to the house again and informed the Earl that he'd betrothed you to the Duke of Mansfield's son and that his wealth and properties would go to you upon his death, unclaimable until your marriage to Andrew.' Effie shrugged. 'Your mother was gone by then. She couldn't have known.'

Once again, a hint of a shiver raced up Annabelle's arms. 'How do you know she was gone by then?'

Effie was quiet for several moments before she said, 'No one had heard from your mother, but she'd had an old tutor who was well travelled and who had left on a trip shortly after your mother had disappeared. She never returned to England, either.'

'What was her name?'

'Elizabeth Stafford.'

Annabelle's heart flipped. 'Lizibet.'

'You knew her?'

Annabelle smiled at the memory of the tall, domineering woman who had visited them several times in Hampton. 'She continued to travel. By land and sea. Sadly, before my mother died, Lizibet died in California, defending her gold claim.'

Walking to the bed, Annabelle sat, let everything settle for a few minutes. 'Did the Earl know about Lizibet?'

'No, and we never told him what we had figured out.' Effie sat down on the bed beside her.

'But he had spies out, especially after the Duke of Compton died. Then they stopped. We all thought you and your mum would be brought home, but that never happened. He emptied out the estate, sold everything and acted as though she'd never existed.'

Annabelle fingered the bootie in her hand, but she wasn't thinking of it, or her mother, or grandfather. Drew was on her mind. She'd been wrong about her reasons for not being able to marry him, but it didn't matter. She still couldn't stay here. Couldn't marry him, even if he ever would want that. Her grandfather wouldn't let that happen. He wasn't as powerful as Drew, but he was far more deceitful, and that scared her.

'I know it's not much, but I could testify about who you are, your true identity,' Effie said.

Annabelle shook her head. 'Thank you, but my true identity isn't important.' She knew who she was and what she had to do.

Every swing of the pickaxe was fuelled by anger. Drew was furious with himself for being tricked. So was Gunner—his pickaxe was ripping into the wood of the door as soon as Drew pulled his axe out. Taking turns, they were shredding the door, but Banks had set this all up. Shortly after the door had slammed shut, the ground had shaken, the walls had rumbled and rocks had fallen from overhead. Not a large amount because the charge Banks had set off had been further back down the tunnel, the way they'd come. They had no idea if the blast had filled the tunnel, completely trapping them, but Drew knew one thing for sure. There wasn't enough air to last long enough for anyone to find them and dig them out.

Jim Banks was working for Westerdownes. Had to be. And Drew was livid for not figuring that out earlier. Westerdownes was desperate to keep his hold on Annabelle's holdings. Drew slammed the pickaxe into the wood again. He had to get out of here for her. She was in danger. Grave danger.

The wood splintered and he felt the axe head fully penetrate the door. It was dark, too dark to see how big the hole was, but he still dropped the axe, found the hole and used his hands to rip away the splintered wood.

Gunner brought both lamps closer, giving him enough light to make the hole big enough for them to climb through. Dust filled the air, telling him exactly what he'd assumed. Banks had let off a charge in this section of the tunnel.

The lamps didn't do much good with all the dust, but he found his axe and then both he and

Gunner felt their way forward, each with a hand on the wall and shuffling their feet to feel among the loose gravel and rocks, cursing.

'I should have known something wasn't right with him,' Gunner said. 'He was too good. Too perfect for what we needed.'

'You aren't to blame,' Drew said. 'I was fooled by him, too. He was at the party yesterday. In the horse race.'

'He was, but I never saw him after that, did you?'

'I don't know,' Drew answered honestly. 'I never paid any attention.' His attention had all been on Annabelle.

His toe hit something solid and he held his lantern out in front of him. A pile of dirt and rock debris blocked their way.

'There's no way to judge how big it is,' Gunner said.

Drew buried his axe into the pile sideways and pulled the dirt backwards. 'There's only one way to find out.'

'Go slow,' Gunner said. 'Keep the dust down as much as possible. Our air is limited.'

Drew didn't need to be reminded of that. Every breath he took felt shallow and his lungs were already burning. His eyes, too. The rest of him was full of anger and regret. He couldn't let

Annabelle down. Had to get out. She'd changed things inside him, things he hadn't been willing to accept and he should have.

He dug until every bone in his body hurt and then dug some more. So did Gunner. Between grunts and curses, they spoke of family, friends, things they wanted to accomplish at the mine and in life, and held other thoughts to themselves. Drew certainly did. All sorts of thoughts about Annabelle. How her eyes sparkled. How her hair shimmered in the sunlight. How sweet she smelled, even when mint had filled the air while they'd rubbed down Champion.

She didn't want to marry a man of the peerage. He didn't have to be one. He could give it up. All of it. Take her back to America and live there with her. Or anywhere else in the world.

Convincing himself that was the answer wasn't hard, until his mind shifted to digging again. Gunner was fighting to get out as hard as he was. Fighting to see his wife and children. If he gave everything up, took Annabelle back to America, what would happen to Gunner? And the others? Westerdownes would cut their wages, increase their hours of working. Make their lives hell.

Or they could all lose their jobs, their homes.

Could he live with that? Knowing he was the cause? Knowing he put his own life, his own happiness, ahead of all of theirs?

All these years, he'd wanted to be alone. Have no one at home waiting for him, because he hadn't wanted to be like his father. Hadn't wanted to fall in love, have a family, because deep down, he'd known the truth.

He was just like his father.

He would always put his duties before anyone else.

Including his family.

'Is there no end to this damn dirt?' Gunner growled.

'Yes, there is,' Drew answered. 'And we're going find it.'

'What if he blew up the whole damn tunnel?'

'Then we'll dig through the whole damn tunnel,' Drew said. He couldn't marry Annabelle, but he could still save her from Westerdownes.

Annabelle stared at the plate before her, moving the food around with her fork. She wasn't hungry. Her mind was a complete jumbled mess of her grandfather's rage, her mother's escape, her own wonderful childhood and Drew. How had she fallen in love with him so fast? She'd only been here a few weeks. They'd only kissed a few times, yet she knew she never wanted to kiss anyone else, ever again. Never wanted to dance with anyone else.

She laid her fork down.

She had to do as her grandfather wanted— leave. That angered her, yet it was the answer. Drew could petition for the betrothal to be voided. Effie would testify that she was Annabelle Smith, not Annabelle Fredrickson—Effie had said she would. Not at first, but she'd finally agreed, and agreed that Annabelle's grandfather wouldn't stop until she was gone.

Drew could then buy out the mine, just as they'd planned. That's why they'd had the masquerade ball. Nothing had changed since then.

No, something *had* changed since then. She'd fallen in love with him. That might prove to be the most foolish thing she'd ever done.

'Excuse me, miss,' Donald said, opening the door to the dining room.

Annabelle had barely looked up to acknowledge him when Effie shot around him, running to the table.

Annabelle glanced from Effie, to Donald, and to Finnegan, Kate, Rosemary and Julia, all standing near the doorway, looking worried, upset. Her heart began to thud. 'What—what's happened?'

Donald moved closer to the table. 'It's the Duke, miss.'

Her lungs stalled. 'Drew?'

'Yes. There has been a cave-in at the mine and he's trapped.'

A ringing formed in her ears and her entire body shook. 'No... No.'

'Yes, my lady,' Effie said, her voice quivering. 'And it's worse. Your grandfather, the Earl, won't let anyone try to rescue him.'

A fog seemed too swirl in her head, making thinking impossible. 'He can't stop them.'

'He is,' Effie said. 'The miners are protesting, but the Earl has men there, stopping them.'

Clarity formed and among the fear and anguish rose fury. Her grandfather had to be stopped, Drew had to be saved! How? What could she do? She had to find a way! Annabelle pressed her hands against the table and, as she stood, her gaze landed on the painting of Champion. He looked regal, powerful, proud of who he was. The steed of a duke.

'Finnegan, saddle Champion for me, please.' As she stepped away from the table, she said, 'Effie, Rosemary, I need you in my room. Quickly. We don't have time to waste.' At the doorway, she made one more request. 'Donald, I'll need the pistol from Drew's study.'

* * *

Within a short amount of time, with her hair coiled atop her head much like her mother's was in the portrait, and wearing the Compton emeralds around her neck, Annabelle mounted Champion. The very power and pride she'd seen in paint was beneath her as they rode out.

Finnegan, as well as several other staff members rode beside her and carriages filled with others followed behind. She didn't have a plan, other than to save Drew's life by whatever means necessary.

She felt the heavy weight of the gun in her pocket and felt thankfulness for the childhood she'd had. One where she'd been pampered and spoiled at times, as well as taught how to shoot and ride and think for herself. To know what was right and wrong and to know what she wanted.

Her parents had insisted she learn how to stand her ground, protect herself and those she loved. They knew they wouldn't always be there, that she would have to become her own person, capable of deciding things for herself.

A great sense of pride, of knowing who she was, filled her as Champion's feet pounded against the ground, racing forward, like the battle horse he'd always been.

She'd never seen the mine and, as they ap-

proached it, she was momentarily awed by the
massive size, the large number of buildings and
housing units, and the crowd. Men were shouting, fighting their way towards the entrance of
the mine, where they were held back by several
armed men.

Slowing Champion enough so people could
move out of her path, Annabelle focused in on
one man as she rode towards the mine entrance.
Her grandfather was shouting to the armed men.
She couldn't hear what he was saying but it didn't
matter. It made no difference.

His face was red, his eyes full of the hatred
she'd seen before as he shouted and waved for
men to get between him and Champion as she
continued to forward.

'Shoot her!' he shouted. 'Shoot her!'

Silence ensued, or perhaps her hearing was
focused only on him. The armed men had guns
drawn, pointed at her, but it didn't stop her, or
her battle horse. Champion moved forward until
she tugged on his reins, bringing him to a stop
as close to her grandfather as possible.

'It's over, Grandfather,' she said, loudly, pur-
posefully.

A low murmur echoed around her.

'I said shoot her!' he shouted.

Champion stamped on the ground, snorted and

swung his head, as if he challenged any man to touch the trigger of his gun.

People around her shouted, claiming no one would dare shoot a woman. They'd go to prison for the rest of their lives.

Despite her surroundings, she felt calm, in control. 'Is there a man here willing to spend the rest of his life in prison because of an old man's hatred for his family?' she asked. 'Willing to shoot his granddaughter?'

The armed men looked at each other warily, then began mumbling about not being told they'd have to kill anyone, especially a woman. There were other mumbles, too, questioning if she really was his granddaughter.

'She's not my granddaughter!' her grandfather shouted. 'She's an imposter!'

'Oh, how I wish that were true,' she replied. 'But it's not, I'm not an imposter. As you can see with your own eyes, I look just like her. Your daughter. My mother. The Duchess of Compton. I am Lady Annabelle Fredrickson.'

'It's true!' a female voice shouted behind her. Effie's. 'She's wearing the Compton emeralds!'

The murmur in the crowd grew louder. 'Duchess' and 'Compton emeralds' were repeated over and over again.

'She stole that necklace!' her grandfather shouted as the crowd grew even louder.

'No, I did not. But you have been stealing everything that was willed to me since the day the Duke of Compton died.' She turned her attention to the armed men. 'Unless you wish to reside at Newgate, step aside. We have men to rescue inside that mine.'

Her grandfather moved swiftly, grasping hold of the gun the man in front of him lowered.

Annabelle pulled the pistol from her pocket, pointing it at him. Cocked it. 'My mother insisted I learn to shoot, to defend myself against anything that might pose a threat to me or my loved ones, because she had been threatened for years, by her very own father.'

As if disgusted, the man pulled his gun away from the Earl and moved further away.

'Finnegan,' Annabelle said to the men flanking her, 'please collect their guns. Donald, please see that the Earl is confined.' As they dismounted and moved to complete her bidding, she shouted to the crowd, 'We need torches, lanterns, shovels and axes!'

Chapter Sixteen

There was no light at the end of the tunnel, no end to the dirt and debris he and Gunner had been fighting against for hours. The air was so thin, so useless, Drew questioned trying to breathe, trying to lift the axe one more time. If not for the image in his mind, he wouldn't have. But she was there, Annabelle, in his mind and in the world where he desperately wanted to return.

He wanted to live. To get married. Have children. All the things he'd thought he didn't want, he did now. He'd make it all happen. Take Annabelle to America. Marry her. That was the first thing he was going to do. Marry her. Beg her to marry him until she finally agreed.

Dropping the axe to the floor, he leaned on the handle, trying to draw in enough air for the energy to lift the axe again. He wasn't sure if he heard something over his wheezing or not, but reaching over, he laid a hand on Gunner. He tried to tell the man to listen, but his throat was too coated with dust to speak. All he could do was cough.

The silence was so thick, he was about to admit he hadn't heard anything when he heard it again. A shout. Faint, but a shout.

Drew tried to shout in return, but again, coughing was all that emitted. Their lanterns had long ago been left behind and he picked up the axe, swung it against the wall until he blindly found a rock for it to ping against.

Gunner did the same and they continued to hit the rocks, over and over, making as much noise as possible.

What happened next, and how it happened, was a mixture of confusion. It was as if he was watching things, doing things, from outside of his body. Voices, faceless men, appeared. He insisted they take Gunner first. Then he was pulled through an opening, half carried and half dragged for what felt like miles, until the air entering his lungs felt sustaining enough for him to draw in a full breath. That caused massive coughing fits, but also gave him the strength to lift his legs. To walk enough to assist his rescuers in getting him out of the mine.

It felt like hours later when he saw light. Not

sunlight, but torches, masses of them lighting up the exit of the tunnel. 'Banks,' he told the men helping him.

'We know, Your Grace,' someone replied. 'There wasn't anyone else in the mine. That was Jim's tag on the board and then he and Westerdownes wouldn't let us search for you.'

Drew sucked in air in order to say, 'Mansfield. Annabelle.'

'The lady is here, Your Grace,' the man said. 'She's right outside.'

'Here?' His footsteps increased and a renewed sense of life filled him.

Cheering filled the air as he moved through the exit. The brightness of the torches made his eyes water and burn. He didn't need to see, not when he could feel her. Feel her arms around him.

'Quickly! Get him in the wagon,' she shouted, her arms around his waist.

'What are you doing here?' His throat burned, but he refused to give in to another coughing fit.

'Making sure you're all right,' she said.

'I'm fine,' he barely got out before a coughing fit took over.

He was put in a wagon, but refused to lie down, knowing that would increase the coughing. Nor would he let go of Annabelle.

She climbed on the wagon beside him. 'No, you're not fine.' She kissed his cheek. 'But you will be.'

He kissed her forehead, leaned his head against hers and felt a great thankfulness to whatever measures had been taken for him to be here right now, with her at his side.

The wagon ride quickly ended and he was ushered inside the main building, examined by the doctor. The fogginess that had overtaken his mind for hours was lifting with each breath he took and he brushed the doctor's hands away. 'Enough.' His gaze was on Annabelle. 'What are you doing here?' he repeated the question he'd asked before.

She stepped forward slowly. 'My grandfather was behind it all. I had to stop him.'

Instantly concerned, he reached for her hand, pulling her closer. She looked fine, beautiful, yet he had to ask, 'Are you all right?'

'I'm fine.' She touched the side of his face. 'I wasn't the one trapped in a mine.'

'Banks.' Drew rose to his feet. 'He needs to be arrested.'

'That's already been handled, old man.'

'What are you doing here?' he asked Roger who seemed to appear out of nowhere.

'I was on my way back to Mansfield when I heard about the mine collapse and came upon what looked like a rider fleeing the scene of a crime,' Roger replied. 'He was. It was Banks. I brought him here and now he and Westerdownes are being escorted to London, where they will have some very serious questions to answer.' Roger nodded at Annabelle. 'Thanks to Lady Annabelle Fredrickson, the daughter of the lost Duchess of Compton.'

Frowning, Drew looked at her.

She shrugged, then asked the doctor, 'Can we take him home now?'

'Yes, my lady. He should be fine in a day or two, once his lungs clear out.'

Roger took a hold of his arm. 'Come on, old man, I'll help you to the wagon.'

Drew pulled his arm away. 'I'm not an old man and I'll ride my horse home.' He then questioned the doctor, 'Where's Gunner?'

'In the room next door, Your Grace,' the doctor replied. 'He'll need to get his lungs cleared out as well, but you'll both be fine.'

He nodded. 'Thank you.' Including Annabelle and Roger in his nod, he added, 'Thank you all.'

She wrapped her hands around his arm. 'Let's get you home. You need a bath.'

He agreed with that. The crowd that greeted

them as they exited the building was massive and loud with cheers. Once they quieted, he thanked all of the miners, and their families, for their heroic efforts, vowing he'd never forget what had happened today.

The crowd cheered again a short time later, as he and Annabelle mounted their horses and rode away from the mine.

'Is there anyone back at the house?' he asked, noting the entourage following them.

'Kate and a few others should be there by the time we arrive.'

He'd noted the horse she was upon as soon as they'd walked outside. 'How's he ride?'

'Like a dream.'

There was a smile and love in her voice and that made him smile, even though it was pitch black and no one could see it.

'He is so fit and fine that he and I could challenge you and Fellow,' she said. 'But we won't. Champion has nothing to prove.'

'Neither did you.' He hadn't been told, but had figured out how she'd revealed her identity to stop Westerdownes. She was wearing the Compton emeralds.

'Yes, I did, but we'll talk about that later. Right now, we just have to get you home.'

He held his silence. His lungs felt heavy, as

though he could never cough enough to clear them, and he wanted to be able to say all he had to say without keeling over in a coughing fit when he told her what he'd decided. That would happen soon. Every moment of having her at his side made him feel better.

A bath was his first order of business upon arriving home and Drew was in the midst of scrubbing his hair beneath the water when a knock sounded on the door. He popped his head above the water just as Roger opened the door and walked in his room.

'Did you find any information about her father?' he asked.

'I did and I figured this was my only chance to talk to you.' Roger waited near the door. 'If you're up to it.'

Drew leaned against the back of the tub and rested his arms on the sides. 'I'm up to it.'

Roger crossed the room and sat in a chair. 'I'm leaving again at first light, for London. Westerdownes is going to try to discredit her and someone needs to be there to advocate on her behalf.'

'Thank you.' Knowing conquest was always first and foremost in Roger's mind, Drew continued, 'I appreciate that, though I can't help but question your motives.'

'Besides the fact that you've saved my life more than once?' Roger asked.

That was true, but Drew kept his gaze on his friend, waiting for another answer.

Roger laughed. 'Not this time, my friend. I know when a woman is off limits. She has been since the moment she stepped foot in this house.' With a nod, Roger added, 'She's all yours.'

A short time ago, he would have denied any alliance with any woman. That was no longer the case. He believed there was a future for him and Annabelle and he wanted that future. 'Not that you are of such good character that I should seek your approval, but I do wonder what you think about that?'

Roger's face held what looked like a sense of wonder before he grinned. 'You've always cared about others, Drew. Even those you didn't need to, but it's different with her. Yes, you care, but you are also happy. I don't know that I recall a time when I've seen that in you. However, it doesn't surprise me. She's not only beautiful, she's genuine and true to her heart, much like you. And I would be lying if I didn't admit that I'm a bit jealous.' He held up his hand demonstrating about an inch of space between his forefinger and thumb.

Drew copied the gesture with his finger and thumb. 'A bit.'

Roger laughed and shrugged. 'Yes, it's more than a bit. But I am happy for you, Drew.'

'There are still a lot of details to work out,' Drew said, more of a warning to himself to not get ahead of things. He knew what he wanted, but it had to be what Annabelle wanted, too.

'Hopefully, what I have to tell you will settle a few things.' Roger leaned forward and rested his elbows on his knees. 'Her father was injured during the fire. The ship that picked him up took him to New Jersey to be doctored.'

That was one step closer. 'Do you know where in New Jersey or how bad he was injured?' Drew asked.

'No, but I know he's no longer there. He found passage on a ship to England.'

'He's well enough to travel?'

'Must be. Should arrive within the next few days. I've hired a coach and left word at the docks that he is to be brought here, to Mansfield, as soon as he arrives.'

It was no use. She couldn't sleep. Annabelle climbed out of bed, pulled a wrapper over her nightgown and walked to the door. Sleep would continue to evade her until she talked to Drew.

She stopped shy of opening the door. He needed rest after what he'd been through. She could just check on him, make sure he was sleeping, or if he needed anything. That might be enough to ease her mind so she could sleep. She had never seen a more wonderful sight than him walking out of that mine.

Mind made up, she opened the door and followed the hallway all the way to the end. There was no light shining under the door and she contemplated opening the door just enough to peek in or going back to her own room.

She knew she wouldn't sleep, so opening the door was the better choice and she did that very slowly, just enough to peer into the room. He was sitting in a chair near the fireplace, which wasn't lit. A lamp was on the nearby table. However, it didn't provide enough light to see if he was awake or asleep.

'You can come in.'

The sound of his voice nearly caused her to slam the door on her nose. It also sent her heart somersaulting. She pushed the door all the way open. 'I just wanted to see if you needed anything.'

'I'm fine.'

'Are you sure? I could get you some warm milk or—'

'A glass of brandy?' He held up a glass. 'I already have one. Come in. Sit down.'

She entered the room slowly, wondering if she had the courage to go through with what she needed to say. It wasn't as if she expected him to feel the same way about her as she felt about him. Nor was it as if she was going to tell him that. She wasn't that foolish.

'How are you feeling?' he asked.

'Fine. I just…'

'Couldn't sleep?'

She nodded and sat in the chair on the other side of the fireplace.

'Me, neither. Want to know why?'

She nodded.

'Because I was thinking about you.'

Her nerves got the better of her and she began to explain, quickly, 'I had to stop him, Drew. I'm sorry. I didn't think of the consequences. Of what people would assume.' She rose to her feet. Paced the floor. Between the betrothal and the Earl's shouting, others now assumed that they would marry. Immediately. Once the searching had started, along with the waiting, the murmurs about that had spread through the crowd like wildfire. 'I'm sorry about that. We can do just as we planned. I'll leave as soon as we hear where my father is and you can have the betrothal voided.'

'Is that what you want?'

'It's what we planned before the masquerade ball.'

He stood and stopped her pacing by stepping in front of her. 'That doesn't answer my question.'

Her heart pounded hard. He was so very handsome. She loved his smile, how it made his eyes twinkle. She loved everything about him. All of him. Everything about him was perfect and she wished things could be different.

'Why are your hands trembling?'

She hadn't realised they were, until he touched them. 'Because I'm sorry for my actions today.' That was a lie. She would do it hundred times over to save his life.

He folded both of his hands around hers. 'Your actions saved Gunner's and my lives.'

'I'm not sorry about that part. I'm sorry that everyone assumes we will now be married.'

'I wasn't aware that is what they are assuming.'

'Yes, it is. My grandfather kept shouting that you'd never marry me and others shouted back that we were betrothed, but—'

He touched the side of her face so softly, so

gently, her insides melted. 'But marrying a duke is not what you want.' His words were barely a whisper as his lips met hers.

The kiss was the perfect mixture of sweetness and warmth, and much more. It was an awakening. Not just for her body that filled with the undeniable need, it filled her mind with the undeniable truth. She could not spend the rest of her life without him. It was that simple. That real. She had no choice but to tell him the truth, the whole truth, no matter how he might react.

He'd be kind, she knew that. He was always kind, but he'd also be honest and at that moment, she hoped that honesty would include that he might be open to considering a life that included her.

Needing to know, she pulled her mouth off his. 'I'm sorry, Drew, I can't—' She bit her lip, needing a moment to get her words right the first time rather than ramble.

'I'm sorry, I was hoping—'

She wrapped her hand around his arm as his hand started to slip away from her cheek. 'Hoping what?'

He rubbed the side of her face, shook his head. 'That I could convince you to change your mind and that's not fair of me.'

Her heart pounded harder and she held on to his arm tighter. 'Change my mind about what?'

His expression was unreadable. 'It doesn't matter.'

'Yes, it does,' she insisted. 'Because I have changed my mind. Or maybe I've made up my mind because I now know the truth. I know now who I am. What I want. What I need. I don't expect you to change your mind, just because I've changed mine, I know that—' She was rambling, which is what she hadn't wanted to do, therefore she cut to the quick. 'I love you, Drew.'

Maybe rambling was better because he stared at her as if shocked. Not blinking. Just staring. The words were out and she meant them. 'I love you,' she said it louder. 'And I don't want to live the rest of my life without you. I don't want to live one minute without you.'

He was shaking his head, but it was the smile growing on his face that held her attention. She tightened every muscle in her body to keep from saying something, to keep the hope rising inside her from bursting out.

'I don't want to live a minute without you either,' he said.

She couldn't stop herself from asking, 'You don't?'

'No. I don't. I changed my mind about that

some time ago. I love you, Annabelle. Love you beyond everything.'

Joy welled inside her and continued to grow as their lips met in a wild frenzy of kissing that included their bodies, their arms, their hands.

'We'll move to America,' he said while running a line of kisses along the side of her face and holding her tight against him.

Snuggled against him and basking in his warmth, his love, it took a moment for his words to penetrate. She lifted her head, touched the side of his face. 'The Duke of Mansfield should live at Mansfield.'

He ran his hands up and down her back. 'I intend to marry you as soon as possible, but that doesn't mean you need to become a duchess.'

'Perhaps, but I want to be your wife, the wife of the man I fell in love with. If that means becoming a duchess, I'll do so with all my heart. That's how I love you. With all of my heart.'

'I love you with all of mine.' He kissed her forehead. 'I never thought that would be possible. Never thought I'd want that. Then I met you. I felt the changes inside me almost immediately. I tried not to, tried not to accept them. I thought I liked my life, liked being alone. That was the life I'd been born into, the life I continued to live because it was all I'd ever known.' He shook his head. 'I don't want that for you.'

The anguish in his eyes tore at her heart. 'We won't be alone. We'll be together.'

He released her, took a step back and ran a hand through his hair. 'That's what I want, but I'm afraid if we stay here, it won't happen that way. I inherited more than the dukedom from my father. His sense of duty kept him from his family. That sense is inside me. I've known it. Felt that dedication while making changes at the mine. Your love is so precious to me, I don't want anything, including my duties, to come between us.'

She felt her love for him growing. The mere fact that he'd admitted his fear said how much he trusted her. His sense of duty, of caring for others, was one of the things she loved about him, but that wasn't what he needed to hear. 'No matter where we live, duty—yours and mine—will keep us apart at some point. For hours, possibly even a day or two. That's life. That's living and we'll rejoice when we are together again. And those duties are what will make our love stronger, because that's love. True love. It's not just between us when we are together. It's there all time.'

He was silent, as if musing over what she'd

said, before he took a hold of her hand. 'How did you become so wise?'

She laughed because she'd only recently understood what she'd just told him. 'My mother. She travelled halfway around the world to find a man she loved with all of her heart and so did I.'

'Your mother took you to America so you wouldn't be forced to marry a man of the peerage. Wouldn't be forced to marry *me*.'

She shook her head. 'I was wrong. My mother left because she feared for my life. She didn't even know about our betrothal. Neither did my father when he sent me here. He, too, did that to save my life. A life they wanted me to have. One where I am free to choose what I want. And I choose you.'

He lifted her hand, kissed the back of it, then held it against his chest. 'I choose you, but there are other people involved. Your father will be here in a few days.'

Air locked in her lungs. 'What?'

'I was informed you were already in bed, or I would have told you right when Roger told me earlier. Your father is on a ship to England. Roger left word at the docks that a carriage is waiting to bring him here, to Mansfield, upon his arrival.'

She stared at him—half in awe of what he'd said, half in awe of him—blinking to gather her thoughts and keep them in line, because the rejoicing happening inside her made her want to hug him, kiss him and never stop. 'He's going to like you and you are going to like him.'

'I'm sure I will.' His expression grew serious. 'He was hurt during the fire. I'm not sure how badly. He saw a doctor before beginning his voyage to England.'

She was shocked for a moment that her grandfather hadn't lied about that, but in this instant, that didn't matter. Her love. Her life from here on out was all that mattered. 'Then I'm doubly glad he's coming. So I can see for myself. Make sure he's all right.'

'I'm sure his main reason for coming here is to take you home. Back to America.'

Knowing her father, she nodded. 'I should have realised that I didn't need to find him, that he'd find me.' She knew something else. 'He won't make me return to America if I don't want to.'

'He made you come here.'

'For my own good, but once he meets you, he'll know that he no longer needs to worry about me. He'll see how happy I am, how much I love you and that I'm in the best hands possible.'

'Keeping you happy and safe will be my main

duties, for ever.' He pulled her into his arms, kissing her.

The smile he bestowed upon her when the kiss ended made her sigh and lean her head against his chest.

Kissing the top of her head, he whispered, 'I'll walk you back to your room.'

She didn't want to leave, to be parted from him.

As if reading her mind, he stepped back and took hold of her hand. 'If you don't return to your bed, I'll take you to mine and that needs to wait for our wedding night.'

'When will that be?'

He squeezed her had. 'We'll wait until your father arrives, so—'

'We don't know when that might be.' She stepped closer to him. 'I want to marry you as soon as possible. I know that's selfish and that I should think of others first, but I can't. Not this time. I don't want to wait.'

'I don't either.' He kissed her, a fast, quick kiss, then led her to the door. 'I'll apply for a special licence tomorrow.'

Chapter Seventeen

Three days later, Drew watched Annabelle walk towards him. Her ruffled silver-coloured gown swayed with each step as she moved past the rows of pews. The pride inside him was nearly as great as the love he had for her. He wasn't perfect, not by any means, but she didn't care. She loved him anyway. He could see it on her face and, grateful for that, he'd strived to make everything for today, their wedding day, absolutely perfect. For the first time in his life, he'd willingly accepted the benefits of his father's lifelong friendship with the Royal Family.

Their wedding was taking place at the private chapel in Buckingham Palace, where he, along with his bride-to-be, had been summoned the day before yesterday. Prince Albert had heard about everything—the mine episode, the betrothal and Annabelle.

Drew took her hand as she arrived at the altar and once again was amazed at how his love for her flowed through him. Continuously. Without a hindrance of his past beliefs.

The service ended with a kiss that he cherished as much as he'd cherish her for ever. He'd vowed to love, honour and provide for her aloud, in the presence of those sitting in the pews, while silently he had vowed to never make her regret giving him her love.

A small reception followed the wedding. They shared their first drink together, their first meal, as man and wife.

As they prepared to leave, Prince Albert met them at the door. He handed an envelope to Annabelle. 'This, my dear, is a wedding gift from me. All of the Duke of Compton's assets have been transferred into your husband's name. The Earl of Westerdownes has been ordered to appear before Parliament and will be encouraged to make restitutions for all monies he's appropriated during your absence. I encourage you to seek my assistance, or that of the Queen in my absence, on any issues that may arise.'

Annabelle curtsied. 'Thank you, Your Royal Highness. I appreciate all of your kindness and your gifts.'

'I appreciate your love for Andrew,' the Prince

responded. 'He's always been considered a member of the family.' He winked at her. 'The one child that didn't give me cause for concern or grey hair.'

Albert then shook Drew's hand. 'Your father would have been as proud of the man that you've become as I am. Now, go, enjoy your lives. The years will go by faster than you can imagine.'

The past three days had moved with an excruciating slowness in Drew's mind. He and Annabelle hadn't had a moment alone together since he'd walked her to her bedroom after they'd confessed their love.

Well-wishers lined the way to the coach and, once inside, they waved out of the windows until the coach had rolled away from Buckingham Palace, then Drew dropped the window shade.

With a laugh, Annabelle lowered the shade on the window near her and looped her arms around his neck. He wrapped his around her waist and they kissed as if no one was watching. For no one was. Finally. Thankfully.

'Oh, Drew,' she said as their lips parted, 'that was such a lovely wedding.'

He chuckled. 'It was your wedding.'

Her touch on the side of his face was as soft and light as her laugh. 'I know and I thank you for that. For marrying me. I'm so happy I could just burst.'

He understood. He'd never been happier or prouder. 'You are so beautiful. So amazing. I must be a very lucky man to have you for my wife.'

'I'm the lucky one.'

A lump formed in his throat. 'I never thought I would need someone, but I need you. Will need you the rest of my life.'

A single tear fell from her eye. 'I need you, too, and I love you,' she whispered. 'So very, very much.'

He wanted to make sure she wouldn't regret not returning to America and had to ask one more time. 'We could move to America after the war ends. It can't last for ever.'

'I hope it ends soon, but my for ever is here. With you.' She sighed, tilted her head sideways as she looked at him. 'How can I convince you that America was my mother's life?'

'It was also yours.'

'It was, but this is my life now. Here. With you. I believe my mother would be very happy with my choice. It's…' She shrugged. 'It's as if her life has come full circle. I'm happy about that, but I'm more excited about our lives. About the adventures we'll have. Building the mine into

something that is prosperous for every employee.
A place they are proud to work. And I'm excited
about building a family. With you. One we can
be proud of.'

He trailed a finger along the softness of her
cheek. 'We will do all that, and more.'

'I know we will.' She leaned closer to kiss
him, but the movement caused her skirt to shift,
increasing the space between them. 'Oh!' She
slapped at her skirt and wiggled. 'The woman
at the dress shop said this would make a lovely
wedding gown and I'd agreed, but this caged
crinoline is the first thing I'm asking you to untie
once we get home.'

The wires beneath the skirt were causing her
dress to take up a large portion of the carriage,
including the seat. 'Would you like me to untie
it now?'

'I wish you could, but I need to take off the
outer skirt in order to lift the dress high enough.
I just don't understand why fashion needs to be
so uncomfortable and inconvenient.'

Neither did he. The wire did make the close-
ness he desired nearly impossible. 'Perhaps you
can start a new fashion.'

'Perhaps I can.' Her eyes shone with a loving glimmer as she stretched to bring their faces
closer. 'I am married to a duke.'

'That you are,' he said before taking her lips in a long, drawn-out kiss.

When they arrived at their town home, they wasted no time in proceeding upstairs to their bedroom, where he did untie the hoop skirt first, then proceeded removing layer upon layer of clothing. 'I hope your new fashion has a few less layers.'

'I promise,' she said with a giggle.

He kissed the side of her neck, felt her body and his own respond. The need inside him had never been so strong.

She turned, faced him, wearing nothing more than her chemise and drawers. 'My turn.' Slowly, she pushed his jacket off his shoulders.

Had he known the level of his control, he might have sneaked into her bedroom the last few nights. Every brush of her fingertips undoing a button was like a caress. A promise of what was to come. He cupped her face. Kissed her softly. 'I love you.'

She smiled up at him, her eyes as full of promises as her touch. 'I love you, too.'

Those were the words that carried them forward, through the removal of their clothing, through heated kisses, caresses, and a union that fulfilled every one of their promises to each other.

He relished each time she whispered his name, each gasp of her breath, each and every nuance she displayed as her pleasure built, and built, until her time came and she clung to him, repeating his name.

Only then, after she'd reached her peak, had given him all she had, did he focus on his own pleasure.

In the past, always aware of the consequences, he'd withdrawn before completion, but tonight, for the first time ever, he spent himself inside a woman. His wife. Annabelle. The Duchess of Mansfield.

Annabelle had known what to expect, but there was no amount of discussion, no amount of explanation, that could have ever explained what she'd just experienced. Drew had been so gentle, kind, loving. He'd never taken his eyes off her. Had watched her every move, her every reaction to make sure she was fine.

She was more than fine.

She was married to the Duke of Mansfield, the most wonderful man on earth.

Eyes closed, she smoothed her hands over his

shoulders, held him tight as he lay atop her, and whispered, 'Don't move.'

He stiffened. 'Why? Did I hurt you?'

The concern in his voice made her smile. 'No,' she said reassuringly. 'Not at all. I'm just sealing this moment in my memory.'

He moaned softly and kissed her forehead. 'It's sealed in mine.'

A soft hum mumbled in her throat. 'Good. Then when we are mad at each other, we can each recall this moment.'

'Why are we going to be mad at each other?'

She opened her eyes, met his loving, yet questioning gaze. 'Because we are married.'

He frowned. 'That's going to make us mad at each other?'

'I hope not, but there will come a time when we are angry with each other, for one reason or another, and that's when we'll pull up this memory. Recall this moment and know there is nothing stronger than our love for each other. A love so strong, so deep, that even while being upset with each other, we'll still love each other. My mother taught me how to do that. How to seal memories and use them.'

'I like that.' He kissed the tip of her nose. 'Your mother was a very smart woman and so are you. You amazed me the first day I met you. When you were hiding in the loft of the stable.'

She knew the moment he was referring to, yet corrected him, 'That was the second time we met.'

'I stand corrected.' He laughed and in one swift movement rolled, bringing her with him so she was now lying atop him. 'I didn't know what to expect when you arrived, but it certainly wasn't this.'

'I didn't either,' she admitted, resting her arms on his chest and her hands beneath her chin. 'I almost feel sorry for the Earl. He must have not considered the possibility that we'd fall in love when he sent me to Mansfield.'

'I'm sure he didn't consider that. He was focused on finding a way to keep you out of sight until he could have you discredited. I was the only solution he could come up with quickly. If you'd arrived later, or the message from your father earlier, he might have had time to find a different place to hide you.' He ran his hands up and down her back. 'I'll be grateful for ever that he didn't.'

She rubbed her hips against his. 'How grateful?'

He cupped his hands over her bottom. 'Do you want me to show you?'

Stretching so their lips could meet, she whispered, 'Yes. I want that very much.'

They left for Mansfield the next morning, along with the entourage of servants who had travelled to London with them, including Effie, who was inside the coach with Annabelle while Drew rode Fellow alongside.

The smile he bestowed upon her each time she glanced out of the window filled her with happiness and exceptionally wonderful memories of their wedding bed.

'Married at Buckingham Palace,' Effie said, shaking her head and sighing. 'I can't get over that.' Growing serious quickly, she added, 'Or the job, my lady. I appreciate not having to go back to the Westerdownes residence.'

'I appreciate your commitment to me, Effie. I have since the beginning. You did send word to Mrs Quinn that there are jobs for any of the household staff that need them at Mansfield, or the London residence if they prefer?' She wasn't sure what the jobs would be, but Drew had agreed they would hire any or all of them.

'Yes, I did.'

'You told them just go to the town house and transportation would be arranged?'

'Yes, I did, my lady. I made sure the message

would be delivered to the kitchen, not the front door.' Effie wrung her hands together. 'I…um… I'm wondering if you'll need help at the estate?'

'The estate?'

'The Compton Estate. You do own that now.'

Annabelle mused on that for a moment. 'I haven't thought of that. I'll have to talk to Drew. It would be better to repair it, use it, than just let it go to ruins.'

'It would.'

Effie's eagerness was stronger than usual, which had Annabelle asking, 'Is there someone else who needs a job?'

With cheeks pinkening, Effie said, 'Well, Grady. He's an excellent coach driver, but he worked in the stable, not the house.'

Annabelle nodded. 'Did you include the stable in your message?'

Somewhat sheepish, Effie admitted, 'Yes.'

'Very good.' Annabelle leaned forward as she asked, 'How long have you been in love with Grady?'

Slapping a hand over her mouth, Effie shook her head.

Annabelle giggled and nodded.

Blushing red, Effie looked out of the window. So did Annabelle and she smiled at her hus-

band as she said, 'Perhaps there'll soon be another wedding.'

'Oh, no, we are much too old for that.'

'No one is ever too old for love,' Annabelle
insisted.

Effie didn't agree or disagree, but changed the
subject, talking about a plethora of things until,
hours later, the coach slowed and then came to
a stop. 'I wonder why we are stopping.'

'I don't know.' Annabelle looked out of the
window, but didn't see a reason for stopping.
'We can't be more than two or three miles from
home.'

Drew rode up to her window, with a grin, and
asked, 'How are you feeling?'

'Fine. Why?'

'Would you care to ride the last couple of
miles?'

She would like that, but questioned, 'Double?
On Fellow?'

Drew shook his head and pointed up the road.

She had to lean out of the window to see the
rider approaching, leading another horse. Champion. The other Mansfield male who had stolen
her heart. 'Yes, I would very much like to ride
the last couple of miles.'

'I'll be right back,' Drew said and rode off to collect Champion from Finnegan.

Annabelle instantly opened the door.

Effie sighed. 'You really should wait for an escort to help you out, my lady.'

'I know,' Annabelle replied, stepping out of the coach on her own. 'And thank you for reminding me of that. I'll expect you to continue telling me the rules.'

'And I'll expect you to keep breaking them,' Effie said with a laugh.

Annabelle laughed, too, and allowed Drew to help her on to Champion, thrilled at how that gave them the opportunity to steal a fast kiss.

She'd loved riding next to him, but today, riding on Champion, in front of the coach as they travelled towards home, she felt something stronger. Something more significant. Glancing at her husband, she felt her smile grow. This was her. Who she was born to be.

'Happy?' he asked.

'Yes, very.' That was the truth. The other truth was that something on his face made her asked, 'What don't I know?'

He pretended ignorance, 'I don't know. What don't you know?'

'Whatever it is you're about to tell me.'

He laughed. 'How do you know I'm about to tell you something.'

'By the smile on your face. The shine in your eyes.'

With a nod, he said, 'You, my lady, have company awaiting at Mansfield.'

It only took only a brief moment before she understood. Excitement filled her. 'My father? He's arrived?'

'Yes. A few hours ago.' He winked at her. 'These horses will get us there much quicker than the coach.'

She needed no further bidding and Champion only needed a slight tap of her heels to increase his speed.

Drew had never been nervous about meeting anyone but had been when it came to Arlo Smith, the man who was now his father-in-law. Annabelle was so precious, such a treasure, he could imagine the man wouldn't want to give her away easily.

However, Drew quickly discovered there hadn't been a need to worry. The man was not only gracious and genuine, he showered Annabelle with unabashed love and was overjoyed at her happiness. Which he openly and sincerely accredited to Drew.

So did the woman with him. Cecilia. Trim, with curly black hair and brown eyes, the woman was just as overjoyed to hear of the marriage.

Arlo's hands and arms were bandaged past his elbows, having been burned while escaping the fires, and, rightfully so, Annabelle was more than worried about his injuries.

'They'll be fine, Belle-girl,' Arlo said. 'Don't worry. Cecilia's been worrying enough for all the rest of us.'

'If it had been up to you,' Cecilia said, sitting in the chair next to Arlo's chair, 'you would have wrapped some burlap around them and kept rowing all the way to England.'

A large man, with permanent laugh lines around his eyes, and dark hair peppered with grey, Arlo levelled a loving gaze on Annabelle. 'I had to get here. Had to make sure my baby girl was all right. I was awaiting word that you'd made it safely to London, but the rebels struck. They were afraid the Union would get a strong hold along the shore. Damn shame. The whole town went up in flames within hours.'

'What about Clara and Abigail? Homer? Suzanne? Did you hear if any of them made it out safely? Or the Parson and his wife, and…' Annabelle was shooting out names so fast no one could keep up, not even Arlo.

Sitting next to her on the sofa in the main drawing room, Drew reached over and laid a hand on hers as her father answered, explaining how some he knew made it and how he didn't know about others.

Seeing her distress, Drew kissed her temple. 'We'll give Roger a list of names.'

The looked she graced upon him glimmered brightly. 'Thank you. That's a wonderful idea.' She kissed his cheek. 'I should have known that you'd think of a way to help. I love you so much.'

'I love you,' he replied. If not for her parent sitting near, he would have proceeded to show her how much.

Her smile said she knew his thoughts and agreed with him. Then she looked at her father. 'Roger Hardgroves, the Fourth Marquess of Clairmount, is Drew's best friend.'

Arlo nodded and, smiling, asked, 'Tell us, Belle-girl, how did you end up here instead of London?'

'It's a lovely home,' Cecilia said, as if not wanting Arlo's question to sound like an insult. 'Extraordinarily lovely.'

'It is,' Annabelle answered, squeezing his hand. 'The estate is called Mansfield and Drew…' She looked at him with pride. 'Andrew Charles Barkly is the Duke of Mansfield.'

She had left his title out of the introductions earlier when she'd proclaimed him as her husband. Drew hadn't corrected her. It was her story to tell. He would step in only when and if she needed.

Arlo and Cecilia shared a pensive look before Arlo said, 'The man who answered the door said the Duke and Duchess were not at home, but we didn't realise—'

'That the Duke and Duchess are us?' Annabelle asked with a giggle. 'It is—we are—and you aren't going to believe this, but we were married at Buckingham Palace.'

'Buckingham Palace!' Cecilia exclaimed. 'How exciting!'

'A duchess. Just like your mother,' Arlo said, nodding. 'She was aristocracy. Full of grace and integrity. I'm sorry you never knew. Your mother thought it best. She didn't want anyone to know. I didn't know until one day when I brought home a stack of newspapers from London. I thought they would be a nice reminder of home, but your real father's obituary was in one. That's when she told me everything and finally agreed to marry me. I bought her the diary after our wedding, asked her to fill it out so that some day you would know the truth. I thought that was fair to both of you.'

'It was,' Annabelle said. 'I appreciate that more than you can imagine.'

Arlo leaned forward. 'I'm sorry, darling. So sorry for how I sent you away. For how upset you were with me. I'd written to your grandfather, planned on sending it and hearing back that he'd welcome you into his home, but then the soldiers arrived and my only hope for your safety was that he'd cherish getting to know you. Everyone who meets you falls in love with you. I thought he'd be no different.'

Cecilia laid a hand on his shoulder. 'We both did, Annabelle.'

Drew would agree with that and gave them both a nod.

'Did your grandfather pass away?' Arlo asked. 'We didn't have a chance to question anyone when we docked. The coach was there and all the driver knew was that he was to deliver us here.'

'No, he has not passed away,' Annabelle said. 'He sent me here upon my arrival in London. To Drew, because we were betrothed.'

'What?' Arlo sat straighter. 'Betrothed. Your mother never—'

'She didn't know,' Annabelle said. 'It happened after she left for America.' Glancing at him again, eyes aglow with love, she added, 'But it was the best thing that could ever have happened.'

'The two of you *had* to get married?' Cecilia asked. 'By law or something?'

'No,' Annabelle answered. 'Drew and I were working together to see that the betrothal was voided, but along the way, we fell in love.'

Arlo was frowning deeply.

Drew didn't blame him. 'There is far more to the story than that, but I assure you, that is the truth,' he said. 'I love your daughter with all I am. The rest of my life will be dedicated to her, to providing for her, to seeing she is happy.'

Arlo nodded. 'I believe you. I saw her happiness as soon as she rode into the yard on that amazing horse.'

Annabelle stood, walked to her father and knelt down before him. 'I am happy, Father. So very happy, and I'm so happy you are here.'

'Dare I believe you've forgiven me for sending you away like I did?' Arlo asked.

The way she embraced her father, insisting that she had forgiven him, made Drew think of her words last night, about how at some point, they would be angry with each other. Life, as it was, most likely would present a time when they were upset with one another, and her preparedness of that, of sealing a memory to remind them of how strong their love was for each other, was the epitome of who she was.

A mixture of calm gentleness and fiery determination.

A mixture of a southern belle and an English duchess.

He wouldn't have it any other way.

Life was going to be an amazing adventure with her at his side.

Epilogue

Stroking Belle's soft fur, and listening to the cat purr in her arms, Annabelle stood at the window, watching the trunks being loaded into the big flatbed wagon. The coach holding her father and Cecilia had left a short time ago and the wagon holding the last of their belongings would soon depart.

Warm, strong arms wrapped around her waist and tightened as she leaned back into the warmth of Drew's embrace. He kissed the side of her neck.

Her eyes fluttered shut and a sigh escaped.

'How are you doing?'

'Fine.' Opening her eyes, she saw snowflakes in the air on the other side of the window. 'It's just such a cold, windy day to be moving.'

'It's not far and they have a lot of help getting the last of their things unloaded.'

'I know.' Having left London, her grandfather's entire household of staff, including Grady and Effie, were helping with the move, and would remain at the estate. Work there.

They hadn't heard a word from her grandfather and they all knew why. Her father had confirmed that her grandfather had known she and her mother had been in Virginia. A messenger, an Englishman, had visited the house in Hampton one day years ago, saying that if her mother ever returned to England, she'd be jailed.

'We can go help them if it will make you feel better,' Drew said, tightening his hold on her.

Having awoken from her nap, Belle leaped from her arms and Annabelle turned around, looping her arms around Drew's neck. 'No. My father insisted they didn't need our help. We'll wait and go visit when they are all settled.'

He searched her face and smiled. 'Tomorrow?'

She giggled, kissed him and admitted, 'Yes.'

Her father and Cecilia had lived with them the past three months, while his hands healed and workers refurbished the estate. She couldn't think of anyone better to live in the manor house. Her father was not only working with Drew at the mine, making changes that were beneficial to the workers, he was helping the entire mining community by assisting shop owners open businesses and acquire merchandise at fair prices. He claimed he'd return to America and she believed he would, some day.

More importantly than that, he and Cecilia were married. She been shocked to learn the two of them had fallen in love after her mother had died, but hadn't wanted her to think they were blemishing her mother's memory by marrying.

She would never have thought that and told them so, along with the fact that her mother's last wish was for Arlo to be loved. That was what she wanted, too. Having found true love herself, she wanted it for everyone.

The only longing she still had was to hear word of her American friends. Roger had found some information, but so far, he hadn't learned anything about Clara and Abigail or Suzanne.

'Tomorrow it is.' Drew kissed her forehead. 'As for today…'

She sighed at the warmth of his kiss, for his touch always made her remember what was right in the world. Her perfect world. Looking up at him, she grinned. 'Do you have something planned today?'

'No.'

She gave his chest a playful slap. 'Yes, you do. I can see it in your eyes.'

'It's not planned. Just an idea.'

The passion-filled smoulder in his eyes told her exactly what he was thinking. She liked his thoughts and her hand on his chest began caressing him. 'Oh, what is your idea?'

'You worked so hard helping them this morning, I was thinking that you might need a nap. It's chilly and damp outside, an afternoon in bed might be nice.' He kissed the tip of her nose and then stepped back, dropped his hands from her waist. 'But if you have other plans, that's fine, too.'

She reached to catch his arm, but he backed further away.

'I can find something else to do,' he said, turning about.

As he began walking away, she hitched her skirt, ran and leaped on to his back, wrapping her arms around his neck and her legs around his waist. 'Oh, no, you won't find something else to do.'

Hooking his arms beneath her knees, he carried her on his back as he continued walking. 'Why?'

'Because I do need a nap.' She kissed the side of his neck. 'So do you.'

'But I'm not tired.'

'Good, because neither am I.'

How could she be tired? She had the best life imaginable.

She was the Duchess of Mansfield. The luckiest woman on earth.

* * * * *

COMING SOON!

We really hope you enjoyed reading this book. If you're looking for more romance, be sure to head to the shops when new books are available on

Thursday 23rd June

MILLS & BOON®

Coming next month

THE DEBUTANTE'S SECRET
Sophia James

'I like rules and manners because these are the only things that keep the world from chaos.'

He laughed at her comment and the sound was not kind.

'I cannot tell you what the secret of a successful life is, Miss Barrington-Hall, but a sure way to failure is to try and please everyone.'

'You think that is what I am doing?'

'Aren't you?'

She took in breath and answered him.

'Perhaps your way of pleasing no one has its flaws as well, Mr Moreland, for the illicit and forbidden have their drawbacks.'

'Ahhh, but they are much more fun, Esther.'

Her name was said informally and in a tone that made her heart lurch. She was prepared for neither his wildness nor his passion, and he knew it.

'I think, sir, that we have come to the edge of patience with each other, but I would like to thank you for the confidentiality you have kept concerning my past.'

'How little you know me, Miss Barrington-Hall.'

She frowned and stood her ground.

'Do you allow anyone to, or do you send people off as soon as they might guess something you may not wish them to know?'

'I've always found distance has its advantages because people can often be disappointing.'

Squaring her shoulders, Esther answered him. 'Nothing hurts more than being disappointed by the one person you thought would never hurt you.'

'Your mother?' Now he looked at her with more interest.

But she was not drawn in to making a confession. 'After disappointment there comes hope.'

'Hope to make a good life?'

'Yes, for without it one is lost, and I have been.'

These words had him stepping back.

'I am sure things will improve markedly, Miss Barrington-Hall, for you are the belle of the season with a choice of fine upstanding suitors who will do everything possible to make your life a happy one.'

She could see him retreat almost as a physical thing, a man who knew who he was and would never change. People had disappointed him, that much was for sure, so he had stopped trying to fit in to expectations and walked a path that was far from her own.

Then he was gone, lost into the throng of people on the busy street. Out of his company she felt the loss of what might have been. Once he had said to her that he wanted her to like him, but now…

Continue reading
THE DEBUTANTE'S SECRET
Sophia James

Available next month
www.millsandboon.co.uk

MILLS & BOON

THE HEART OF ROMANCE

A ROMANCE FOR EVERY READER

MODERN

Prepare to be swept off your feet by sophisticated, sexy and seductive heroes, in some of the world's most glamourous and romantic locations, where power and passion collide.

HISTORICAL

Escape with historical heroes from time gone by. Whether your passion i for wicked Regency Rakes, muscled Vikings or rugged Highlanders, awa the romance of the past.

MEDICAL

Set your pulse racing with dedicated, delectable doctors in the high-pres sure world of medicine, where emotions run high and passion, comfort love are the best medicine.

True Love

Celebrate true love with tender stories of heartfelt romance, from the rush of falling in love to the joy a new baby can bring, and a focus on th emotional heart of a relationship.

Desire

Indulge in secrets and scandal, intense drama and plenty of sizzling hot action with powerful and passionate heroes who have it all: wealth, statu good looks…everything but the right woman.

HEROES

Experience all the excitement of a gripping thriller, with an intense romance at its heart. Resourceful, true-to-life women and strong, fearless face danger and desire - a killer combination!

To see which titles are coming soon, please visit

millsandboon.co.uk/nextmonth

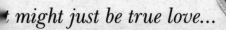